-DARK-

COVENANT'2

H. L. RANDALL

Dark Covenant'2

H.L. Randall

Universal Battles Books RPG

Alpharetta, GA 30004
Universalbattles.com

First published by Universal Battles Books RPG 2020

ISBN 978-0-9862928-6-6

Dedication

Book two is dedicated to my fans of the first book in the Dark Covenant Series, Dark Covenant: The Berwick Witches.

Acknowledgment

I would like to thank my editor C. J. Skye for her valuable knowledge of the written word and her contribution to my book. My appreciation also goes to my book designer SelfPubBookCovers.com/Kreativecovers.

CONTENTS

NEW BERLIN, ILLINOIS

POPULATION 5,767

CHAPTER ONE

"Dig faster, Naomi!" Jewel shouted over the roaring thunder. A bolt of lightning tore a cloud to shreds, and rain fell like blasts of water from a thousand hoses. Fearfully and repeatedly looking into the dark afternoon sky, Naomi lifted her shovel and stabbed the earth with flashing speed. Both knew it was no ordinary storm. Digging up that forbidden book sent a clear message to the demonic world that their diabolical deeds were required once more. Nothing tells demons, *I need you,* like a mystical storm.

"Jewel, there it is!" Naomi blurted.

Jewel bent and pulled the huge, human-skin-covered book from the earth; it was crawling with fat worms. She scraped the dirt and worms from the plastic covering the book and carried it to the trunk of her car. The two settled in the front seat, and both breathed hard observing one another and speaking with their eyes: *damn glad that's over.*

As they drove through the storm, the car skidded several times, once almost colliding with a utility van. Jewel had to pull over to the side of the road to wait until the rain fizzled then stopped. When she tried to pull back into highway traffic, the right rear wheel became stuck in mud, and the two spent the next half-hour digging the car out.

Finally, in the safety of Jewel's house, they changed into dry clothes while Aunt Vera prepared each a hot cup of spice tea. Naomi stayed the night and agreed with Jewel that they'd wait until morning to tackle the difficult task of finding a spell to free Jesse from the Mirror Dimension, where Corina had magically banished him.

Starting the next morning, and in the days after, the three of them poured over pages of spells, but the one they needed didn't seem to exist. A week went by, and Aunt Vera remembered something; she revealed to Jewel the existence of a notebook taken from Corina centuries ago. Perhaps if she could get her hands on it, she might discover the incantation Corina had used. The notebook was locked in a vault in the sacred library. Only high council members had access to it. And getting it seemed almost as impossible as freeing Jesse.

"Naomi, *you're* a council member. Surely you're allowed in that library?" Jewel asked.

"Of course I am, but only *elite* council members possess the combination to the vault, and I can't ask for it without raising suspicion. I'm already in heart attack mode as it is with that damn grimoire. Don't ask me to stick my neck out any further."

"Come on, Naomi."

"No. You've got to find another way."

"Naomi, it can't hurt to ask if you can look at the thing," Vera said.

"Knowing Corina," Naomi replied. "That notebook is full of dark magic. And they're going to wonder why a Covenant witch would want to see it."

"Oh, she's right, Jewel," Vera said. "I wasn't thinking."

"Well, I've got to get my hands on it," Jewel scolded. "There has to be a magical way of getting into that vault."

"How on earth are you going to use a spell against the council?" Naomi asked. "Their combined magic will sniff out anything you send in an instant."

"Not if I use a dark incantation, it won't," Jewel said with a bit of mischief in her grin.

Vera and Naomi's eyes glittered.

"That's right," Naomi said with a chuckle. "With this book, we *are* stronger than they are, aren't we?"

"So, are you going to stand there looking silly or help me find a spell?" Jewel teased.

Vera, Naomi, and Jewel once again pored over the grimoire until they found something they thought might work. Vera wondered out loud about a Plan B if the notebook didn't pan out.

"The notebook *is* Plan B," Jewel answered. "Plan A was the grimoire. But let's not get ahead of ourselves. Right now, we'll concentrate on getting that notebook—then we'll go from there."

"I'll drink to that," Vera said, tapping her teacup against Jewel and Naomi's cups, which were sitting on the table. She tossed her head back, drained her cup then flashed a smile.

The next night, a mystical, thin, blue fog hovered above the sacred library building. All the security guards surrounding the building suddenly yawned and lay their heads on their steering wheels. Three watchdogs stationed near the wooded area behind the building lay snuggled against each other and began to snore. A dark shadow appeared to walk straight through the library's locked door.

Inside, there was more yawning, and the heads of the night crew lay next to monitors that showcased every area of the building. The dark figure dashed about—up the stairs, down the hall, around corners, and through more locked doors. A female security guard exited the ladies' room, and as soon as she inhaled the blue mist, she tumbled to the floor and curled into a deep sleep. The blue mist thickened, and only the glare from ceiling lights was visible.

After a few minutes, the dark figure seeped out of the sacred room door's keyhole like black smoke. It held something under what seemed like an arm. It dashed around a corner, down a long hall, down the staircase, past the beddy-byes, and out the door, merging with the night.

Shortly afterward, the thick, black notebook materialized on top of the grimoire, which Jewel had placed on a large table in her private library. It was as if someone in Jewel's home had hit the Lottery when they rejoiced after reading through the notes and finding many spells that could free Jesse. It was just a matter of which one would do it more effectively.

"We'll test it on a cat," Jewel said, "and cast each spell to see which works."

But Naomi didn't think it was that simple. Whatever was in there with Jesse probably wouldn't object to freeing a cat, but would, no doubt, put up quite a fray to keep Jesse. Magic would be the only means of getting him out. Corina had no way of knowing that a Covenant witch had access to Dark Magic, so whatever incantation Corina used at that time, she used it knowing no White Magic could undo it. It proved to be one of Corina's many mistakes.

*****

Across town, Ward Burges had just sat down to a plate of spaghetti with meat sauce and a glass of red wine, when a louder-than-usual knock sounded on his door. "Who the hell?" he said, rising from his chair. He strolled to the door and glared through the peephole. "Jewel?" he mumbled. He opened the door to her, Naomi, and Karl standing in the doorway like statues.

"Well, are you going to let us in, or stand there with your thumb up your butt?" Karl asked, brushing by him and not waiting for an answer. Ward stood puzzled until he noticed Jewel carrying a big book under her arm and a small, black one in her hand. He smiled when he recognized the writing on the spine of the big one that read, The Grand Grimoire.

"Hell, it sure took you long enough," Ward said. "It's been several weeks. I thought you said you were done with that thing."

"We dug it up the same night we left here," Naomi said.

"You mean you've had that book all this time and didn't tell me—with poor Jesse trapped in that godawful mirror?"

"We couldn't take a chance on *anyone* knowing," Naomi said.

"Not only that," Karl weighed in, "we had to bury the damn thing then dig it up again after getting tipped off the council was launching a locating spell for forbidden things; we couldn't have it traced to Jewel. It was tiresome, to say the least."

"*You* knew about this?" Ward asked, glaring at Karl.

"Don't, Ward. We made him promise not to tell," Naomi interjected.

"Threatened me was more like it."

"Oh, stop. We weren't really going to banish you into oblivion. We just wanted to keep you quiet," Jewel said. "And as for you, Ward, if you had known, you would have been a real pain in the ass—bugging me every five minutes about how close I was to finding a spell."

"No, I wouldn't have."

"Oh, yes, you would've. But pain in the ass or not, I couldn't live with myself if I didn't help you. We go back too far."

"Yes, we do. I'm not going to lie—I was hurt when you left here that night. But I never doubted your loyalty. You're here now. And that's all that matters."

"I told you, I will always be here for you, Ward."

"As I said, I've never doubted your loyalty, Jewel."

Karl smacked his hands together. "Jewel, I'm touched by you and Uncle Ward's tender moment here, but ...can we get started?"

"You...you mean now?" Ward asked.

"Lead the way," Jewel said, pointing to the basement door. Ward smiled widely and led them down the dark staircase.

They entered the dimly lit basement, where Jewel stood in the middle of the concrete floor like a queen ordering her subjects. They listened and obeyed. Ward uncovered the mirror and dragged the heavy antique to where Jewel pointed, but she changed her mind several times. An exhausted Ward didn't complain. Karl struggled with a large table he'd taken from the attic; Jewel needed one wide enough for the grimoire, candles, and other tools of her craft.

Naomi, the only one capable of traveling in and out of dimensions safely, prepared to go inside the mirror. But according to Ward, that mirror realm could prove more dangerous than any other realm in which she had traveled. He said whenever Jessie appeared banging and pleading for help, he bore fresh bruises and scratches on his face, neck, and hands. Then the mirror would turn smoky, and Jesse would disappear.

After several days of this, Ward couldn't take it, so he'd covered the mirror and never returned to the basement. "Poor Jesse," he said. "What could I do?"

The Mirror Dimension was as old as the Earth itself, a parallel dimension that mirrored Earth's plane of existence, complete with the same surroundings, but different inhabitants. Users of dark magic would gain free access to the mirror. Advanced sorcerers often used it to test dangerous spells without them directly affecting the real Earth.

Humans magically placed there, could not exit its gate without a mystical object worn about the neck, wrist, or finger. Those who channeled extradimensional power from a dark realm were twice as powerful in the mirror. Getting Naomi inside with the green stone ring Jewel had conjured for Jesse to wear was simple enough; getting Jesse out before whatever was attacking him killed him was quite another matter. Since the mirror's dimension of New Berwick was a replica of *Earth's* New Berwick, Naomi felt hopeful she'd have an easy time locating Jesse.

Jewel lit the candles and let her Athame bathe above the flames until currents, like tiny lightning, ran along the blade. She held Naomi's hand and pulled the blade's edge across her palm. While Jewel spoke the incantation, Naomi placed her bloody palm on the mirror, which suddenly vibrated and shot out lights like blinding sun rays. It sucked Naomi into its dimension; then, a thick gray mist appeared, and she vanished.

Inside the dimension, Naomi looked back. She was outside Ward's house, and it was leaning forward. Everything was leaning forward: The buildings, cars, buses, people walking—all appeared to be leaning. Yet no one seemed to be off-balance. The sky looked the same—a flat blue plane as far as the eye could see, but no airplanes, helicopters, or birds, at least, not yet.

Naomi didn't feel like she was leaning, yet the pavement seemed much closer to her body as she walked. Jewel's locating spell tracked Jesse to an old abandoned house near a deeply wooded area. "I need to catch one of those cabs," she mumbled.

"Taxi!" The cab pulled over, and Naomi got in. Then she thought, *"Money—good Goddess, is the money the same here?"* When the driver pulled up to the old mansion, she handed him a bill. He didn't seem to mind the bill, but when he lifted his eyes, he frowned at her.

"Lady, you sure you want to go in there? You want me to wait?"

"No. I'll be fine. Keep the change."

"Okay, Miss," the driver said, widening his eyes. He shook his head and drove off.

Naomi stood in front of the dilapidated house, which looked as if it were about to topple over on her, but of course, it wouldn't; it just leaned like everything else in that dimension. The old house still bore good bones, though its exterior had long fallen away from it. The balcony floor appeared rotted through, and the garage packed several feet high with old boxes. White paint on the front door appeared flaky, and the knob left a smear of rust on her hand when she turned it.

The door whined when Naomi pushed it inward. Inside, an icy chill brushed over her as she made her way through the darkness, the wooden floors squeaking under her weight. Stained and faded walls and furniture littered the room. Hung portraits wore hideous stares and sinister smiles that sent a jolt up her spine. Tattered drapes covered the windows while the cold fireplace overflowed with gray ashes. Next to it, a portable heater sat broken beyond repair. The hallways and staircases were thick with dust. The elevator door was missing, and the bathrooms had become miniature swamps.

"Jess," she called softly each time she poked her head in the doorway of a room. She walked to the staircase, looked up at the dim frame, and dreaded climbing to check the bedrooms. As she did, the eyes on the life-size portraits that lined the staircase lifted with each step her feet touched. Naomi swallowed hard and kept in mind that her magic was stronger in that dimension.

After searching three bedrooms and two baths, she reached the fourth bedroom at the very end of the long hall and immediately seemed taken aback. "Jesse?" she inquired, gazing at the pathetic figure curled in a fetal position on the closet floor. Jesse looked up and whimpered like a little child. He lay naked, covered in deep, bloody scratches on his face, neck, and torso, down to his chained ankles to the bottom of the bedpost. She noticed bald spots as if someone had yanked out his hair. He flinched and moved away from her hand when she reached for him.

Naomi magically removed the chains and then spoke to him softly until she gained his confidence. He allowed her to help him to the bed. She saw that Jesse's mind was practically gone, and the mystery of the scratches and bald spots was solved when she pried open his fist and saw the bloody roots of his hair and skin under his nails. He had lost a considerable amount of weight. The bedroom was in shambles with solid objects thrown about the floor—all near the heavy mahogany, antique mirror, as if he had tried breaking it in the hope of escaping.

Using telepathy, Naomi contacted Jewel, and after a short victory of cheers and high-fives, Jewel prepared the spell in reversal. Naomi gathered up Jesse's tattered clothes, dressed him then prepared him for the rescue.

Jesse stood leaning against Naomi in a daze wearing the greenstone ring on his right index finger. He didn't acknowledge her presence, speak, or appear to know where he was. Jewel spoke the incantation, then placed her cut hand against the mirror so that the blood made a total print of her hand on the dimension side. Naomi placed her hand in the outline of Jewel's handprint and spoke the same spell. Both continued to speak the incantation until the mirror glowed, sparked, disappeared, and materialized again and again.

A sudden wind surrounded the mirror in both dimensions, and it whipped the witches' hair, but there was no wind anywhere else in the basement or the dimensional bedroom. Their chanting became louder and louder as the roar of the wind whipped around them. Ward and Karl stood amazed—their hearts pounding in their chests as that spectacular sight unfolded before their eyes.

Suddenly there came a crashing sound, like a massive kick to a door heard coming from the dimension hallway of the mansion. Jesse jerked, looked over his shoulder and spoke in a frightened child-like voice, "It...its...coming.... gotta get out...its coming...gotta get out."

Naomi couldn't hear Jesse over the wind but felt the vibration of the floor thudding, like the distant thundering feet of a Tyrannosaurus rex. Jesse freaked out, but Naomi continued to chant as the thundering feet got closer. Jessie's body shook violently when a deafening thud cracked the cciling causing pictures to fall from the bedroom walls and the chest of drawers to tumble over onto the floor.

Then a large, smoky outline crashed through the bedroom wall just as Naomi and Jesse were sucked through the mirror, but not before it ripped Jesse's left arm out of its socket as he crossed the dimension. The rip happened so quickly, and the pain so severe that Jesse did not scream but tumbled, passed out, onto the basement floor. Blood gushed from his side like a crimson tide as he lay in the thick, red pool. While the rest grabbed towels to stem the flow, Jewel quickly blurted an incantation that closed the dimension gate so nothing else could get through.

She learned from Naomi what things Jesse had done to himself due to his mental state, and that attempting to leave that dimension had been the only real threat to his life. They managed to control the bleeding and took an unconscious Jesse to a shock trauma unit. He remained in the intensive care unit under a fake name for many weeks. His physical therapy continued for months, and his out-patient psychiatric care lasted for several years.

CHAPTER TWO

Four years later

Fourteen-year-old Russell Sooner lay naked in a fetal position with a temperature of a hundred and five. An elderly woman had discovered him in her backyard after she thought she'd heard a dog howl then noticed a peculiar figure near her greenhouse.

A few miles away, Matthew Porter drove cautiously, hoping to spot the boy after learning he was missing. The phone rang. Matthew clicked the speaker and answered, "Yes, honey."

Kayla Morrison Porter, Matthew's wife of eighteen months, sounded frantic. "Matt," she said, "I know where Rusty is. I just got off the phone with Veronica. She mentioned a call Sheriff Tilbert got from some woman in the 1600 block of Koloric Road about a nude male she found lying in her backyard. The sheriff and several deputies are headed over there now. Honey, you've got to get there first."

"I'm on it. Thanks, precious."

Matthew veered off Kingston Road, pushing 85 mph. He felt he had failed his fellow wolves *and* Russell for not telling the boy he was a werewolf and guiding him into his new existence. But Russell *was* a late bloomer. Werewolves had always experienced their first transformation between the ages of six and thirteen. Perhaps the boy's unique way of becoming a wolf contributed to his late start, Matthew wasn't sure. As he pulled onto Koloric Road, he saw a couple of patrol cars and an elderly woman talking to Sheriff Wayne Tilbert and two of his deputies.

"Dammit," Matthew blurted.

Sheriff Tilbert stood holding a pad and pen. "Now, Mrs. Baines, you reported seeing a naked teenager?"

"Yes, he was right there," she said, pointing to a spot near her greenhouse. "He was as naked as a new-born baby. Why, I've never been so startled in my life. What's wrong with these darn kids anyway?"

"Hm," Tilbert uttered, looking in the direction of the greenhouse. Then turning back to the woman, he said, "Did he look drugged out? Say anything? Threaten you?"

"Drugged? I don't know. He didn't say a word…just lay there. I turned away from the window to grab my phone to call you, and when I turned back, he was gone."

"Just that quick?"

"Just that quick," she replied.

Sheriff Tilbert sighed. "Well, he won't get far without being noticed, that's for sure. If you should see him again or hear anything suspicious, be sure to lock your windows and doors then notify us."

"I will, Sheriff."

Tilbert and his deputies got into their patrol cars and headed off. Matthew had long left the location. His keen wolf ears had picked up everything. He pictured Russell wandering around naked in a haze of confusion. *But where the devil 'is' he?* he thought. His phone rang.

"Honey," Kayla spoke hastily. "Were you in time? Did you get him?"

"No."

"No?"

"Tilbert beat me to it. But the kid had left."

"Great Zeus, Matt, this is dangerous. He could hurt someone."

"I know. If he does, it's all my fault."

"Now stop it. No one has ever become a werewolf the way he had. Who could know *when* he'd turn?"

"Thanks, honey."

"Think you'll find him before dark?"

"I hope so, baby."

Matthew drove for hours, often retracing his path. He spent a further few hours searching on foot—walking along the outskirts of a wooded area near the Koloric River.

Back at the sheriff station, Tilbert scratched his freshly grown short beard. He sat at his desk. Bob Wilson sat across from him, waiting for him to speak.

"What's up with that *damn* kid?" Tilbert finally said. "At ten-years-old, he disappeared then showed up weeks later with amnesia, now four years later, here we are again."

"How do we even know it's him, Wayne?" Bob asked. "Maybe it's some other kid."

"What other kid? No one else has reported a missing teenager fitting his description."

"True," Bob said, settling back in his chair.

Meanwhile, Matthew had grown tired of walking. He stopped and rested on a stool-sized tree stump. With his back to the forest, he allowed his wolf-vision to take in all of the blue beauty of the Koloric River when suddenly he heard a deep growl from the dark, dense growth behind him. He turned slowly to find a snowy, white wolf with greenish-gray eyes staring at him. Its lips were curled, and saliva streamed from sparkling white fangs.

Before Matthew could gather himself, the wolf leaped, knocking the wind out of him as he hit the ground. The crushing weight of the animal took Matthew's breath away—

yet he used every bit of strength he could muster to keep the needlepoint fangs from ripping out his throat. The two tumbled and scrambled until a small dustbowl developed around them. The wolf's growl vibrated loudly against Matthew's ear and its saliva half-covered his face.

Then a stabbing bite to the side of Matthew's head triggered his own transformation. He quickly shapeshifted and lifted the white wolf that was now half Matthew's size and tossed it through the air as he would a stuffed toy. Landing hard on its back, the white wolf appeared stunned, then scrambling to its feet, turned, and bolted.

Matthew took off after it on all fours. He caught up to the pale one, leaped, and pinned it to the ground. The white wolf, too stunned to struggle, stared at Matthew; it watched as Matthew released him, stood on hind legs, and transformed back—his naked body with ragged clothing hanging from his neck, wrist, and legs. Then slowly, Russell transformed but stayed curled up on the ground.

"Wha...what's happening to me?" Russell asked in a small, trembling voice.

"Come on," Matthew said, sympathetically holding out his hand. "Don't be frightened. I'll explain everything."

Russell took his hand and rose. The two wolves walked to Matthew's car, where he kept extra clothes and shoes in the trunk. He handed Russell a pair of jeans, a sweatshirt, and a pair of Nike shoes. The teenager dressed in total silence while keeping an eye on Matthew. Sitting next to Matthew in the front passenger seat of the car, Russell experienced a startling Deja vu, though nothing else made much sense. Matthew started the car and grabbed his phone.

"Kayla."

"Yes!"

"I have him."

"Thank the Goddess," she said.

Matthew drove around for nearly an hour and explained to Russell how, when, and why the boy had become a werewolf and many other details. Suddenly, Matthew slowed the car after seeing Russell scramble out of his seatbelt and opened the door.

"Rusty, wait," Matthew said, watching the boy hop out. "I told you, you have to control your anger. Now look at you— you're growing fur. Get back here. Rusty!" The boy scurried across the highway—horns blowing, motorist cursing— vehicles barely missing him and quickstepped toward a wooded area. Matthew pulled the car to the shoulder of the road. He jumped out and tried to overtake the teenager.

Russell stopped and sharply turned to Matthew. "You had no right!" Russell shouted. "It was my life, and you had no right! You and your damn witch-aunt..." The youngster's eyes burned with fury; he looked hideous standing there, a young boy with white, pointed, furry ears on top of a crop of dark brown hair—at the end of one arm, a hand, at the end of the other, a paw.

"Now, Rusty, calm down."

"No!"

"Get in the car before someone sees you."

"No!"

"All right, I'll kick your little stubborn ass and throw you in. How 'bout that?!"

Russell shifted from one foot to the other. He studied Matthew's face then looked at the ground. He gazed up all around him, appearing not to know what to do. Finally, he yelled, "Damn you! Take me home!" He stormed to the car and climbed in. Matthew followed and started the car.

"I'm not taking you home yet. It's too dangerous. There's more you need to know."

"I would never hurt my parents or my friends if that's what you think!" Russell snapped.

"You don't know *what* you'll do. And it's your enemies I'm worried about." Matthew pulled into the highway traffic. "You have to understand," Matthew continued, "not even our worst enemies deserve our kind of deadly force. You must control your anger. And fasten your seat belt."

"Why? What does a werewolf need with a seat belt? You said only silver can hurt us."

"How about putting it on, so I don't have to hear that damn warning sound?"

Once the boy fastened his seatbelt, Matthew took off toward the mountains. It was a long trip, and Matthew wanted more time with his werewolf apprentice.

Russell asked multiple questions, and Matthew answered them all. His curiosity exhausted, Russell sat back in his seat and peered out the side window. "Why are you pulling in here?" he asked, gazing back at Matthew.

"Just get out. I want to show you something." He and the boy left the car and walked along a sidewalk to a little building on a slight hill. The sign on the building had strange symbols and Greek markings.

"Is this your place?"

"No. You'll see."

Matthew knocked on the door. A boy about Russell's age opened it and grinned. "Hey, Matt," the boy greeted moving aside, so the two could walk into the room.

"Hey, Dell, this is Rusty Sooner. Rusty —Dell Slogan."

"Hi, Rusty."

"Hi," Russell said awkwardly.

"Your dad around?" Matthew asked, looking about.

"Yeah, he's out back cleaning the pool."

Matthew turned to Russell. "Relax. I'll be right back," he said quickly leaving the room.

"Want a beer?" Dell blurted.

"I'm...fourteen," Russell said, raising his eyebrows.

"So am I."

"But Matthew said alcohol could trigger me. Make me dangerous."

"Not when you get used to it. Besides, Matt doesn't have to know everything."

"But he threatened to kick my ass if I don't do what he says."

"Aw, Matt talks that way to all of us. He's really pretty cool. Come on, meet the gang."

"The gang?"

"Sure....this way." Dell led Russell to a back room where about fifteen young wolves between the ages of thirteen and sixteen sat around several tables gaming. Some rocked to earphones, some watched sports TV on a huge wall monitor, while two sixteen-year-olds shot a game of pool. Another group sat texting their girlfriends. Dell's father operated the small center for the young wolves to keep them occupied and out of mischief.

Closing the door behind him, Dell said rather loudly, "Hey, I want you guys to meet Rusty Sooner." The abrupt quietness of the room made Russell swallow a lump in his throat. He flashed a half-smile, but as his eyes scanned the room, their faces remained stoic. The young wolves didn't consider Russell one of them. His strange journey to werewolfdom made him an outsider. They were grateful that his sacrifice had given them more control over their lives, and that it meant they were not subject to turning at every full moon.

But it was Jewel Porter who was their hero, not him. Russell sensed they didn't like him making him want to run from the room. Dell stood behind Russell and gave his young wolf-brothers an evil look. Finally, one young wolf put down his pool stick and walked over to Russell and held out his hand, "Hi, I'm Randy." Russell shook his hand and nodded. Then one-by-one, they all came and coldly introduced themselves.

When the teens went back to their games and texting, Russell appeared forgotten, as if he'd never been introduced at all; he stood there awkwardly. Dell didn't quite know what to do next. He had promised Matthew he'd help with welcoming Russell into the group, but it didn't seem to be working. Dell clenched his teeth at Randy, which prompted him to blurt, "*So*, Rusty...you play pool?"

"Not very well. Look, it was nice meeting you guys." Russell turned and hurried from the room. Dell followed, and once in the other room offered him a Coke.

"Forget the Coke. What about that beer?"

"But I thought you said, Matt..."

"Screw Matt and make that beer to go. You can tell him I'll be outside."

After Dell brought him the beer, Russell walked out and leaned on the car. A few minutes later, Matthew came storming out of the building. "Are you drinking, you little bastard? Thought I told you..." Matthew stopped short and ducked as an empty beer bottle sailed past his ear. "Boy, what is wrong with you?"

"Why did you bring me here?"

"Why...what happened?" Matthew asked, glancing back at the building.

You screwed up my life, that's what happened, you and your damn witch-aunt. I'm not like anybody anymore...not my family...not my friends. And those things in there who are just like me," he said, pointing to the building, "want nothing to do with me! I hate this shit, and I hate you!"

Dell stood in the doorway. He and all the teens had stopped everything and heard Russell's rant. Their face showed sadness for the boy, yet none disputed his claims. Matthew tried to console Russell as the boy stood with his backside against the front passenger door—his arms folded, looking at the ground. Fur covered parts of his body, and his face had slightly elongated.

"They're not shunning you, Rusty. They just view you as being uncomfortably different, that's all. They'll come around. Besides, _I_ like you. I have a thirteen-year-old brother who's dying to meet you. You'll have two families—yours and mine. I'm always going to be here for you. I promise."

"Yeah," Russell said with a bit of a cry in his voice, "until I do something wrong, and then you'll kick my ass."

"No," Matthew said, inching up to him. "That was just talk. I would never hurt you. Not ever." He got close to the boy and gently grabbed his shoulders. Russell fell against his chest and sobbed.

CHAPTER THREE

Matthew held the sobbing teenager, speaking softly, and gently patting his back. A troublesome mood swept over the boy like a dark cloud.

"No!" Russell blurted as if suddenly coming to his senses. He pushed away from Matthew, turned, walked past the car, and onto the shoulder of the road.

"Now what?" Matthew snapped. "Where are you going?"

A pouting Russell kept walking. Matthew caught up to him and grabbed his arm. Russell jerked away and turned to him. "*You* did this. You're the one who bit me, then pretended to be a Good Samaritan who just happened to find me wounded."

"Rusty, I didn't want to, I swear. I fought against it. I did."

"Bullshit! You didn't have to do it."

"If I hadn't, one of the other wolves would have."

"But why me?" Russell asked, hitting his chest with both fists. "Of all the damn kids in this town, whose idea was it to pick me?"

Matthew dropped his head and looked up at Russell. The guilt in his eyes flashed under his dark lashes, and his lips parted slightly.

Russell's eyes widened. "Oh my god! You son of a bitch!" He turned sharply and stormed off down the shoulder of the road. Matthew stood speechless, awkwardly shifting his weight as he watched the boy walk farther away.

*****

An hour later, Matthew pulled into his driveway and parked next to Kayla's red Chevy Malibu. He held the steering wheel, rested his head upon it, and let out a hard sigh. Kayla, having heard him drive up, watched him from the window. He got out of the car and slowly made his way to the front door.

Before he could touch the knob, Kayla swung the door open. He stopped and bent so she could kiss him, and then he strolled into the family room. Matthew sat wide-legged with his head down, pulling on his chin. Kayla stood before him.

"Well?" she said sarcastically.

"Well, what?"

"What do you mean...'well what'? Where's Rusty? Did you get through to him? Take him home? Is he all right?"

"No. He's angry...wants nothing to do with me, and no, I don't know if he's all right."

"What do you mean you don't know?"

"I don't know. Okay?"

"You're telling me a fourteen-year-old, pissed-off, immature werewolf is prowling around out there somewhere, and you just left him?"

"Kayla, honey, I've had a really rough day. I don't need this shit right now," he said rising. "I'm going to take a shower." Matthew stomped up the stairs.

"Matt, I'm sorry...I just..." She cut off after noticing a slightly-raised wound on the left side of his head. She watched as he turned the corner at the top of the stairs.

*****

Russell wandered around for a while then headed for home. He walked into his house and got halfway up the stairs when his mom, hearing the door slam, came running from the kitchen.

"Rusty, oh honey, thank God! Where were you?"

"Mom, I'm okay." He walked back down the stairs, and she grabbed and hugged him tightly.

Mr. Sooner heard Russell's voice. "Sheriff, I think I hear Rusty now." He clicked off his phone and rushed out of the room. "Son, where have you been? Me and your mother were worried sick. What happened? Did someone try to grab you again? Are you hurt?" He placed his hand on Russell's shoulder and examined him.

"Mom, Dad, I apologize. But I'm fine."

"Fine? Where were you? Why didn't you call? Son, you can't do that. It was like four years ago all over again and..."

"No, Dad, stop. This is not four years ago...even though I don't remember. Look," Russell said, thinking up a quick lie, "I...I was jogging, stumbled ...hit my head and...."

"Hit your head? Oh, honey!" she said, reaching up and touching his head. "Maybe we should get him to the hospital." Mr. Sooner turned to rush off.

"No! Dad, don't. It's no big deal. I'm fine, really."

Mr. Sooner turned back. "Are you sure, son?"

"Have you eaten?" Mrs. Sooner asked.

"I'm not hungry. I told you I'm fine. I'm going up to take a shower," Russell said, turning and walking up the stairs. "I'll eat later, okay?"

"Sure, honey," Mrs. Sooner said, her eyes lifting with every step he took.

"All right, son," Mr. Sooner said, "if you insist."

Russell walked down the hall and into his room, where he peeled off the clothes Matthew had given him and stepped into the shower. Standing under the flow of the water, Russell prayed it would wash his ugly truth away. He had once been a boy, normal and happy; now, a hideous thing spawned from the lips of a witch.

*****

Feeling bad about her behavior, Kayla walked into the bedroom to find Matthew lying on his stomach upon the bed, naked and scented from his shower. She eased beside him and gently touched the raised bruise on his head. "Did Rusty do that?"

"It's nothing," he said solemnly.

"I'm so sorry I lit into you. I should have asked you how things went before jumping on you like I did." She leaned, kissed his bruise, and attempted to rise from the bed. He gently grabbed her hand.

"Don't go," he said. She eased back down. "I just need more time with the kid, that's all." He sat up, still grasping her hand. "You can't blame the boy. I mean, look what we did to this kid."

She cupped his hand, and her eyes stared tenderly into his.

"You should have seen his face when I explained what had happened to him and why. We were selfish to use this poor kid like that. He had no say—it's like we just ripped his whole life from him. I know he'll never forgive the part I played. But I can't let him run around with all that hate inside. Honey, I don't know what to do."

"Why, Matthew Porter, I have never *seen* you act so defeated. And you're *not* defeated." She cupped his face in her hands. "Honey, keep trying. I know you'll get through to him. Remember how I acted when I found out about you?" I despised you at first. Then I remembered how sweet and kind and loving you were, and I came around. Remember?"

Matthew grinned and nodded. "But Rusty's not you. It's not the same. He's not a girl."

"No," she said, rather coyly. "But, you could introduce him to a few." She smiled.

"You mean..."

"Exactly," she answered.

"Are you sure? I don't know if that's the answer. I thought introducing him to wolves his own age would help him, but it didn't."

She leaned into him, displaying all of her sex appeal. "But sweetheart," she said, "you're underestimating the power of the female."

Matthew, finally realizing her plan, smiled widely. "Oh, no, I'm not," he said, pushing her back onto the bed. He climbed on top of her. "I'll get right on it. As soon as I get off you," he teased. He kissed and fondled her while she giggled.

*****

Russell, fresh from his shower, lay back upon his bed, looking up at the dull sword hanging above it. His thoughts echoed with Matthew's voice and the way he had become a werewolf. This New Birth had changed him completely, and there seemed nothing he could do about it. No one could know—not his parents, and certainly not best friends Mark and John. He wanted nothing to do with Matthew or the wolves but feared he couldn't stay a lone-wolf forever.

Downstairs, Tray and Caroline Sooner sat trying to understand what was happening with their boy. Was it like before when he went missing? Caroline was beside herself. Tray wanted to talk to Sheriff Tilbert about putting an ankle bracelet on Russell.

"Oh, no! *That's* what you do to criminals. Our boy is *not* a criminal!" Caroline snapped.

"Honey, we simply have to do *something*, or one day he'll just wander off, and we'll never see him again."

"God, no. He wouldn't do that...would he? Tray, I'm so worried."

Tray pulled her to him and wrapped his arms around her. The two sat hugged together, while upstairs Russell struggled to find a way to cope with his strange new existence.

CHAPTER FOUR

After several months, including that of his fifteenth birthday on October 25th, Russell still struggled with the terms of his new life. Although he loathed Matthew, taking his advice on managing his anger gave Russell full control over his shapeshifting. His parents proved to be a real pain, though checking on his every move—lecturing him on what time to be home—calling him, what seemed like every few minutes when he wasn't.

At school, he found it wasn't as hard to focus on his studies anymore. And hanging out with Mark and John eventually brought Russell a sense of normality though he hated not sharing his secret with them. One particular factor disturbed Russell greatly; if he wanted to hide his secret, keeping his unusual strength under wraps, especially when playing sports, was essential. Once, he'd broken a couple of ribs of a boy he'd tackled during football practice and jumped nearly seven feet off the ground while catching a high fly ball during a championship game.

Russell managed to play it off by ignoring the surprised gasps and praises but was forced to endure whispers and stares in the locker room and school hallways. Mark and John wouldn't let him forget it until Russell one day snapped at their relentless astonishment for his unusual performance so viciously they never mentioned it again. *Thank God his mom and dad missed that particular away game,* Russell thought.

Earlier in the week, Russell had searched online for others like himself. He encountered people from all over the world who claimed to be werewolves but turned out to be a bunch of phonies, like the ones that set up a Go Fund Me for a cure. Some phonies Russell didn't mind, like the girl werewolves looking for romance. *Now she's hot,* he thought smiling at a cute brunette on the screen. *What if I showed up...a real werewolf? That'd make her day.* Russell chuckled at the thought. *But what would happen to...*

"Rusty...honey, come and eat," his mom yelled.

Russell ended his search and watched his screen flip to Marvel Comic wallpaper. He locked his bedroom door then descended the stairs.

*****

Resting quietly at home, Jewel and River enjoyed a glass of Mourvèdre. After five years of recuperating, Jesse Carter left Illinois for North Carolina and moved in with relatives. A year earlier, he had turned himself in to police custody. He knew the court would never believe the truth about his doppelganger attacking Karl and some witch trapping him in a floor-length mirror, so he lawyered up and claimed mental illness and amnesia.

Karl had refused to press charges against his friend and testified on Jesse's behalf. Jesse was found guilty because of temporary insanity and sentenced to undergo treatment. With Jesse cleared and safely with relatives, it seemed the only thing left on Jewel and River's To-Do-List was the task of convincing the young wolves to welcome Russell into the pack.

"You know, that kid could screw everything up for us," River told Jewel.

"I know. Corina is gone, but she sure left a mess for us to clean up."

"You're right. Corina *is* responsible for this. It was her curse that made us kidnap the boy in the first place."

"Not to mention all the deaths she caused," Jewel replied.

"Thank the Goddess she's gone," River said. "Now, all you've got to do is get rid of that damn grimoire."

"Don't worry. Naomi magically banished it and won't tell me where it is."

"Think we'll ever need it again?" River asked.

"No. I've studied enough of that grimoire to protect my family and friends for a lifetime."

The Porter household had recently shrunk to just Jewel, River, the two younger girls, Aunt Vera, and five-year-old Merchant. Chelsea, who earned an MBA from Emory University's Goizueta Business School in Georgia, accepted a position in Atlanta and decided to live there.

Abby, who attended the same university, moved in with Chelsea. Dria and Becca did well in high school and were very popular with the boys—something River dreaded. Jewel poured more Mourvèdre. She and River sat sipping their wine while Aunt Vera home-schooled little Merchant in the next room.

*****

Russell felt around for his buzzing phone among the textbooks and papers spread out over his bed. He grabbed it and folded his lips at Dell Slogan's name. "Dell," Russell said unenthusiastically.

"Rusty, finally."

"What do you want, Dell? I'm kinda' busy right now."

"Dude, come on. How long are you going to keep avoiding me? I'm not the one you should be pissed at. It's not fair."

Russell shoved the books and papers aside and rolled onto his back. "Look, I know you're trying to help, all right? But stop pushing...either they accept me, or they don't."

"I'm not pushing. And my call has nothing to do with them."

"Then, what?"

"I just thought you'd be interested in a double-date."

Russell hopped up and sat on the edge of his bed. "Really...with you?"

Dell, hearing the change in Russell's tone, winked at Matthew, who sat across from Dell's dad. "Aw...yeah. You interested?"

"You mean...girls?"

"Unless you like boys," Dell chuckled.

Russell scooted around on the edge of the bed. "Aw...these girls...do... they know about... I mean that we're...?"

"Werewolves?" Dell said with a slight smile. "Of course. So, are you interested?"

"I might be," Russell said, trying not to sound anxious.

"Dude, either you are, or you're not."

"Ok... when?"

"I'll pick you up at six."

"Fine...see you then."

Russell stood and ran his fingers through his hair. He lay the phone aside and turned about like he was confused. Should he lay out his clothes first, or take a shower and then decide on something to wear? He wasn't certain. Finally, he elected to shower first.

With a slight grin, Russell felt giddy. The thought of girls knowing what he was and not caring stimulated him beyond his composure. And Dell...he *had* been relentless in reaching out to him. As the water rolled down his muscular body and the hot steam engulfed him, it suddenly came to him that Matthew could be behind it. But Russell was finally in a calmer state of mind after finding out what he was, and he didn't want to spoil it by giving a damn.

After dressing, he seemed pleased at what he saw in his mirror and slipped his arms through the sleeves of his sport coat. He moved his head from side-to-side further checking his appearance. Satisfied, Russell turned from the mirror and crossed the room to his bedroom door.

"Rusty," his mom called to him as he got midway down the stairs. "You going out?" she asked, her eyes dancing over his attire. Mr. Sooner peered over his glasses but didn't speak.

"I thought I'd hang out a while with some friends."

"Well, honey, I wished you had told me; I would have had dinner a little earlier."

"Mom, it's okay. I didn't even know until a little while ago. I'm sure we'll stop and get something on the way. And stop making me eat all the time," he teased, kissing her on the cheek. "You're going to make me as fat as Dad," he said, walking away grinning.

"I *heard* that!" Mr. Sooner said loudly from the family room.

"Need your dad to drop you somewhere, sweetie?"

"No, I'm good. Dell is picking me up. I'll just wait on the porch," Russell said, stepping outside.

Mrs. Sooner stood frowning then said loudly, "Don't stay out too late and call if you do." Russell mumbled something affirmative before closing the door.

*****

A light blue Ford Fusion rolled up at 6:05 p.m., but Dell wasn't driving. He sat hugged up in the back seat with a luscious blonde. Dell beamed a hardy smile watching Russell's reaction to the blonde as he climbed in the front seat. But Russell's reaction to the backseat beauty was nothing compared to the glow on his face when he saw who waited for *him* behind the steering wheel.

"Hi," Russell managed to say. Dell introduced the girls, Massie, Dell's date, and Heather, the Ava Gardner look-a-like who flashed her green eyes from under her long dark lashes and greeted Russell in a soft, sultry voice. Russell momentarily forgot to breathe, then forced himself not to look uncool as he smiled and greeted her a second time.

Russell couldn't figure out where a fifteen-year-old like Dell could have found such beauties. One thing for damn sure, these weren't teenage girls, and if they were, they were probably overly-matured eighteen or nineteen-year-olds.

"Where would you like to go, handsome?" Heather asked Russell sweetly. Russell turned his head slightly toward the back seat.

"Hey, Casanova, can you come up for air and tell Heather where we're going?"

Dell eased out of a passionate kiss. "It's a…a place called Eagle's Nest right off of Moon Hawk Drive. Me and some friends checked it out a couple of weeks ago. It's really cool. You and Heather will love it."

Dell immediately went back to kissing and feeling up Massie while Heather entered the name and location into the GPS.

Eagle's Nest lived up to its name. It was a popular hangout for mostly New Berwick's rich college kids, but a few other young adults attended as well. It sat high on a hill well-guarded by a private security force. Wherever those rich college kids were, there was bound to be some illegal activities.

From the hill, the guards could see everyone coming and going, especially the law. Its name signified safety like an eagle's nest far up from the danger of land animals or other birds that could harm its chicks. Eagle's Nest also had a secret tunnel for quick get-a-ways.

The guards were there to prevent kidnappings since the law had long given up on raiding the place. Their parents had smart, well-paid lawyers whose clients could afford any fines. Also, their parents were active board members and supported numerous charities and organizations, like the policemen's fund in many parts of the region; so, giving those kids any jail time was out of the question.

Heather parked the car, and Russell ran around to the driver's side and opened her door. He slipped a nervous hand into hers, and the foursome walked up to the dark brown cabin with push-out wooden windows and wooden French doors. Massie knuckled a secret knock. The door opened, and a short, stocky guard with a grim face recognized her and moved aside.

Russell figured the only reason the guard examined him so closely was that he was the newest patron. Marijuana hit their noses the minute they walked in. Russell was taken aback by how well lit the place was given its illegal activities. The floors, walls, and ceiling were polished wood. It had round tables for two, four, and eight people and a long mirrored bar with high-back red leather bar stools.

It also housed an area for large parties, two rooms for smaller parties, and three private dining suites. Massie seemed to be someone of importance because, without a word, the minute the waiter spotted her, he hurried over and escorted them to a private dining suite. She tipped him a large bill. He smiled and nodded before walking off.

The private suite was beautiful, with an over-stuffed, multi-colored sofa, love-seat, and chair. A heavy, shiny mahogany cocktail table and two end-tables with green globe lamps and beige lamp shades complimented the room.

Russell admired the colorful throw pillows scattered around one wall. A round mahogany dinner table centered with gold candlesticks and green candles surrounded by green velvet chairs sat in the far corner under a sparkling chandelier.

Heather adored the cold fireplace, and Dell stroked a life-size black sculpture of a nude couple that stood near one of the bedroom doors. The room emitted the scent of fresh flowers, and on a nearby waist-high table sat hors d'oeuvres and champagne. They sampled the hors d'oeuvres until a waiter brought Massie's order of burgers and fries. Russell had never eaten gourmet burgers and fries before.

"This sure tasted good," he told Dell.

An hour later, the waiter came back for the dishes. "Merci, mademoiselle," he said to Massie after palming an enormous tip.

Soft music played in the background. Heather and Massie sat chatting while Dell stood eagerly pouring champagne in four glasses.

"Dell," Russell whispered, "these girls are a lot older than fifteen or sixteen."

"Yeah, so?" he answered, pouring.

"Well, how old are they?"

"Twenty, twenty-one...I don't know. Dude, relax."

"But, they could get into trouble."

"Who's going to tell?" Dell asked irritably. Dell brushed by him with the tray of drinks and held it before the girls. "One for you, one for you," then he looked over his shoulder at Russell and frowned. Russell hurried over, grabbed a glass, and sat next to Heather.

Dell, grinning from ear-to-ear, made up a silly toast, and the clinking of glasses filled the air. Russell was a little skeptical of the champagne. Matthew had warned that until he could control himself, alcohol could trigger his transformation. But observing how well Dell handled *his* drinking made Russell feel more confident.

Heather crossed her shapely legs that showcased her six-inch black pumps. She held her drink to her face, her long, dark red nails stood out against the sparkle of the glass, her jaded eyes practically hypnotizing Russell as they peered over the narrow rim. Dell and Massie kissed and fondled each other like Heather and Russell weren't even there; then they rose and hurried off to one of the bedrooms—kissing and giggling as they closed the door.

"So, I hear you're very athletic," Heather said, bringing the glass down from her plump red lips.

Russell felt silly discussing high school stuff with such a mature beauty. "Yeah, I...ah ...play baseball and football. It keeps me in shape." Feeling awkward, he changed the subject by asking if she wanted more champagne. He rose but quickly sat again when she shook her head menacingly and with a sultry stare, slowly circled the rim of her glass with her index finger.

She dipped her finger into the champagne, leaned in and smeared it over his lips, then leaned in further and sucked it off. Russell immediately felt an erection growing and tightening his pants. Everything she did after that seemed in slow motion. They kissed passionately, and then Heather set her glass aside, rose, and took his hand. She led him to the other bedroom. A lump rose in Russell's throat. He knew what was coming, but given his inexperience, could he handle such a beautiful task?

Heather closed the bedroom door and led him to the queen-size bed. She turned, took off her jewelry, and kicked off her shoes. *Even her feet are gorgeous*, he thought. Russell felt stupid just standing there. Should he take off *his* clothes or hers?" Russell managed to slip one arm halfway out of his jacket when she stopped him. "No. I'll do that."

She glided to him—her curvy hips moving like the smooth slither of a snake and finished sliding the jacket down his arms, all the while staring into his blue eyes. Russell thought he would faint. She loosened his tie, unbuttoned his shirt, and tossed them on a chair. When she got to his pants, his face flushed with embarrassment when she had trouble unzipping it due to his enormous erection. Finally, he stood naked—his erection as straight as the barrel of a gun.

She kept her eyes on his exquisite pole—backed away and unzipped her black, mini dress, letting it spill to the floor and pool around her feet. She unfastened her bra, held her arm out, and let it slip from her fingers. Then slowly, she rolled her panties over her plump hips, past her shapely thighs and legs, down to her perfect ankles, and stepped out of them like a seasoned stripper.

Russell stood dumbfounded as she climbed onto the bed. She rested back against a pillow—her white skin silky and smooth like that of a baby. Feeling a little less nervous, he climbed on top of her and lowered himself—slipping his throbbing penis inside her. Her hot flesh surrounded him and gripped him tightly. Russell feared he'd prematurely burst, and so he froze. She pulled his face down to hers and whispered an incantation in his ear that would keep him from ejaculating.

"YOU'RE A WITCH!"

"Shhh," she said. "I'll release you when I'm satisfied."

Locked in a passionate embrace, Russell began to mimic the man he'd watched on a porn flick one afternoon when he and some schoolmates had played hooky at an older teen's house. After a few moments, he realized he must have had a pretty good memory because Heather began to moan as he bit and nibbled her neck and ear while gently thrusting against her soft flesh. His body moved like rushing waves, and every stroke brought Heather's sultry voice up a notch as her body jerked and trembled beneath him.

He gently grabbed her hair and pried her mouth open with his tongue, then sucked her lips into his mouth. The sweet warmth of her lips made the room spin. She slipped her tongue between his lips, and he eagerly sucked it. She forced him over onto his back while still gripping him inside of her—their bodies now as one moved like the flapping wings of a bird in slow motion, soaring higher and higher. His desire to burst forth and the thrusting of her hips had him at her mercy.

But she held him, ignoring his quiet pleading. Then her voice hit a pitch that rose throughout the private dining suite. Finally, she released him, and he blurted words that made absolutely no sense as his body quivered, and he flooded inside of her." She fell to one side, both panting and smiling at each other, and they lay silently for a while. After catching her breath, Heather lit a joint, inhaled, and passed it to Russell. The two talked and giggled well into the night.

*****

It was a little past 3:00 a.m. when the Ford Fusion rolled up to Russell's house. Dell and Massie had been dropped off first. Heather wrapped her arms around Russell's neck and melted into his kiss. They parted, and Russell got out of the car. He stuck his head in the window, and they exchanged sweet goodnights. She pulled off, and Russell bounced up the sidewalk, up the porch steps and into the house. Mr. and Mrs. Sooner, clad in their bedclothes, walked briskly toward him and began to scold.

"Look, cut it out," Russell snapped, "I'm not a baby. See I'm fine. I'm going to bed now. I suggest you do the same.

Love you." He kissed Mrs. Sooner on the cheek and bounced up the stairs. After hearing his bedroom door close, Tray and Caroline looked puzzlingly at one another then with their mouths still partly opened, turned their heads slowly, and stared up at the empty staircase.

CHAPTER FIVE

November came with much fanfare as usual. Russell's mom and dad planned a family reunion Thanksgiving dinner with relatives traveling from different parts of the East Coast to attend. Little Rusty, as they called him, endured numerous "Come and give your 'whatever' a kiss," "I remember when you were just yea high to a duck," and "He's a Sooner man all right—look at those muscles."

After greeting several cousins he'd never met, Russell took them to his bedroom to play Fortnite, while his dad showed off his last year's high school football and baseball trophies. Soon the adult talk drifted to politics, and the women, having none of it, scolded the men causing them to take their disagreements to the clubroom on the lower level.

Later in the evening, while yet light, Russell left his cousins absorbed in the online games and slipped out to meet Heather at her apartment. Instead of staying in, they walked along the Norwick Forest then climbed a steep hill.

When they reached the top, they found a large crate someone left there, and they sat on it looking over the lake.

"Why on earth would someone leave this here?" she scolded.

"Perhaps they knew a strikingly handsome dude, and his beautiful lady would come here," he said, branding a boyish grin.

She leaned to him, and he wrapped his arm around her. They kissed for a moment and watched the pillars of gray move across the sky. The air cooled, and clouds formed. A distant deep hum grew closer. Heather pointed up, and a helicopter zoomed right over them as tiny raindrops, like transparent strings of beads, fell upon their heads.

"We better be heading back," he said, taking her by the arm. They returned to Heather's apartment, where he spent a good portion of the night.

From that night came many more nights, and their relationship blossomed well into May. They became inseparable, and Russell knew he deeply loved her. She often pretended to seduce him like she had the first time they'd met, but his once shyness and immaturity, though she seemed to relish it, proved no comparison to his well-developed body and what he could do with it when pleasing her.

One night as they cuddled beneath the covers, she rested her head upon his chest. "I love you," she said. "You complete me the way no one ever has."

"I wanted to say that to you many times, but my tongue seemed to get twisted when I tried," he said, gently fingering a lock of her hair. "I guess because I've never said it before, except to my parents."

She rolled onto her side to face him. "I know it's not a long time, but after months of being together, I haven't sensed any lapse in our affection. Have you?"

"No," he chuckled, "whatever that means," he teased, referring to her articulate way of phrasing it.

"Oh, you know what I'm saying," she said, playfully punching his arm. "I feel so lucky to have you in my life. I sometimes wonder where I'd be right now if I hadn't been your date that night."

"Worse than that—imagine if Dell had given me Massie and kept you for himself."

"Oh, dear goddess," she blurted, trying to keep her composure. "I adore Dell, but um...no...he's a little too overheated for me. I like my studs at room temperature," she said seductively. I like driving up their temperatures myself."

"Oh, you do...do you? Well, you've only got one stud. Get that straight. And come here."

She slid into his arms, and they made a second go of it as if sex an hour ago didn't count, as if they hadn't seen each other in weeks; or he'd been deployed to the Middle East and returned hungry to hold her at last. Finally, he and Heather fell apart. Exhausted, they lay panting. She lit a joint and shared it before they snuggled and fell asleep.

*****

He and Heather's love played like a well-tuned orchestra—full of soul and music. Then the last week of July, she upended his world when she abruptly left New Berwick without a word. For several months, he wrestled with her sudden departure, and it puzzled and hurt him deeply because he thought their relationship was solid. *Had he unknowingly done something wrong?* He thought. Text and phone messages went unanswered. It was as if she'd fallen off the edge of the earth.

Meanwhile, after much debate—the junior wolves reluctantly accepted Russell into the pack. Russell felt it was too little too late since the woman he loved wouldn't be joining him to celebrate that diabolical victory.

One morning, while Mr. and Mrs. Sooner were out, Russell lay across his bed listening to music. It was another October—another birthday. He was sixteen, but Russell didn't feel much like celebrating; the memory of Heather's green eyes and plump red lips filled his mind. A knock came at the front door. Russell hurried down the stairs and opened it. "Oh, Christ, what do *you* want?"

"Now, is that any way to greet your mentor?" Matthew teased, knowing Russell couldn't stand the sight of him. "Aren't you going to ask me in?"

"You know I'm not."

"Okay. So how are you?" Matthew asked.

"I'm just fine." There was a pause with the two staring at one another. "Waiting for me to ask how *you* are?" Russell smirked.

"Let me guess...you don't give a shit."

"Exactly."

"You know... you've become quite an asshole lately?" Matthew said provokingly. "What happened to you? You use to be so cute...so fuzzy and warm. That's why I chose you."

"I know what you're doing. You want to see if I'll get all angry and start prematurely transforming. Well, I won't."

"I'm impressed," Matthew said.

"Are you through?"

"No...I mean it. I didn't choose you carelessly. I know you're angry with me. But there's not a kid in this town or maybe even the world that could have adjusted to this life as well and as quickly as you have. Rusty that speaks volumes about your character."

"*Now*, are you through?"

Matthew's mouth tightened, and he leaned into the doorway. "Damn you...you little punk," he yelled. "The junior pack is right; you're not like us. We have a heart. And we know how to get over shit and move on."

"Well, I'm sorry. It seems my heart and everything else good about me got sucked out right along with my freaking mortal soul, you bastard. Don't come here again."

He slammed the door in Matthew's face while Matthew's muffled voice yelled, "You're going to need me, you stupid moron. You don't know everything."

"Don't hold your breath!" Russell yelled. Right then, someone knocked on the back door while the phone rang. Russell saw Mark through the window, and Dell's image appeared on the phone. "Damn, why am I so popular today?"

He grabbed the phone, "Dell, hold on, someone's at the door." He opened the door. "Hey, Mark," he said with the phone to his ear. Mark walked in and settled in a chair. "Dell...can I call you back?" He turned to Mark. "What's up, buddy?"

"Oh, nothing just wanted to know if you wanted to hang out. I thought maybe we'd take in a movie."

"That's right...a new Jurassic Park movie is out. What is this...Jurassic Park eight?" he joked.

"I've lost count, but it can't be too many for me."

"Yeah, me either," Russell said. "But can I get a rain check? I'm going to be kind of tied up all week."

Mark eyed him disappointingly. "I haven't even said when we were going. Seems to me you've made up your mind no matter *what* day I chose."

"Why would you say that? Where is this coming from?"

"You've changed."

"No, I haven't."

"We haven't hung out in months. Every time me or John call, you got something else lined up for that day," Mark said. "No matter what day it is, you've got something else lined up."

"Dude," Russell chuckled. "You sound like a jealous girlfriend. I haven't been avoiding you. I swear. I would never let anything or anybody come between us. You and John are like my brothers. You know that."

"Really? What about that guy Dell? You seem to be spending an awful lot of time with him."

Russell chuckled. "Come on, you're creeping me out. Are you really arguing with me for spending more time with another guy?"

"Don't give me that shit. You know very well what I mean."

"Mark, I hope you're not trying to make me choose. You and John are irreplaceable, and Dell is a really cool guy."

"Fine. Bring him around. The *four* of us can hang out."

Russell knew that could never happen. Dell could be pretty reckless at times. He wasn't accustomed to being around ordinary people—maybe bumping into them on occasions, like on the street, at the mall, or brushing by them to make his way to an Eagle's Nest's private dining suite; but to make it a point to hang out with them was out of the question.

Russell struggled to find the words Mark would accept without suspicion. The words finally formed, but Russell had taken too long to answer, and before he could expel them, Mark snapped, "Forget it!" He hopped up from the chair and started for the door.

"Mark, wait! We can go whenever you say. How about this weekend...okay, bro?"

Mark turned slowly while still holding onto the knob. "What about Dell?"

"I'll ask him to join us," Russell lied. "I'm sure he'll be cool with it."

"Okay," Mark said, appearing pleased. "See you then." Mark closed the door behind him, and Russell hurried to call Dell, hoping he could get out of whatever Dell had planned. But Dell was pissed. "I made reservations, you prick."

"I told you I would get back with you," Russell said.

"Fine!" Dell snapped, ending the call.

*****

The weekend came. Russell had to admit it felt good sitting in the theatre with Mark, John, and a couple of hundred normal kids his age. He hadn't transformed in months, which helped father his temporary illusion of being his old self. He sat like the rest of them—throwing back popcorn, sipping soda, and peering up at computer-generated dinosaurs gobbling up several dozen Hollywood extras in their path.

After leaving the theatre and feeling exuberantly frightened, John suggested they walk to the Science Center right down the street and visit the dinosaur section. Still high from the movie, each took selfies hanging from the dinosaur's mouths and a few kissing T-Rex on the lips until a guard caught them touching the exhibits and chased them out.

Back on the street, they acted like twelve-year-olds, giggling and high fiving each other so much, so they blindly walked right into the path of an on-coming car. The blast of the horn startled them. The threesome hustled back between parked cars—all the while laughing.

The incident should have been over. Instead, slamming on brakes had caused the plastic top on a cold drink to fly off and the contents to spill all over the middle-age driver. He jumped out of the car, cursing and pointing to the mess on his white shirt, tie, and pants. The boys, one-by-one, said they were sorry, but the guy wasn't having it. He spat foul language at them and threatened to bash in their faces.

"Look, asshole," Mark snapped, "We said we were sorry."

"Yeah, on your way, Gramps," John said.

"Who the hell you calling Gramps, you little pissy bastard?" the man bellowed swiftly walking towards John with clenched fists. "I should go get your mother; tap that ass...as payment for my suit."

John's face reddened, and he jerked forward to attack the man, but Russell quickly stepped in front of John.

"Why don't you just get in your car and go, mister?" Russell said calmly.

"And which one of you retards gonna make me? Maybe I should follow *you* home, get *your* mama to pay for my damn clothes," he said to Russell pumping his hips and grabbing his crotch.

Russell grabbed the man so fast, the guy stumbled sideways and tripped over his own foot. He practically lifted the man off the concrete and shoved him into the driver's seat of his car. Russell moved his face in so close he smelled the loudmouth's liquored breath.

The guy gasped when Russell's eyes turned yellow, and he drew back his lips, revealing long needle-point fangs. Then Russell spoke in a deep growl. "Leave, or I'll rip your goddamn throat out."

The man nodded nervously. Russell stepped back, and the man yanked the door shut with a bang and locked it. He fumbled turning the key—the wheels squealed as the car recklessly tore away, shot through a red light, and dashed around a corner. Mark and John cackled loudly.

"What the hell got him so scared?" John asked.

"Yeah," Mark asked. "What did you say?"

"I turned into a werewolf and told him I'd rip his goddamn throat out if he didn't shove off."

"No, for real Rusty," Mark chuckled. "What got him so scared?"

Russell continued making up lies that kept them laughing. And he, Mark and John horsed around just like old times. Russell felt genuinely happy again, and from then on, he vowed to himself, that he would never again neglect to spend time with his two best friends.

CHAPTER SIX

It was the junior wolves' annual gala at Perry Hall in Kingstone Valley, east of New Berwick. Outside, the young wolves and their dates worked the recently laid red carpet like it was Oscar night. The multi-color rocks on either side of the pathway, stone-carved statues, year-round plants, and a breathtaking view of the Koloric River presented the perfect location to host the years' junior fest.

Massie, gorgeous in a sequined burgundy dress, played hostess to the lively assembly, while waiters quick-stepped elegantly among the young guests. That was Russell's first engagement as a member of the wolf pack. He hesitated to attend at first—but once Dell made up his mind about anything, he was hard to resist.

Russell stood scanning the room in a formal, black suit, white shirt, a royal blue vest, and a matching blue tie.

"Rusty," Massie called to him. "You look fabulous," she said, eying him up and down.

"Thank you. And I see *you're* lovely as ever."

"Aren't you sweet," she said, looking about. "Dell is around here somewhere." Then she spotted him. "Oh, there he is." She turned back to Russell. "Now, Rusty don't just sit alone, mingle."

"Yeah, yeah," he said. She smiled at him and hurried off.

Russell grabbed a drink off the tray of a passing waiter and stood with the glass in one hand and the other hand in his pocket. He scanned the room, and his eyes fell on several small groups that were laughing and talking among themselves. Russell felt awkward because he knew most of the pack felt pressured into accepting him.

Mingle? Russell thought. *Oh, no. I'm not making a fool of myself twice.* He decided to do exactly what Massie told him not to do. He found a cozy seat away from everyone and sat taking in the beautiful sights and sounds of the evening. After sitting awhile—still nursing his first drink, Russell noticed Dell rushing over to him.

"Rusty, what on Earth are you doing sitting here all by yourself?"

"Look, don't start. I came all right?"

"At least go and get some food."

"I will. Now go on back to your guest. I'm just fi..." Russell's next word stuck in his throat. *No, it couldn't be,* he thought. But it was. In the doorway, Heather stood breathtaking in a sleeveless, pale-green, cocktail dress. She wore an emerald necklace and matching dangling earrings that glittered against the dark canvas of her long, auburn hair that lay curled on her white shoulders. The hem of the dress hugged her thighs and showed off her long elegant legs right down to her green satin stilettoes. Clutching her silver purse, she spotted Russell and Dell and made her way over to them.

"Heather," Dell said, kissing her cheek, "this *is* a surprise."

But Russell wasn't buying it. He had gotten to know Dell's expressions well enough, and he knew a phony look of surprise when he saw one. Russell stepped to Heather and kissed her cheek, then offered to get her a drink.

"No," Dell said. "You two sit there, I'll send a waiter over." And he rushed off. Heather sat, and Russell eased beside her.

"Dell didn't tell me you were going to be here," Russell said.

"He wanted it to be a surprise."

"I figured as much," Russell replied.

"You know Dell. Always dramatic," Heather said, smiling.

The waiter came with a tray of champagne drinks. Russell placed his empty glass on the tray and took two and handed one to Heather. He watched her bring the glass up to her dark red lips—her green eyes flashing at him from under her dark lashes.

He wanted to ask her how long she would be staying this time, but decided against it. A part of him was glad to see her, and another part regretted it. He couldn't be sure if he could stand her leaving again. But then, out of the blue, she said, "I guess you wondered why I left so abruptly."

"Actually, it never crossed my mind," he said sarcastically.

"I had to rush off. A family matter."

"Hope it wasn't *too* serious."

"Oh, *it* was. But nothing we couldn't handle," she said deviously.

A chill rushed through him when she had said that. Russell loved that spark of danger and mystery about her—it had heightened their sexual passion. But that rush proved something far different; he had never felt such coldness from her before.

"Let's dance," she said, taking his glass and placing it beside hers near the leg of the chair. She grabbed his hand and pulled him onto the floor. Russell held her close as the slow music seemed to hover above them. She placed her forehead against his cheek; they danced like they were the only two people in the room. And, if the snooty junior wolf-pack pretended not to notice Russell before, they certainly couldn't ignore that notorious outsider's appeal to the most beautiful creature they had ever seen.

*****

As late evening eased into midnight, for once, Russell felt good about letting Dell talk him into something he hadn't wanted to do. Being with Heather again made his werewolf existence all the more bearable. They left the hall in separate cars. Walking Heather to her hotel room door, he watched her dig in her purse for her key card. He politely took the card and swiped it. He stood back and watched her push open the door.

"Will I see you again?" he asked, rather sadly handing her back the key card.

Heather eased it from his fingers. Her emerald eyes darkened when she flashed them up at him. And with a sexy pout that no male creature could resist, she gently pulled him into the room by his lapel—all the while backing toward the bedroom. She let go of his lapel and kicked off her shoes, followed by other pieces of clothing. Russell smiled and followed suit stepping out of shoes, socks, tie, and shirt.

By the time they reached the bed, they were beautifully naked and heavily panting. Russell knew her desires and satisfied each with gentle thrusting, passionate kissing, and stings of erotic biting—lapping up tiny streams of blood from her long, elegant neck. Their loud moans echoed throughout the night.

The following morning, Russell woke to the sound of a vacuum cleaner in the next room. Heather had forgotten to place the Do Not Disturb sign. He yawned then turned to see her still sleeping. God, she was beautiful; not even with her hair all disarray and smeared make-up could keep her from being a vision of loveliness.

"Oh...sorry," the housekeeper said after bursting in. She quickly pulled the door closed. *You would think their trail of clothes leading to the bedroom would have given the idiot a hint*, he thought.

When the housekeeper left, Russell called for breakfast. He and Heather sat in the dining area with small bottles of energy drinks waiting for their food. When the food arrived, they ate and chatted. Russell was beside himself. All morning he tried to steer the conversation back to the night she slipped away without a word—only to have her quickly change the subject. Now, the utensils hitting the dishes moved in and out of total silence.

"I can't stand it," Russell blurted. "Are you staying or running off like last time?"

"How many times do I have to tell you no?"

"As many times as I need convincing."

"Great stars, I'm not running off and leaving you."

"How can I be sure?"

"I told you, I only went off that way because of an urgent family matter that needed my immediate attention."

"You could have called, texted...left a note."

"It was a pressing matter," she gritted out.

"Too pressing to return my messages? What sort of matter?" Why so much secrecy? I thought we knew each other well enough not to *keep* secrets. You know everything about *me*."

Heather became highly irritated as she set her glass aside. "If you must know...it was a matter of an old enemy who needed to be taught a lesson."

"What sort of lesson?"

"Oh, goddamnit!" She jumped up and walked swiftly toward the bedroom. "This is why I left without telling anybody. People ask too many damn questions." She slammed the bedroom door and locked it.

"People! I'm not people, damn it. Is that what I am to you...people?" Russell banged his empty glass down on the table. Then after seething for a moment and fearing she'd leave again because of their spat, he attempted twice to console her, but she refused to unlock the door.

"Heather, how many times do I have to say I'm sorry? Will you let me in?" He pleaded for nearly an hour but heard only silence from beyond the door. He sat on the sofa with his feet crossed on the glass cocktail table.

After two hours, Russell heard a click. He turned and saw Heather ease through the door wearing a black, see-through negligee. The pale white of her voluptuous curvy body broke through the sheer fabric and beckoned him. He smiled widely—walked to her and cupped her face in his hands.

"Heather...I promise never to pressure you again into revealing anything you don't want to reveal... Just don't ever run off like that. Okay, baby?"

She nodded coyly. "I didn't mean to be cross with you. I just..."

He interrupted her by placing his finger over her lips. "You don't have to explain a thing," he said. He kissed her passionately then scooped her up in his arms. She pushed the door shut with her barefoot, and he carried her to the bed.

CHAPTER SEVEN

Bob Wilson removed the sterile gloves, mask, and gown. He washed his hands, wiped them on a sterile towel then tossed what was soiled into a biohazardous container. Sheriff Tilbert seated patiently in Bob's office, scanned the walls covered with science degrees and medical certificates.

"Wayne," Bob called out, smiling as he stood in the office doorway.

Wayne's eyes followed Bob over to the big leather chair behind his desk. Bob's smile faded when he noticed his friend's troublesome stare. "What's going on?" Bob asked.

"I've been thinking about something, Bob...it's really just a theory. I wanted to see what you thought."

"Okay, shoot." Bob eased down in his chair.

"I can't stop thinking about that Sooner kid...past and present. You know... the way he disappeared six years ago and then turned up with no memory. Then a couple of years ago... disappearing around the same time that naked kid showed up in Mrs. Baines's backyard; and his parents giving some cockamamie story about where he was during that time."

"You think there's a connection?"

"I'm beginning to. But it's crazy."

Bob scooted around in his chair as if such an action might stir up some part of his brain that could give Sheriff Tilbert the answer he needed. "Why not question him?" Bob asked. "Your instinct may not be as crazy as you think."

"That's not going to do any good. He doesn't remember anything."

"Maybe he didn't when he was ten. An incident like that can be very traumatic for a kid."

"You think he might remember something now?"

"It's possible. Want to know the crazy thing *I* think?" Bob smirked.

Tilbert looked at him puzzlingly.

"I think the kid's a werewolf," Bob blurted.

Sheriff Tilbert stared at Bob momentarily then said softly, "Bingo. That's exactly what I think."

Tilbert leaned forward and appeared relieved now that Bob shared his bazaar awakening. Tilbert grew excited as he spoke further. "Something happened to Russell Sooner that night, Bob. He didn't just forget...something or someone made him forget. What if what happened to this kid years ago... is back to bite us *all* in the ass?"

"Damn," Bob said looking like he felt a chill. "I always thought it kind of strange that Matthew Porter was the one who spotted Sooner wandering on the side of the road that day. No other driver ever reported seeing a boy in a baseball uniform walking alone."

"Wandering around on the side of the road my ass. I never believed him, but I couldn't prove he was lying. And the fact that those wolves got away with butchering the Winters girl *and* my deputies haunts me to this day."

"Then don't let them get away with it," Bob urged. "Use the weapons the Shadow Hunters sent you."

"And do what?" Tilbert said, leaning back. "So... we go after the Wolves, then that stirs up the witches to protect them...then arcane energy from the witches' magic hits the air and alerts the Shadow Hunters. You remember what the hunters said? If they come back here, they swore to destroy everything not human. Bob, New Berwick wouldn't be the same after such an attack."

"Okay, so you *don't* go after the wolves. What are you going to do about the kid?"

"Damned if I know."

"Well, what about hauling his ass in for a little old fashion interrogation," Bob said smacking the palm of his hand with his fist.

"No, that's call child abuse. And anything less would make him suspicious...too prepared. If I decide to go with interrogation, I'd rather catch him off guard."

"You mean show up at his house unexpectedly. Hm...I don't know, Wayne. That'll mean dealing with his parents."

"Shit! His parents... I forgot about them." Then Tilbert quickly glanced at his watch and mumbled, "7:15."

"Why does that matter?" Bob asked.

"Have your secretary call the Sooner house. If my guess is right, the kid's alone."

"How do you know?"

"I believe there's another Fund Raising event at Valley West tonight. His parents always attend."

Bob did what he asked and after a minute or so, his secretary informed him that the Sooner's son said his parents were out. "Okay, Columbo," Bob said, "care to tell me what you're up too?"

"We might can use this kid."

"For what?"

"Tell you on the way," Tilbert said rising from his chair.

*****

Around 7:45 p.m., Russell sat curled up on the sofa with a bag of chips and a soda grinning and talking quietly to Heather on the phone. Before the Sooners left, Mr. Sooner had given Russell the big lecture about what not to do while they were gone.

"Someone's at the door, hold on." Russell hustled to the door and pulled it open. "Sheriff Tilbert?" Russell asked frowning. "My mom and dad are not here. Can I help you with something?" Bob stood beside Sheriff Tilbert and eyed Russell curiously.

"Actually, it's *you* we're here to see. Got a minute?"

"Ah..." he stammered, "what's it about?"

"May we come in?" Tilbert asked.

Russell slowly, reluctantly moved aside and Bob and Tilbert walked past him and stood.

"I have someone on the phone," he said hurrying towards the sofa. "Please," Russell said looking over his shoulder, "have a seat."

Bob and Tilbert followed him to the family room and took a seat on the sofa.

"Heather, sorry, someone's here to see me." Then lowering his voice, he said. "I'll get rid of them as soon as I can and get back with you."

"Okay, sweetie," she said.

Russell turned and took a seat opposite Bob and Tilbert. "So, what do you want to see me about?"

Bob chewed on his bottom lip and stared at Russell—waiting for Tilbert to speak.

"Rusty, I know we've been over this a dozen times, but I need to know if you have recovered any of your memory about that night you disappeared following the baseball game."

"Are you kidding me? That was ages ago."

"More like six years ago," Tilbert said.

"I don't remember anything. I told you guys that a thousand times."

"Are you saying that in all this time, nothing has come to mind about that night? *Nothing?*"

"No, nothing. And you're bringing this up again.... *because?*" Russell asked sarcastically.

Bob leaned forward. "Because we were hoping maybe some tiny thing had jarred your memory," Bob said.

"No, it hasn't," Russell said irritated. "Is that all you stopped here for...because I was on an important phone call before you guys came." Russell stood. "I have nothing to add to what you guys already know. So, if you would excuse me..."

Sheriff Tilbert slowly looked up at Russell and stared into his eyes without blinking. "Rusty, where were you two years ago when your father frantically called me? And don't tell me you don't remember. We're talking about just *two* years ago."

"What is this?" Russell snapped.

"Where...were you?" Tilbert repeated.

"What difference does it make? I...I might have been hanging out with some friends."

"Might have been?"

"All right, I was."

"Was what?"

"Hanging out with some friends."

"What friends?"

"Just friends."

"Human friends?"

"What the hell does that mean?"

Sheriff Tilbert stared at Russell. "A naked teenager fitting your description was discovered by Mrs. Baines and called into my office. He was lying in her backyard. The woman was scared out of her wits." Tilbert hesitated. "Was that you?"

Russell's heart pounded and his mouth swung open. He looked from Bob to Tilbert and just stood there. "No. No! Of course, it wasn't me. What makes you think I'd run around naked?" he snapped.

Bob frowned. "Son cut the crap. You're a werewolf."

Sheriff Tilbert and Bob watched the smirk leave Russell's mouth and panic covered his face like a murky shadow.

Russell stepped back and eased down on the overstuffed sofa. He couldn't close his mouth as he searched both their eyes. "I...I don't believe you guys...You're, you're crazy," he said with a nervous chuckle.

"Son," Tilbert said. "We don't think you're a bad person. Just a victim of a terrible incident."

"Yeah," Bob interjected. "We know there's a connection to what happened to you six years ago and you showing up naked in Mrs. Baines' backyard."

"What part of that wasn't me don't you get?" Russell said his voice rising.

Tilbert looked at Russell sympathetically. "Son, don't," Tilbert said shaking his head. "We're on *your* side. We want to help you. Nobody blames you for what happened. You were just a kid. Just don't insult our intelligence. That naked kid was you. You're a wolf. Admit it?"

"I'm not admitting shit. *You're* nuts. Everybody knows there's no such thing as werewolves. Now you get the hell out of my house." Russell shot up from his seat.

Sheriff Tilbert and Bob exchanged looks then Tilbert looked up at Russell. "Son, you're living in the only place in the whole, wide, world that *does* know werewolves exist. So sit down and don't give us any more of your shit."

Russell flopped down and hesitated before he spoke. "But that doesn't mean *I'm* one. Even if I were, you couldn't help me. No one could."

"You're right...we lied," Bob said.

"Then why are you here? If you're not going to lock me up or anything..." Russell suddenly broke off. "Oh wait! You're here to tell my parents."

"Your parents don't know you're a wolf?" Bob blurted.

"Of course they don't know...I...I mean...there's...there's nothing *to* know."

"They could be in danger. You could hurt them." Tilbert warned.

Russell freaked. "You go to hell. I would never hurt my parents! You...you're trying to confuse me. And don't you dare confront my parents with this lie. My parents go into a panic mode every time I leave the house because of that night six years ago. I won't have you shocking them with this werewolf talk!"

"All right, son, calm down," Tilbert said. "We'll keep this conversation between us. But don't think for a split second that we don't know what you really are. It's too many strange things about you that keep adding up."

Bob rose and took a step forward. "There *is* one way to settle this. Make all of our so-call false allegations go away," Bob said waving his hand. "If you're not a wolf, then you won't mind giving me a little blood sample. It will only take a minute."

Bob and Tilbert watched Russell's eyes dart back and forth. Bob pulled from his inside coat pocket a small clear plastic bag with syringe, needle, phlebotomy package and rubber gloves.

A lump rose in Russell's throat. "I need you to go." He swept his arm out towards the front door.

Sheriff Tilbert rose. "Son," Tilbert said. "You've just confirmed everything we needed to know. You have a nice day."

"Wait!" Russell said. "What happens now?"

"Well, I'm glad you asked, son. As I stated before, we'll keep this conversation between the three of us. Your parents and no one else needs to know. And in the meantime, being the decent kid that you are, well, maybe you could keep an eye on the other werewolves and from time to time alert us to any witch activities you deem suspicious and report that information directly to me."

Russell laughed. "A rat...you want me to be a rat." He chuckled again. "You guys beat everything, you know that? You'll tell the whole world I'm a werewolf unless I rat on some people. Even if I was what you say...I'm no rat. And besides, that's blackmail. And you're supposed to be a lawman."

Tilbert and Bob glanced at one another.

"I won't do it," Russell said. "I don't even like Matthew Porter and I wouldn't rat on *him* if I suspected something."

"This is not blackmail, Rusty," Sheriff Tilbert said. "We just thought you might want to get back at them for what they did to you...that you might want to help keep them in check so they don't do this to anyone else, like your loved ones or even your friends."

"Help you...keep them in check?" Russell suddenly felt a connection to the wolves though they treated him like crap. He couldn't admit to being one but felt a need to protect them. He told them that since they believed in this myth about werewolves that they might be interested in a little story circulating; it was about a witch discovering a moon cure that kept wolves from shapeshifting during a full moon and going on a killing spree the way they had for centuries. Russell further said wolves could still turn at will, but that the cure had rendered them relatively harmless.

"Werewolves? Harmless? And you believe that?" Bob asked rather smugly.

"I said it was just a story."

Tilbert shifted his weight. "Thanks for that piece of information. And don't worry, we'll keep your secret."

What secret? I told you I'm not what you say!" Russell blasted him.

"Sure, son. Sure," Tilbert said amusing him. "If you should ever need us, I mean it, for anything, we're here for you."

Russell looked away from them. "Please go. My parents will be home soon."

Sheriff Tilbert and Bob thanked Russell for his time and left. As soon as the patrol car pulled away, Russell phoned Heather.

"Great Goddess, Rusty," Heather said. "This is not good. You have to tell the wolves."

"I can't. They don't trust me as it is. If they knew I was asked to rat, the first time something got out, they'd blame me. Heather, you can't tell anybody."

"I won't, sweetie. But this is definitely not good."

"Rusty, you home?" Mrs. Sooner called out.

"Damn gotta go, my parents are back. I'll see you later on tonight...love you."

"Love you too."

"Rusty, why didn't you answer your mother?" Mr. Sooner scolded entering the room.

"Dad, I was on the phone. So, did you guys have a great time?"

"It was fine, honey," Mrs. Sooner said. "Raised a lot of money. Did you eat?"

"Mom, stop it."

"I just asked. Don't have to take my head off."

Russell kissed her on the cheek and brushed passed her towards the stairs. "I'm going up to shower. I'll be hanging out for a little while. Don't wait up," he said trotting up the stairs.

"Our boy is growing up," Mrs. Sooner said sadly, still looking up the staircase.

"Honey, I'm afraid there's nothing we can do about that."

They walked into the family room and Mr. Sooner half-filled two glasses with Bourbon and water. They relaxed on the sofa with their drinks.

"I wonder what Sheriff Tilbert was doing in the neighborhood this time of the evening?" Mr. Sooner said. "He seldom comes himself unless it's something serious."

"And he had such a worrisome look on his face as he rode passed us and waved," Mrs. Sooner added. "Hope everything's okay in the neighborhood," she said. She took a sip of her drink.

Upstairs, Russell stood in the shower and second-guessed himself about telling Sheriff Tilbert and Bob Wilson so many details about the wolves, even though he had said that it was only a story. Was he really trying to protect the wolves or himself?

"God, I hope I did the right thing," Russell said letting the water wash over his head.

CHAPTER EIGHT

Russell drove his new, bronze Chevy Malibu, a birthday present from his parents, past Norwick Forest on his way to Dell's house. He had talked of wanting a Toyota Camry, words that went right over the head of his conservative father who strongly believed 'Buy American' wasn't just a tagline. He pulled up behind a black Buick LaCrosse, one of several cars parked in the Slogan's driveway, and walked around the house to where Dell was backstroking in the family pool.

"Hey, Rusty," Dell said flipping over on his belly and swimming toward the edge of the pool. "How about grabbing two of those beers," he said climbing out and scooping up a towel. Russell pulled the beers from a cooler and handed one to Dell who flopped on a lounge chair. Russell slid into a chair next to him and took a gulp of his beer.

"So, birthday boy, what's up?" Dell grinned turning the bottle up to his mouth.

"Nothing much...just thought I'd take my new wheels for a little spin." Russell nodded toward the house. "Sounds like quite *a la fiesta* your parents are having," Russell said showing off his Spanish lessons.

"Yeah, another one of their boring cocktail parties, Dell said. "I saw you pull in past the gate just before I slipped out. Nice ride. But what happened to that grand Toyota you always talked about?"

"Toyota is a synonym to un-American in my house. Got tired of defending my patriotism to my dad every time I mentioned that damn car."

Dell chuckled. "Dude, I feel you. You see what's parked in our driveway. Besides, get a job...buy your own car. Right?"

"Sure," Russell said solemnly looking off.

"Okay, Rusty. I know that tone...talk to me."

Russell drained his bottle of beer and hesitated for a moment, then blurted, "What do you know about Heather?"

"Heather? Dude, you're the one sleeping with her. Why you asking *me*?"

"You've known her longer."

"No, I haven't. I met her the same night you did."

"But, I thought you guys were friends."

"No. She and Massie met at the hair salon. We needed a date for you that night and Massie asked *her*."

"You never told me that."

"I didn't think it was necessary. Why all the concern now...you guys having problems?"

"Kind of," Russell said. "After she came back from wherever the hell she popped off to, things went great for a while; then I questioned her about why she'd left like that without a word. She kept explaining, but her explanation just wasn't cutting it, so I kept pushing. Bad idea... she snapped...we argued and almost broke up. I don't think I ever saw her that pissed before."

"Damn, that's messed up," Dell said. He drained his beer then strolled to the cooler and pulled out two more. He handed one to Russell and eased down in the chair. "All that just because you asked her about skipping out without telling you?" Dell asked frowning.

Russell, with a worried look, didn't answer, but asked, "And you're sure Massie doesn't know anything more about her?"

"I can ask her."

"No," Russell said anxiously. "I don't want Heather to know I'm prying. I promised her I wouldn't."

"I'll tell Massie not to mention you."

Russell grinned. "How many female friends do you know can keep a secret from each other?"

"I see your point," Dell chuckled. "So, what are you going to do?"

"I don't know. I'm really into her, and I know she feels the same way. But ever since she came back, I've sensed this weird aura about her. First, I thought it was all in my head. But I'm not so sure anymore."

"What kind of weird aura?"

"Not an aura exactly...it feels more like a cold breeze hugging me... like it's alive. I...I don't know how else to explain it. But, Dell it's...it's really creepy."

"Damn, that *is* creepy. Did you mention it to Heather?"

"Yeah, a couple of times. But she just dismisses it like I'm nuts or something. I don't know."

"Wow, Dude, sounds like some serious shit."

Dell hesitated for a moment then leaned forward. "Rusty, now, I know what I'm about to say won't sit right with you, but just hear me out...okay? I know you've got a thing against the witches, but Heather and Massie are witches and you trust *them*. Look if..."

"Heather and Massie are different," Russell interrupted. "They're not like the others."

"All right, you say they're different, I get that. But, Rusty, what I'm trying to say is...if anybody can give a reason for this mysterious feeling...this aura as you call it, it's another witch. They know this stuff."

Dell could see signs of fury sparking in Russell's eyes. He saw Russell's eagerness to jump in and rip his advice to shreds. "Rusty, calm down. I understand. But I'm telling you...you need to consult a witch about this. I can't help you. I wish I could."

Russell turned his face away slowly and blew his breath out hard. Dell watched the rapid way Russell's chest moved in and out then after a few moments of what seemed like soul-searching on Russell's part, Dell noticed a spread of calmness on his face.

"Maybe you're right," Russell said. "Maybe another witch would know what it is." The sudden switch pleasantly shocked Dell. Then Russell frowned and jerked his face toward him, "But not that bitch, Jewel...anybody but her."

"Oh... hell no! I agree," Dell said eagerly. He seemed glad that Russell was willing to reach out to a witch for help. And he knew just the one, Melvita Burkison.

Melvita was a bit of an outcast herself and well understood the arrogance of rejection. The Burkisons were a family of rebellious witches that had been forced out of the Covenant along with Corina two centuries ago. A battle had ensued over who would head the new coven—Corina won and the Burkisons for the second time found themselves rejected and banished.

Crawling back to the Covenant witches proved embarrassing; the Burkisons begged to be taken back into the sacred circle—expressing their utmost remorse; stating that Corina had led them astray, but the Covenant witches stood their ground and refused to accept them back.

Forced to wander without magic, food or shelter, the Burkisons, with what little they could steal, divided the spoils among the children. At ten-years-old, Melvita's great, great grandmother had watched as her adult family members slowly succumbed to sickness and starvation.

After learning how Corina and her followers had regained *their* magic, the younger Burkisons used that knowledge to regain theirs as well. But the magic came too late to save their parents. In 1900, a new and more powerful generation of Burkisons settled in a region of Illinois called Rigousville. Although burning with anger against the Covenant witches, they managed to live a very quiet and non-revengeful life, though the bitterness of what had happened to their ancestors lingered well into the 21st century.

*****

Russell agreed to accept Melvita's help, and Dell made many calls within several days to her before he and Russell set out for Rigousville. Rounding the curve near Bone Creek, Dell drove cautiously in this unfamiliar region, while Russell's sudden cold feet put Dell's nerves on edge.

Russell still couldn't shake the hatred he harbored for Matthew and his witch-aunt Jewel. Because of what Jewel had done to Russell, outside of Heather and Massie, he remained wary of witches.

"Rusty," Dell snapped. "We're almost there. For the last time...I'm not turning back. I didn't force you to do this, you know."

"What else do you know about this witch? I mean, how can we be sure I can trust her?" Russell asked.

"I told you, she's not *down* with the Covenant witches. That should be proof enough."

"I...I don't know. I just feel queer about this."

"Rusty, come on. Relax."

Russell took a deep breath and nervously fingered with the seatbelt strapped across his chest. Looking out the window, he saw many fine homes with green lawns and luxury cars parked in two-car drive-ways. Towering several hundred feet behind the houses, stood a dark green forest alive with different species of birds flying over it.

The car swerved and Dell pulled into a driveway. The two climbed out of the car and walked slowly up to a two-story, brick detached house with a dark green door and a gold knocker shaped in the face of a lioness. They ascended white, stone steps and Dell lifted the lioness head and struck it against the metal three times.

Moments later, the door opened. An attractive, blue-eyed blonde, about thirty, stood eying Russell up and down, her hair curled upon her shoulders. She stood elegantly in a collarless, white, long-sleeve blouse and loose-fitting black slacks that tightened at the ankles complete with black, three-inch pumps.

"Come in," she said stepping aside. Dell and Russell walked into the foyer and stood.

"Melvita," Dell said. "This is Russell Sooner. As I said over the phone, he really needs your assistance."

Melvita closed the door and turned back to them. "Russell," she greeted nodding.

"Melvita," Russell greeted back with a quick nod.

"Follow me," she said leading them through the foyer, down a narrow hall, and into a medium-sized, dimly lit room with dark, hardwood floors and tan scatter rugs throughout. A small home wine bar and cabinet with three brown leather bar stools sat middle-way against one wall of the room. A long, dark brown, leather sofa, loveseat, and chair stood out against the multi-colored green and beige drapes that graced a large picture window.

The sparkling, glass end-tables held round, forest-green, globe lamps with mint-green lamp shades. A long, glass, cocktail table with a gold plated box, cigarette lighter, and two large ornaments sat in front of the sofa. The leather chair sat two feet from the cold brick fireplace; above it, a life-size, early 19th-century, wedding portrait. The bride bore a strong likeness to Melvita and the dark-haired groom stood tall and handsome.

"Please sit," she said. "I'd offer you a drink, but given your ages…" her voice trailed off.

Dell wanted a beer but thought she was much too refined to have brew in the house. "No thank you," Dell said. "We're fine."

Melvita sat across from them and crossed her legs.

"Mind if I smoke?" She looked from Russell to Dell.

"No!" they both said in unplanned unison.

Melvita held her hand up and near her face then spread her index and middle finger. The gold box top flipped back and a thin, brown cigarette floated toward her and settled between her fingers. The top came down and the tip of the cigarette suddenly glowed red. Melvita took a draw and blew a stream of smoke into the air above her head.

"Far, freaking, out," Dell said in a harsh whisper. She used no spell book, no incantation. Dell never saw a witch do magic without saying or doing *something. Not even a wave of her hand,* Dell thought. He looked at Russell and saw that a 'stay or run' uncertainty had crept upon his face. Dell reached and touched Russell's hand. Russell turned to him and Dell shook his head and exaggerated a frown meaning: I know what you're thinking about doing and…don't. Then Russell settled back.

Melvita, thinking she had done something wrong, leaned forward. "Dear Goddess, I didn't mean to frighten you," she said to Russell.

"No. No. It's okay," Dell assured. "We're fine, right, Rusty?"

Russell swallowed a lump. "Ah...yeah...sure."

"So, Rusty. I can call you Rusty?"

"Of course."

"So," she began looking directly at Russell. "You welcome my assistance?"

Russell took a deep breath and leaned forward.

"Exactly why do you need my help?"

Russell explained to Melvita about Heather leaving town abruptly one night without telling him, and then after she'd returned—those odd feelings he got from being near her

"One night, after we fell asleep. I was holding Heather in my arms," he said. "Suddenly, I felt the mattress slowly sink right in back of me, then a cold breath on my neck. I swear to God, I wasn't dreaming. Anyway, something held me and I couldn't move. I tried to yell, but I couldn't speak. Finally, after what seemed like forever, I broke free. I scrambled out of that bed so violently I knocked poor Heather to the floor. She, in her anger when I told her what had happened, yelled every curse word in the book at me then stormed off to sleep on the sofa. I understood her fury...this had happened a few times before."

Russell, looking agitated, ran his hand through his hair. Dell appeared calm having heard the story before. "I can't take it, Melvita," Russell exclaimed. "Am I crazy?"

Melvita didn't answer. She wanted another cigarette, but this time she manually pulled it from the gold box and lit it with a lighter. "Hm..." she uttered. "Sounds like your girlfriend is into some really dark stuff. It sounds familiar, though. If it's what I think it is...and I do. We actually call it the sewer hole of magic."

"Sewer hole?" Russell repeated.

"Yes, we call it that because once a witch conjures that deeply into Dark Magic, like a sewer, it's hard to get rid of the scent or in your case, the aura."

"What do you mean?" Russell asked frantically. "Is she in danger?"

"Not danger," Melvita answered. "It's like a pesticide you spray just once. You can empty the can and throw it away. But the invisible residue leaves a killing action behind that last for weeks. That's the way some Dark Magic works. It lingers long after the demonic deed is done. The aura stays with the user. It doesn't hurt the user or those who interact with her. But the after-effects are felt by all who become intimate with the user. In Heather's case, you."

Russell, still worried, said, "Then, could she be in some *future* danger? I mean, this dark stuff is bound to take a toll...don't you think?"

"The longer she stays away from this dark magic the sooner this presence will disappear. Let me put it this way. There are different levels of Black Magic and the Deities of Darkness control them all. Unless Heather is willing to belong to the Dark Lords of that world, I'm afraid, magic that potent is best left alone. Not even the most powerful sorcerers of ancient times dealt with it because the Lords always insist on something in return. Something they know you can't bear to part with. Something they don't wait for you to give them. It's theirs and they take it in due time."

"But why would she need something so dark?" Dell asked.

"That's exactly what I was thinking," Russell stressed. "Magic made me a werewolf—got rid of the moon curse—it also lit your cigarette with no effort from you. Why can't that level of witchcraft be sufficient for Heather? Why does she have to fool around with stuff so dangerous?"

Melvita sat back with her legs crossed and took a draw from her cigarette. "Heather could be dealing with something that requires that level of power. Or it could be just plain greed. Simple magic is often not enough for some witches. Look at Corina...she was the victim of her own greed for power beyond White Magic. So were my ancestors who blindly followed her."

Melvita looked Russell straight in the eyes. "Rusty, you came here for my help. I'm going to dig into Heather's magic and her choice of demons...find out as much as I can. Slogan and I talked for a long time, mostly about you. I hope you don't mind. He really cares about you and he wanted my opinion about a few other things." Russell glanced over at

Dell and back to Melvita like he felt it was no big deal. She continued. "Do you trust me, Rusty?"

Russell thought a moment. "I admit I was skeptical at first. But, yeah, I think I do."

"Well, I'm going to tell you something. You have a perfect right to be angry with Jewel *and* Matthew Porter for taking your normal life away. But I've got to be honest with you. Jewel did what she thought was right for the people she loved. And I know that's no consolation. But it's only fair for me to tell you that if I were in her shoes, I would have done the same thing. Only I would have done it smarter. Putting a teenage boy in charge of you and letting you go back to your neighborhood, to your family and friends, where you could have been a danger to everyone you loved? Then risking you to shapeshift in broad daylight—where humans could see you and report you...was sloppy witchcraft...real amateur stuff. And you can tell her I said so."

Russell chuckled. "I like you, Melvita. You're honest."

Dell smiled and touched Russell's shoulder. The three talked for a while longer then Melvita walked them to the door.

"Rusty, I'm going to discuss Heather with my sister and brothers. With a little time, I should know what Heather is up to. And once we know more, the sooner we can get her away from the darker stuff, the sooner things will return to normal between the two of you."

Then she turned to Dell. "And Slogan, thanks for bringing him here."

"Oh, of course. Where else would I take him? You're the smartest witch I know."

"Better not let Massie hear you say that," Russell teased. "And thank you, Melvita, for seeing me. I really do appreciate it."

"I'm glad I can help. You guys have a great day now."

Driving back, heading for New Berwick, Dell turned to Russell. "Tell the truth, was that so bad?"

"No, you were right. Melvita *is* pretty cool."

"I told you things would work out. Now, aren't you glad I suggested it?"

"I have to admit I feel a whole lot better knowing a little more about what's going on with Heather."

"And...your mistrust of all witches, excluding Heather and Massie, of course?"

"Okay, I admit not all witches deserve my wrath. But I'm not ready for a Kumbaya moment with them either."

"Well, that-a-boy. I'm proud of you... I bet that *hurt*," Dell teased.

"No. Actually, it felt pretty good."

"Really?"

"Yeah. But I'd still like to shapeshift and catch that bitch Jewel Porter on a dark roadside some night."

"Dude!" Dell chuckled. "You're hopeless."

CHAPTER NINE

While waiting to hear from Melvita, Russell decided to do a little research on his own. Two relatable questions circled his mind. Why do witches have to search for strong magic? And why is the strongest magic frequently ancient?

During an extensive web search, Russell happened upon a small town magazine article written by a young college student in 1996. He thought it rather strange that the student was so open about such a hush subject among normal people. The article dealt with magic.

She wrote: It seems a common problem in the world of magic that the most powerful spells are ancient and no longer in practice. Whether it be forbidden or forgotten, today's witches know basic spells, but have to (sometimes literally) dig up more powerful, ancient, and sometimes, dangerous forgotten ones. Unlike science, which achieves improvement from one generation to the next, magic, for some odd reason, appears to have weakened and stalled over time.

The article was a half-page long, but the first paragraph heightened his interest in more information on the subject.

After several hours and several more extensive articles, there it was. "The Rise of Christianity" written by Christofur Vale.

Vale stated that with the rise of the Christian faith came the destruction of major temples of gods and goddesses who had dated back thousands of years. Those temples were the spiritual sources for witchcraft. Christians called for the stoning of priests and priestesses, causing temple worshippers to scatter; those who stayed either converted to Christianity or pretended to convert for the sake of their vast wealth that was stationary or too large to carry off.

Later centuries saw anti-witchcraft laws pop up all over the Western part of the world; witches were on the run, separated from their families, covens, unable to draw knowledge and strength from their leaders. The tools of their craft were destroyed or stolen; they were unable to teach spell-casting to their offspring, who were sometimes taken from them. In the eighteenth century, Grimoires were discovered tangled in spider webs and covered with ancient dust.

By the mid-twentieth century, the *decline* of Christian influence was as devastating to witchcraft as its rise. For the decline came with the onslaught of Atheism. A new generation, denying the existence of a spiritual realm was unaware of their magical or divine potential. Christianity helped pave its own way to destruction with only a little push from outsiders. Because the faith had shifted from spirituality to corporate capitalism and greed, people barely attended services, if at all. With the rise of social media, the scam was on and many church leaders rose to multi-millionaire status with no thought or heart toward world conflicts, hunger, poverty, and disease.

Vale ended his article by stating that New Agers wanted to believe in something, so they settled on believing in nothing: If you can't see it, smell it, taste, hear or feel it—well, it doesn't exist. By the time witchcraft rose again, witches were just a few, scattered and continents apart. Many found each other, studied their craft, and became powerful once again, but the rules for engaging magic had changed.

The witches, nobler now, placed a spell to make it difficult, almost impossible to access the realms of Dark Magic; anything having to do with the summoning of the dead, fallen spirits or demons was forbidden and punishable by death or ex-communication and permanent loss of magic. Only White Magic was deemed legal. Witches operating outside of legal magic, the Covenant considered an enemy and a threat.

Russell's eyes grew tired and he rested his back against his chair's soft cushion. He yawned and tried blinking away the glare of his computer screen from his eyes. His phone rang. "Hey, Dell," Russell said, stretching.

"Are you sitting down?" Dell asked.

"No. I'm standing on my head...what?"

"I have some news."

"Jewel Porter fell off her broom and broke her ass?" Russell chuckled.

"Dude, I'm serious."

Russell straightened. "Okay, now you're scaring me."

"Massie said that Heather has left town and said for her to tell you she'll see you in a couple of months...maybe longer. Massie said Heather explained that she didn't want to tell you face-to-face because she knew you'd be upset." Dell heard an uneasy silence.

Russell slammed his fist down hard. The bang jilted his mouse causing it to fall onto the hardwood floor. "She told *Massie*? She told *Massie*?" Russell repeated angrily. "She could have told *me*. That's bullshit! See what I have to put up with? I'm sick of this shit! You know what...I'm done."

Dell heard a crash. "Rusty, I'm sorry... you want me to come over? Rusty... Rusty?"

"Russell's phone lay smashed on the floor near the wall baseboard. He sat with his head in his hands for nearly an hour just thinking and wondering if he should even consider continuing a relationship with Heather. He felt numb.

*****

Early the next morning, someone leaning on the doorbell startled Dell out of his sleep. He stumbled half-awake down the stairs and flung open the door.

"Rusty, what the hell...it's five in the morning."

Russell brushed by him and stood looking around. "I need Massie, where is she?"

"She's asleep, where everybody should be this time of the morning."

"Well, wake her up."

"Whoa...you don't get to storm into my girlfriend's place and order me around!"

"Dell, it's important."

"Nothing is that important at five a.m."

"Dell, please."

"No!"

"What the hell is going on down there?" Massie yelled over the banister. "Rusty...is that you?"

"Massie, I've got to talk to you," Russell stressed.

"Now?" Massie snapped.

"Please, I need you to do something."

"Do what? You know what time it is?"

"Massie, you may as well come down," Dell said. "Nobody's getting any sleep until he gets whatever it is he wants. You know this is about Heather."

"What about Heather?"

"Baby, just come down," Dell told her.

Massie, barefooted, in bikini panties and an oversized short sleeve sweatshirt that came down to her knees, slowly descended the stairs. Her golden blonde hair, a bit disheveled, hung midway her back. She pulled on the hem of her sweatshirt and stared into Russell's troublesome eyes. "Apparently this couldn't wait for a decent hour, so here I am," she said.

"I want you to cast a locating spell on Heather."

"Great Zeus, Rusty, that's not an easy spell. You know how long it'll take me to set that up?" Massie saw the disappointment flash in Russell's sad, blue eyes. Dell saw it, too and while walking toward the kitchen quickly said, "Honey, take your time; I'll make us some egg and bacon sandwiches. Russell crossed the living room to follow Dell.

Massie entered the doorway to the next room where she would prepare the spell, but stopped and turned quickly, "Oh, wait," she said. "Rusty, do you have any items of hers?"

"Items...what do you mean?"

"I can't do a locating spell without something personal like hair from her brush or a piece of clothing."

"Aww, Massie! I didn't know."

"Well, how the hell am I supposed to...wait," she remembered. "I think I still have that blouse she loaned me a while back. I'll go see if I can find it." She hurried from the doorway and climbed the stairs.

"I'm sorry to be so much trouble," Russell yelled up to her.

"It's okay," she said, her voice trailing off as she entered her bedroom.

Russell paced at the bottom of the stairs while the aroma of fried bacon hung in the air. After fifteen minutes, Massie bounced down the stairs. She had pulled on a pair of jeans and was holding a wrinkled, bright, yellow blouse.

"Oh, great, you found it," Russell said. "Will it be enough?"

"*It* and your blood."

"Why my blood?"

"Because you're the one looking for her," she said, entering the dark room.

Russell stood staring at her back as she entered the darkness then he turned and joined Dell in the kitchen.

"Did she find something?" Dell asked, filling two glasses with apple juice. He placed the plate of egg and bacon sandwiches in the middle of the table.

"Yeah, she found a blouse Heather had left here."

"Good," Dell said, sitting across from Russell and sipping his juice.

Russell grabbed a sandwich and the remaining glass of juice. The two talked about things unrelated to Heather for nearly an hour then Russell said, "Dell, I know I've been a real pain in the ass about this thing with Heather. I'm sorry.

You're the only friend I've got...that is...the only wolf friend. *You* know what I mean."

"Sure I do. Look, dude, if you can't wake up a *wolf friend* five in the morning, who can you wake up?" he said, smiling. "Forget about it." Dell took a big bite of his sandwich. Talking with his mouth full, he muffled, "I've got an idea... how about I bite Mark and John then you'll have three wolf friends."

Russell froze with his glass of juice inches from his mouth. "Is that supposed to be funny?"

Dell cackled.

"I'm serious, man. You think that's funny? Mark and John are like my brothers."

"Rusty, chill. It was just a joke."

"Maybe to *your* kind, it's a joke, but not to me. That's how *I* became what I am."

"For heaven's sake, I would never do anything like that. I was just trying to take your mind off Heather."

"You couldn't think of anything better?"

"Holy shit! I'm sorry, okay?" Dell angrily stuffed the other wedge of sandwich into his mouth.

Dell and Russell sat without talking for nearly a half-hour, while Massie busied herself in the far end of the apartment. The sun broke through the pale sky, and Massie placed a dark covering over the drapes so the room would stay dark.

"Rusty," Dell said breaking the silence. "Dude, lighten up. I didn't mean to upset you."

"How could you not know speaking that way about my close friends wasn't funny? A third-grader would have known better."

"Man, you can be such an *asshole* at times," Dell snapped.

"Asshole! Really?"

"Hey, you two," Massie said, popping her head in the kitchen doorway, "I'm ready."

Russell scrambled from the table; he and Dell followed Massie into the dimly lit room. "Russell, you sit here," she said, pointing to a chair directly in front of her. "Dell, over there," she said, nodding to her left. The three took their seats at a square table—twice the size of a card table. Four tall, gold, candle holders with ancient markings held thin white candles.

In the middle of the table, a map of Illinois and in front of Massie was an opened spellbook. Massie lit the candles and placed each one at a corner of the map, then used shears to cut pieces of Heather's blouse into a small bowl. She picked up her ceremonial blade.

"Give me your hand," she told Russell. He placed his hand in hers,' and Massie pulled the sharp blade across his palm. Russell loudly sucked air through his teeth but didn't cry out. She held his hand over the cut pieces in the bowl and watched the blood flow until the yellow pieces turned dark red.

"Here," she said, placing a white towel over the cut. "Put pressure on it." Russell withdrew his hand and wrapped it tightly in the towel.

Dell and Russell looked on as Massie slowly closed her eyes and slipped into a trance. As she eased deeper and deeper, her breathing grew noisy. With her eyes still closed, she slowly lifted both hands, held them over the bowl, and chanted an incantation in Hungarian. The candles began to flicker, and a light, cool breeze blew over them. Massie continued chanting—louder and louder and the breeze grew colder and stronger.

The bloody items caught fire. The bowl rose and spun in midair. The fire turned into red smoke. Dell and Russell looked on, their eyes wide as pinballs taking in the strange action that appeared before them. Dell's mouth gaped open. Russell, too excited about finding Heather, seemed surprisingly calm and reserved.

Massie stopped chanting and opened her eyes; she appeared to still see, though her irises had disappeared and only the white sparkled. The bowl tilted and a stream of red smoke spilled out onto the map and began to slither like a serpent.

"Massie, what's it doing?" Russell blurted.

"Quiet! You idiot," Dell snapped.

The serpent-like substance slithered east of the map—so far east, it nearly crawled off the table, but didn't. Instead, it stopped and melted into a red arrow that pointed to a small black dot on the map. It wasn't a town or a city—just a heavily wooded area. It didn't even have a name.

"Is that where she is?" Russell blurted.

Massie, still half in her spiritual state, blinked to focus on the area. "I have no idea where that is, she said in a rather husky voice.

"How are we supposed to program the location into the GPS?" Dell asked.

"Is that all your magic can do? This is nothing. You've done nothing!" Russell said angrily.

Massie's face darkened and her lips parted to say something. Dell saw the danger. Witches could be unpredictable when coming out of a deep trance. They were mediums and still in the grips of powerful spirits that temporally took them over.

"Ah...Rusty," he interrupted. You really don't want to do this, dude."

Russell glanced at Dell, who was staring at Massie. Russell's eyes also shifted to Massie. He saw traces of the darkness still in her mannerism. He suddenly realized Dell's warning.

"Oh...no...Massie, I...I didn't really mean it like that. You've been great. Really you have. Russell dropped his head and tried to hide his disappointment. "I didn't mean anything by it. It's just if I don't find Heather soon," he said his voice faint, "I'm going to lose it. I've got to find out why she keeps running off like this. I know what Melvita said, but I still sense she's in some kind of danger. And I don't know what to do."

Massie's eyes returned to their normal color and they softened when she looked at him. "We'll find her, Rusty," she said.

Russell looked up at her with relief and smiled.

Massie blew out the candles and rose from the table. Dell and Russell followed suit. "Go on home and get some sleep," Massie told him. "Dell and I will figure this out." They walked Russell to the door.

Russell turned to Massie and gave her a hug then turned to Dell and hugged him. Russell walked out, got into his car and gave a quick wave before pulling off.

"Poor thing...I'm almost sorry I introduced him to her," Massie said, closing the door.

"No. They really care for each other. We'll get to the bottom of this." Dell slipped his hand into Massie's, and they climbed the stairs together then disappeared into the bedroom.

*****

Well into the night—within the silence of a dark forest, which earlier had appeared as a dot, a no-name place on a map, Heather stood. A black, hooded robe covered her nude, white body. She was a part of a large hand-holding circle. Among them, her brother Sky, her sisters Brook and Wendy, close cousins, Brink, Coleen, Dave, Reese, and Josh, plus fourteen extended family members, in-laws, and friends—each nude save for the black robe.

Heather led them in a rhythmic chant. Moonlight bathed the landscape. Its streaks of silver shot through the trees and rested upon their shoulders. In the middle of the huge circle blazed a tall barn-like fire. The fire split the logs, and sparks, like fireflies, danced out from the flames. Those were no ordinary flames, but fire from the belly of a forbidden hell.

Clawed feet and hands reached from beyond the blaze. The expenditures were pale and leathery and matte, like tarnished copper; its claws curved like scimitars. That strange and hideous entity, imprisoned for a damn good reason, no doubt, seethed from within the flames; and whatever its purpose, their ongoing chanting appeared on the edge of setting it free.

CHAPTER TEN

Russell went home and immediately went to bed. Four in the afternoon the same day, he rose with a thumping migraine. Groggy from sleep and pain, he made his way to the kitchen, pain pills in hand, to make a cup of hot chocolate. While the water heated in the microwave, he tossed the pills into his mouth then turned the orange juice carton he'd plucked from the refrigerator shelf to his mouth and drowned them.

Russell poured the steaming hot water into the cup and added two teaspoons of the chocolate powder. As he sat and sipped, he heard his new phone ringing from the bedroom. Russell got to his phone on the sixth ring and grew excited at the name.

"Melvita?" Russell greeted.

"I have some news," she said.

"I'm surprised you got back to me so quickly. What did you find? Oh...first, let me say I had Massie, that's Dell's girlfriend, use a locating spell to find Heather and she did.

Only we still don't know any more than we did before. It's just a dot on the Illinois map. The place has no name."

"It has no name because it doesn't exist in Earth's realm. You magically looked for her so it magically showed up on the map. But if you'd look at the map now, you wouldn't see a trace of it."

"You mean it won't even show up as a dot."

"Correct. She's in another realm...a very dark realm."

"What the hell is she doing?"

"That's why I'm calling. You need to brace yourself."

"Oh, Christ!" Russell heard himself say. He hadn't said that name with any meaning since finding out what he'd become. Or, rather, what Jewel Porter had forced him to become. He wasn't sure if he any longer had the right to mention Christ's name. He didn't *feel* evil, yet, he wasn't sure of his religious upbringing anymore.

And he still loved and respected his mom and dad. Any rebellion he executed against his parents was really to protect them from finding out what he was. He didn't know how long he could keep up the charade, but he'd protect them as long as he could.

"Rusty...you still there?"

"Oh, yeah. You said for me to brace myself? Look...before you say anything. Tell me...is Heather all right?"

"Heather is more than all right. She's the least of your worries."

"Then, what?" Russell asked.

"Heather, along with a whole host of her powerful family members and friends, are trying to release Corina. I don't think they can. But if the hunters who put her there get a whiff of what they're trying to do, it will start a supernatural battle that this region won't be able to sustain. She and her cronies must be stopped."

"Holy shit! Why is she doing this?"

"That's for you to find out. You're closer to her than anyone of us."

"But, for me to stop her, I'd have to reveal to her that I've been talking to you and snooping around. Once she finds out I've been prying..."

"Rusty, this is no time for you to be concerned about Heather's feelings. So she finds out you've been snooping and she breaks up with you... so what? This is serious. You've got to choose sides now."

"You mean, choose against Heather...make her my enemy? And what if that means harming her? No, there's got to be another way."

"If the hunters find out what she and her group are up to, they won't only harm her, they will destroy her. These hunters don't use magic...they use divine weapons. No level of magic is a match for them. If they go after Heather, the rest of us will fall like dominos."

"What do we do?"

"My family and I will help as much as we can to keep her from making this diabolical blunder. But if the hunters find out, you're on your own."

"In other words, you and your family will bail—leaving the rest of us hanging."

Melvita ignored his remark. "As I said, my family will help as much as possible."

Russell, hearing silence on the other end, slowly pulled the phone down from his ear. His drink was cold. He walked into the kitchen and placed it in the microwave.

Around eight o'clock that night, Russell got up enough nerve to phone Dell and Massie with the news. Both seemed stunned and said they needed to inform the Covenant witches. Russell hated the idea. In his mind, he was pitting Jewel Porter against Heather. He knew what Heather was attempting was dangerously wrong. But siding against Heather in favor of a witch he despised was sickening.

"Maybe I need to go away," Russell told Dell and Massie. "I can't be a part of this."

"You don't have to, Rusty," Dell said. "Massie and I understand."

"Do me a favor," Russell urged,

"Sure, anything," Dell said.

"Give me a little time with Heather before you tell the Covenant and the wolves."

"How much time? We don't even know how to find her. It may be already too late."

"God, no. Don't say that. Then that means I'll have to go find her myself."

"Rusty, that's brave, but I wouldn't be your friend if I didn't say that's also stupid. Dude, we don't even know what we're dealing with here. Listen to me, you stay put. I know how you feel about Heather, but it's out of your hands now."

"Ah, Dell."

"I know, buddy. You love her...I understand. Go spend some time with Mark and John. Pretend to be human for a few days. That always makes you feel good."

"Yeah...thanks, man. I think I will."

*****

Days went by. Russell spent the weekend hanging out with Mark. John had gone out of town with his parents to a cousin's wedding and wouldn't be back for a couple of weeks. Russell tried to remove the mystery of Heather from his mind. He enjoyed the time with his friend, but Mark knew him better than anyone and sensed something was bothering Russell.

"Hey, Rusty, I gave you some space. I didn't want to crowd you, but it's been two days, and you need to spill."

"Spill?"

"Come on, Rusty."

"Boy, I never could fool you."

"What's wrong?'

"It's my... it's Heather."

Mark chuckled. "Aww...woman trouble," he said with relief. "That explains it. You guys aren't breaking up?"

"No. It's a little more serious than that. But I don't want to worry you with my problems. Besides, it'll work itself out."

"Oh, *well*...if you don't want to tell me...it's okay. I didn't mean to pry."

"Come on...I didn't mean *that*. You know nothing is too private not to discuss it with you and John. It's really nothing. I don't even know why I'm stressing." Russell smiled widely and gently slapped Mark on the back. "Come on," Russell said, "Let's take a boat ride across the lake. We haven't done that in ages." Mark smiled and agreed.

*****

Meanwhile— an exhausted, Heather, along with her fellow cohorts, sat sprawled on the stone ground. Some, bone-tired, had fallen asleep. The huge blaze, all but dim now, had trickled down to flames no more wild than those in a cozy fireplace. The spell had failed miserably. Perhaps the clawed hands and feet reaching to be set free was just an illusion.

After all, the spell did call for a special potion to be drunken minutes before the chanting. Mass illusion was possible, but to see the same sight and at the same time was neither possible nor probable. Nevertheless, the spell had failed, and it was back to searching the grimoires for a stronger one.

It had been months since Heather left, and she dreaded facing a pissed off lover. She wasn't sure what she would find in Russell's eyes. Would he greet her...accept another explanation? Would they argue...break up? She felt more passion for Russell than any other lover she'd ever known. He had once been human, maybe that was the appeal. Humans were equally as forgiving as they were demanding— something she'd found missing in past lovers.

She never cared about it before. She hadn't known about such pure unselfishness. But once she had experienced it with Russell, she found she didn't want a relationship without it. She just had to make Russell understand. Heather wondered if she had worn out his patience. She walked through the door of the apartment they shared on week-ends and called out to him.

Russell thought he heard his name. The steam rose around him, and the foam washed into his ears as he worked the lather into his hair. There it was again, he thought and with a cool breeze this time. Russell peeped through the narrow slits of his eyes that were now stinging from the shampoo suds streaking down his face. He made out the hourglass figure.

Russell didn't stick his head out, but turned toward the shower spout and let the water wash over him. Heather gently pulled back the shower door for him to see her, but he continued to rinse and not look her way. Heather stood for a moment until finally getting the message. She closed the shower door, her eyes staring down at the floor, and slowly walked back to the bedroom.

Minutes seemed like hours as she unpacked, found the sexiest negligee she had, and positioned herself on the bed like a Greek goddess waiting for Odysseus. Then she thought, *No. This is so corny...he'll never fall for this.* She jumped up, took off the negligee, and put on a flowered lounging set, then sat in front of the mirror primping and brushing her long dark hair that graced the middle of her back.

The bathroom door opened and her muscular lover walked through with his lower torso wrapped in a navy blue towel. His dark hair shiny and wet, he turned his back to her and sat on the edge of the bed drying his hair with a hand towel. Then he rose, pulled off one towel, let it slip to the floor and tossed the other aside. He pulled on boxer shorts, drew back the covers and climbed into bed. She continued brushing her hair and watching him through the mirror—her emerald eyes dancing.

Heather rose, slipped into a nightie and climbed into bed next to him. She lay still for over an hour and thought how best to tell him what her family had forbidden. How could she tell him about Holly, Corina's sister? The hunters had blasted her into oblivion or so everyone thought. Holly was nowhere, yet everywhere. Wherever she was, her magic was alive and well. They saw no visible body but her voice could be heard and felt.

Heather's parents were kidnapped and magically trapped until Heather and her family found a spell to release Corina's spirit from the mystical prison of the damned. Holly's magic wasn't strong enough for such a difficult task. Corina, herself, could not be released by magic, but her spirit could survive outside her body long enough for Holly to absorb all of Corina's magic. Holly would then free herself—recreate Corina's evil empire and reign in her place.

And just *why* had Heather's parents been the target? The continuous greed for more powerful magic seemed a common plague among some witches. Despite warnings and the number of witches having paid an enormous price for this rapacity, it proved a-never-ending temptation that could snare even the kindest of witches.

Heather's parents, Grant and Rita Marshall happen upon a demonic book that required the blood sacrifice of small animals. Not realizing the consequences, both were suddenly and violently pulled into the pages of that book. The terrifying expressions that froze on Grant and Rita's faces proved that they had realized, much too late, the error of trusting the unknown. The Marshall family was summoned from every part of the country. Grant and Rita would remain a living photo unless the family did what Holly demanded.

Heather knew, that time, the only way to save her relationship was to tell Russell the truth. And she would promise never to leave again without telling him first. From now on, she wanted to include Russell in every aspect of her life. Her family would just have to understand. With this decision, Heather closed her eyes and fell asleep.

Nearly noon, the next day, Russell gently shook Heather. She opened her lids to a thin veil of sleep that clouded her vision. After blinking, she saw a clearer picture of Russell's deep, blue eyes peering angrily at her.

"Get up! We need to talk...downstairs," he snapped then walked bristly out of the bedroom.

Heather rose and stumbled sleepily across the floor to the bathroom. She yawned, scratched, and examined her face in the mirror. After brushing her teeth, she splashed cold water on her face. In the bedroom, she exchanged her nightie for a bright, pink lounging pant set then made her way into the kitchen where Russell had prepared hot chocolate and toast. Heather eased in a chair across from him and the two sat silently sipping the hot drink and crunching on buttered toast. Finally, he broke the silence.

Heather allowed Russell to rant on and on—swearing, shouting, insinuating, sometimes insulting, and threatening to end their relationship after every other sentence. Then he shocked Heather with information about her whereabouts as well as what she and her family and friends were up to. He had consulted not one, but two witches concerning her.

"Well," she said appearing indignant. "Seems you've been quite the detective."

"Don't you dare talk to me about snooping. Damn right I did...and I'm not going to apologize. What the hell do you think you're doing? You're not only endangering yourself but what you're doing could destroy all of us. Not only that..."

"Rusty..." she tried to interrupt.

He ignored her. "....did you know I was told to side with the Covenant witches against you? How do you think that made me feel...huh?"

"Rusty...sweetheart, I'm trying to tell you something."

"Tell me what...more secrets...more lies?"

"Honey...I'm trying to tell you...you're right — no more secrets — no more lies. You found out *what* I'm doing. Now, let me tell you why."

Russell listened—stunned, while she filled in all of the empty pieces of the puzzle that had plagued their relationship for over a year. He searched her glassy eyes as she gave meticulous details of that horrible year she'd spent away from him and the many failed attempts to find the right spell that would save her parents. Part of his heart went out to her— the other half burst with anger at her for not telling him sooner. He reached across the table and held her hands as she wrapped up the story with the uncertainty of being able to find the right spell.

Russell placed a thumb over a tear that slid down her cheek. "Baby, it's going to be all right. I understand...you were just doing what your family told you. But I'm in this thing now. And one way or another, you're going to have your parents back safe and sound. Don't worry... okay?"

Heather's emerald eyes brightened. She strained a smile and nodded.

CHAPTER ELEVEN

One Year Earlier

Holly lingered somewhere breathing. In the shadows of her entrapment, she tinkered with what was left of her magic. *Could she manage enough to get free?* she thought. Sending out magical feelers, Holly waited patiently. The wait was intense, stimulating to a fault, but the perilous trap was set. Then like clockwork, there came an old woman who lived under a walking bridge near a cottage where Heather's parents, Grant and Rita Marshall lived. Because the small country-side was loaded with Marshalls, outsiders jokingly called the place Marshallville. Heather, before leaving, had shared a cottage with her sisters, Brook and Wendy; her brother, Sky lived with cousins Dave and Josh. The rest of the family lived further down the path near a wooded area by a creek. Many of the Marshall's close friends didn't live in the area but were only a twenty-minute drive away. The old woman was seen many times by the folks in the region, pushing a food cart loaded with trinkets and yelling the names of her items for sale.

Rita Marshall had bought a few things off the woman; she didn't need them—just wanted the old girl to be able to buy food. For months, Rita had heard the old woman yell out things such as gold hairpin boxes, jewelry boxes, earrings, necklaces, things the woman had found or made and polished up for sale; so Rita's surprise was justified when one afternoon she heard the old woman yell, "Ancient book of the dead!"

"What the devil did she say?" Rita thought out loud. She scrambled to her cottage window and pushed both halves outward. "Hey!" Rita called. "Let's see that book."

The woman kept a snail's pace up to the window. It was ninety-degree weather, and the woman wore layers of clothing but not a bead of sweat claimed her brow.

"How much...and where did you get it?"

"Twenty dollars and I don't reveal my suppliers," the old woman graveled.

Rita believed the book wasn't worth that but didn't want to argue with her. "I'll get my purse," she said, grabbing it from the dining table.

"Here," Rita said, placing four five-dollar bills in the dingy palm. The woman rolled the bills and stuffed them in her bosom. She handed Rita a thick book covered in brown animal fur. Embedded on the front in a font much like that of old English was a Hungarian word Rita couldn't pronounce. She took the book and pulled the window closed. Strangely, after that day, no one ever saw the old woman again.

Rita sat and opened the book to a blank page. Seeing no reason why the first page shouldn't have been blank, she flipped through a couple more, a few more and a few more...and... "Damn! Why, that deceitful old biddy," Rita blurted. Every page was blank. She tossed the book in the trash and stormed off to the kitchen to prepare dinner before Grant got home. Cursing under her breath, Rita pulled lettuce, tomatoes, onions and other ingredients for a tossed salad from the refrigerator. Her arms full, she turned to place the items on the island and gasped when she saw the furry book, sitting in the middle of the island and...breathing. She put the vegetables aside and picked up the book; it pulsated in her hand feeling warm and alive like a cat or a small dog. The book also felt a little heavier. Needle sized blue veins and red arteries crisscrossed every blank page.

A few hours later, Grant walked into the house and smelled the aroma of baked chicken and onion gravy. A large, clear bowl of green salad sat near a smaller bowl of homemade dressing. "Rita!" Grant called out.

"I'm in here!" she yelled from the den. Searching a secret coded site accessible only to witches, Rita had discovered the secret of the furry book. Why it was called the book of the dead, Rita wasn't sure; it was, however, a book full of ancient spells that could unleash powers Rita could only imagine.

Almost without a breath in between, she told Grant about the old woman, and what secrets the book held—how this could be their ticket to power and wealth beyond their wildest dreams. Grant was skeptical. They debated all through dinner about using or not using the book. But Rita wore Grant down as usual.

Reluctantly, Grant spent the next two days catching field rats and squirrels—putting them in cages and preparing them for the sacrifice. Each sacrifice would reveal a little more of the spell that would bring them closer to riches and triple their magical powers.

They had sacrificed all the squirrels and were down to two rats. "I think we're close," Rita said excitedly—unaware that minutes away, she and Grant would tap into a pocket of the universe where a dangerous witch lay rotting and scheming. All Holly needed was contact from another entity to cast her weak spells from her timeless tomb. Her magical feelers had finally latched on to someone, and they weren't letting go.

"Look! Grant said. "There's writing. The book is trying to communicate with us."

"Let's answer," she said.

"No," Grant snapped. "I don't like this. We don't know who or what it is."

"Grant, come on. We're just going to communicate. It can't hurt anything."

"Oh, all right, honey," he said begrudgingly.

The communication started casually. At first, it was a little difficult to read with all the veins and arteries scrambled about the page. Rita wrote a short bio, where they were from, their family members and friends. Holly magically scribbled she was chosen by a goddess to help witches improve their craft and greatly increase their magical capabilities. "All you have to do," Holly further wrote, "is cast this spell and all will be yours."

Grant anxiously pulled the last rat from the cage and slit its throat. The rodent squealed and squirmed as Grant held its dripping throat over the written spell and Rita spoke the incantation. Instantly, the room grew dark and misty. The chandelier twirled violently as the windows and walls slowly breathed in and out.

"What's happening!" Grant yelled.

"I...I don't know," Rita stammered.

Suddenly, the rat yanked its head free and bit the top of Grant's thumb, nearly severing it. Grant cried out and the rat jumped on his chest and edged half its body into Grant's mouth. Rita screamed when the rat's tail slipped from her fingers and quickly forced its way down her husband's throat. Grant gagged and his face turned blue while he frantically scratched at his throat. Rita continued screaming his name all the while beating him on the back—desperately trying to dislodge the rodent. Then Grant's neck swelled the size of his head, and his whole body trembled violently. Rita, still screaming Grant's name, grabbed him and she too began to tremble. Both turned pale blue and blinked off and on like someone playing with a light switch. Then they blinked off a full thirty seconds. But when they blinked on again, they were permanent fixtures on a page in the furry breathing book; a look of horror stained their faces. Grant—his mouth wide open, a thin tail sticking out past his tonsils and laying on his tongue—and Rita, holding on to him for dear life, eyes bulging. Scribbled under the picture read: *If you want to know how to release Grant and Rita, write the Hungarian word three times then wait for reply.*

Holly Brewer...

Heather had been staying in New Berwick when she received news that her brother made the horrifying discovery after not hearing from their parents for several days. It became the Marshalls' worst family crisis in a century.

*****

Throughout Falcon Haven, news of Heather's kidnapped parents used as pawns in Holly's diabolical scheme hit the Covenant witches like a bullet to the gut. Because Heather was Russell's girlfriend, many teen wolves blamed him for drawing their region into a possible head-on collision with the inimical Shadow Hunters.

"Didn't I tell you? I knew those assholes would find a way to blame me for this shit."

"I'll talk to them, Rusty," Dell said.

"No. I want them to say it to my face."

"Let Dell handle it, honey," Heather said loudly from the bedroom. She was pulling clothes from Russell's duffle bag and placing them neatly into drawers. School would be out in a couple of weeks and Russell was moving in for the summer.

"Great goddess, Rusty," Massie snapped. "Don't we have enough to contend with—you want to start something with the wolves?"

Russell just stared and sulked. Then Massie walked across the living room and stuck her head in the bedroom door. Spotting Heather still busy sorting Russell's clothes, Massie asked, "You want me to start dinner?"

"Oh, would you? You're a doll. I left lamb chops thawing on the counter."

"I'll see if they're ready," Massie said.

Later that evening, Matthew drove from his home in Southern Greyscott Falls to River and Jewel's place to give them first-hand news. He knew they would see his presence as a sign of respect even if they had already heard about it. As head of the Northern wolf pack, this was the respect that River deserved. Jewel was napping and the girls, Dria and Becca were still away at boarding school. They would join River and Jewel when school was out. River bought Matthew a beer then flopped opposite him on the sofa.

"I knew that kid would be trouble...I could feel it," River told Matthew. "I don't want Jewel having anything to do with this. We're expecting our second son and the strain of difficult spell casting is not good for her right now."

"Why don't you take Aunt Jewel away from here until things blow over?"

"I'd sure like to, Matt...but will you and Dex be okay? I hate leaving you."

"There's really nothing you, I, or any of the wolves can do. This is strictly witch business," Matthew said.

"The things witches get themselves into..." River said, shaking his head.

"Tell me about it," Matthew said. "And we have to be the ones to get them out of it."

"Wait now...to be fair, they have saved *our* asses quite a few times."

"Be fair, hell?" Matthew said. "They saved us from shit *they* started in the first place." River laughed.

*****

For several days, the same scenes repeated. Massie made dinner, Dell and Russell watched sports TV, and Heather unpacked more of Russell's clothes, toiletries, and his Playstation4 for the online game, Fortnite. After dinner, they all sat near the cold fireplace with pie and ice cream.

"Why haven't we heard anything from the Covenant witches? You think maybe because I'm an outsider they don't care?" Heather asked.

"Of course they care," Russell exclaimed. "They'd better care—Holly has an ax to grind with them. They can't afford not to help us."

"You're right. That's probably why Holly wants to be free," Dell said, "so she can enact revenge for her and Corina."

"There's a part to this I don't understand," Heather said. "If the Shadow Hunters made her disappear then how is she's still able to exist and wield such power?"

"Who told you that?" Massie asked. "The hunters didn't make her disappear; they shrank her until she was just a dot in the wind. Where she went, nobody knows."

"They shrank her?" Heather asked surprised. "If they shrank her then she's still in this realm."

"Yes, and?" Russell smirked.

"And—we can do a locating spell," Heather said.

"Hey, that's right," Dell blurted. "Find out where that tiny bitch is. Why didn't *I* think of that?"

"I'm glad you didn't," Massie told him, "because that would make you as wrong as she is."

"How's that?" Dell asked.

"Can't do a locating spell on someone unless you have something personal that belongs to them...you know that," Massie said.

"Oh, yeah...I forgot," Dell said.

"Well, that was fun while it lasted," Russell joked.

"Wait a minute," Heather said wide-eyed. "We could do an advanced search."

"Aww, no. No, no," Massie said, shaking her head.

"Why not, Massie?" Russell asked.

"Because it requires really dark magic. And Heather is already up to her eyeballs in it as it is."

"How dark?"

"Dark dark, like summoning the deceased from the pits, dark."

"Holy 'Walking Dead,' Batman," Dell blurted.

"Dell, stop joking. This is serious. That spell is dangerous, and I've never done it before."

"I've seen it done," Heather said. "I'll lead you through it."

"Heather no."

"Massie, I'm begging you."

"No! I won't do it."

"Massie, please, they're my parents. Please."

Massie looked around for support for her refusal and saw only pleading eyes staring back at her. She turned and shrugged. "All right, I'll go set everything up," she said solemnly.

Across town—in Northern Greyscott Falls, little Merchant Porter waved bye-bye to his cousins Matt and Kayla, Uncle Dex and Aunt Jan from his car seat. Beside him in the back seat, Aunt Vera struggled to open a variety pack for her and Merchant to snack on during the long trip. Jan leaned in the front passenger side window and hugged Jewel for the fourth time. "You take care of yourself, honey," Jan said, "and don't worry; I'll see to it that Dria and Becca join you and River as soon as school lets out."

"Thank you, Sweetie," Jewel said misty-eyed.

"Dex, are you and Matt sure about this? I really hate leaving you guys," River stressed.

"How many times do we have to repeat this? You know as well as I do, that what might be coming won't be good for Jewel and the baby. So, leave already," Dex scolded.

"As I said, Uncle River, this is a witch thing. I think the Covenant got this."

"And if they need wolf backup," Dex said. "We're just a stone throw away. So—get out of here...go."

River shot his hand through the window and bumped knuckles with Dex. He pulled off with little Merchant waving like crazy and Jewel and Vera yelling good-bye repeatedly from the front and backside windows. River's three-hour drive would end at Ziggley's Air Field where a private plane waited to whisk them off to Knowles Island, a witch resort known and occupied only by Covenant witches and their families. There—the girls and soon-to-be-born son, Bridge Porter were to stay for several months to a year.

Back at Heather's apartment, the women busied themselves preparing for the advance search that would reveal the location of Holly. But Heather got cold feet. Finding Holly couldn't be that easy, could it? *Holly had to have known someone would get the idea to use a locating spell*, she thought. Heather reasoned they'd all know soon enough as Massie completed the preparations for the summoning.

"Heather, you sit here, Russell here, Dell there," Massie said, pointing.

CHAPTER TWELVE

Massie and Heather did what they had thought was impossible. With the advanced locating spell and a few close calls with the Undead, they found Holly in a subzone of the Biosphere. The Biosphere was a narrow zone where the earth's three realms: lithosphere, the realm of land; hydrosphere, the realm of water, and atmosphere, the realm of air—all connected to support living organisms. Holly lay trapped in a small pocket of the subzone. That subzone, called Withersphere was where debris from the three realms: land, water, and air flowed and settled. Holly had survived a hunter's deadly blow from his divine weapon, but she had been slowly wasting away until her magical feelers connected her to the lithosphere giving her new strength and hope. But it would take superior witchcraft to shut down that hope. Still, Heather couldn't stop thinking of how easy it all had been. Would Holly be waiting for them when they came for her? Was that her plan all along? Heather had to voice her opinion. After all, it was *her* parents and she was the only one who had something to lose if things went wrong.

Russell held his phone and placed his thumb on Melvita's face on the screen.

"Wait!" Heather said, touching Russell's hand. She turned to Massie. "I know it was my idea, Massie. And I don't mean to throw cold water on this victory, but I have concerns."

"Concerns...about what?" Massie frowned.

"Don't you think it was a little *too* easy finding her?" Heather asked.

"Easy! You call brushes with the Undead, easy?" Massie griped.

"Okay, easy is the wrong word. I mean the fact that we discovered her at all. I can't believe a smart witch like Holly would have let that happen."

"So what?" Massie snapped.

"Heather," Dell weighed in. "What are you talking about? So, it was easier than we thought. We found her, didn't we? Isn't that what you wanted—to save your parents?"

"Yeah, Heather," Russell said. "Why are you putting the brakes on this? Let's take care of this bitch and free your parents."

"You don't understand," Heather said.

"Understand what?" Massie asked irritated.

"Don't you think Holly would have anticipated us using a locating spell? She's not stupid." Heather said.

"How do we know she's not stupid?" Dell asked. "She's been lingering in a subzone sewer for over five years. How do we know she still has all of her brain cells?"

"Now who's stupid?" Heather snapped. "She's a goddamn witch. It was magic, not some elaborate scheme from a brilliant mind that has my parents trapped in an ancient spellbook. And you guys are acting like this is going to be some cakewalk."

Russell eased to Heather's side and put his hand on her back. "All right, baby, calm down. I get it now. You think we could be walking into a trap."

"Exactly," Heather said a bit shaken. "If we don't get this right, I may never see...see my parents again," she stammered, her eyes filling.

Massie's face softened. "Okay, honey," she said to Heather. "Let's all sit down and figure out the best way to approach this."

"I've got a better idea," Dell said. "Let's hear what Melvita thinks."

"I agree," Russell said, touching Melvita's face on the screen.

*****

Across town at Southern Greyscott Falls, Matthew was visiting with his dad. "Why haven't Dell and Rusty reached out to us, I wonder?" Dex asked Matthew.

Matthew flopped across from Dex and handed him a beer. "Ah, he's still pissed at me and Jewel—all of us really, about being a wolf."

"You'd think he'd moved past it by now," Dex said, swilling his beer.

"Well—we've never been human so, we can't know how the kid feels."

"Yeah, I guess you're right. Poor kid," Dex said. "But I got to tell you," Dex continued, "I'm not sorry one bit that I don't have to worry about a damn full moon anymore."

"Neither do I. I'm just sorry the kid chooses to live with so much hatred."

"Well, that's *his* problem," Dex said. "Life's a bitch." Dex walked over to the minibar. "How about something a little stronger?" he said. "Scotch and water?"

"Yeah—a little heavy on the water. I think I'll drive over to Russell's girlfriend's place. That's where he stays most of the time. I'll try one more time to get him to at least act civil toward me."

"You *like* beating your head against a brick wall," Dex said, handing Matthew his drink.

"We've got a nasty witch putting pressure on his girlfriend's family to release Corina. And if I have to *stay* in his face, I've got to convince him to put his hatred aside so we can tackle this mess together."

"Good luck," Dex smirked then drained his glass of scotch.

"What do you mean good luck? You're coming *with* me." Matthew drained his glass and stood. "Come on, Grandpa."

"Grandpa?" Dex asked, following Matthew to the door.

"Yeah, didn't I tell you—Kayla is pregnant."

"No, you didn't tell me—and don't call me grandpa."

"Ok, Gramps," Matthew teased. The two bickered all the way to Matthew's car.

When Matthew and Dex arrived at Heather's apartment complex, Matthew spotted Russell's car on the parking lot. Inside the complex, they looked for the apartment. "Hm— 204, 206, Matthew mumbled reading the apartment numbers, "216 must be around the corner," he told Dex.

Hearing the buzzer, Massie walked to the door and peeked through the peephole. "Great Zeus, you're not going to believe this," she said, turning to them.

"Who is it?" Heather asked.

"Let me put it this way," Massie smirked. "Rusty, it's for you."

"Me?" he said, marching to the door. He looked through the peephole then rolled his eyes before snatching open the door. "You have got to be kidding me," Russell snapped.

Before Matthew could respond, Dex blurted, "We don't give a damn how you feel about us. What your girlfriend is doing can affect us all." Dex forced past Russell intentionally bumping his shoulder and causing Russell to slightly stumble to one side. Matthew kept his head down and smirked as he passed Russell in the doorway.

"Now wait just a damn minute," Russell said, but suddenly ignored when Dell grabbed Dex in a bear hug.

"Dex, boy am I glad to see you and Matt." Then turning, he said, "This is my girlfriend Massie and this is Heather."

"Nice to meet you," Dex said. "This is my son Matt." Matthew nodded to the women. Heather told Dex and Matthew to sit wherever they felt comfortable and Massie offered them something to drink which they declined. Russell, feeling a bit betrayed by Dell's fawning over the Southern wolf leader, struck an intimidating pose against a far wall and folded his lips throughout the ongoing conversation in which he chose not to participate.

"So, you guys have any plans for how to handle this situation?" Dex asked. Dell weighed in and brought Dex and Matthew up-to-date on the location of Holly and told them about Melvita and her powerful family.

"Melvita?" Dex repeated. "You mean as in Melvita Burkison?"

"Yes," Dell answered surprised.

"Well, that's going to be a problem," Dex warned.

"Yeah, the Covenant witches will never trust a Burkison witch," Matthew said.

"But the Burkisons are powerful. We can use their help."

"Don't matter," Matthew said. "The Covenant witches would rather dance with the devil then even *speak* to a Burkison."

"Well, that's a fine thing," Heather said, standing. "Russell hates Matthew; Melvita can't stand the Covenant witches; the Covenant witches won't work with the Burkison witches, and the Burkisons plan to abandon all of us at the first sign that the Shadow Hunters have gotten wind that my family is tampering with releasing Corina." Heather's eyes filled and her voice rose. "While you all are hating and fighting with each other, my parents are stuck in some goddamn spellbook!"

Russell frowned and stepped out of his pose. Massie rushed to Heather's side. "Honey, it's going to be all right," she said, placing her hand on Heather's back.

"Don't tell me that," Heather snapped at her. "You don't know that—nobody does. Why don't you all just get out! Me and my family will keep trying spells until we get the right one then give Holly what she wants."

"You mean releasing the spirit of Corina?" Matthew blurted.

"Are you nuts?!" Dex snapped.

"What choice do I have? You guys are too busy hating on each other to help me."

Seeing the hurt on Heather's face, and the pain he knew she carried, Russell understood what he had to do. Heather was right. It would have to be a team effort if they had any hope of freeing her parents from a fate that seemed worse than death. He stepped to the middle of the room. "Matt," Russell said. "Nothing much is going to change between me and you, but I *am* willing to work with you, Dex, and if necessary, the Covenant to take out Holly. Russell stuck out his hand. Matthew, a bit shocked, hesitated, but then grabbed his hand and shook it. Russell stepped to Dex and did the same.

Heather walked to Russell, all smiles. She hugged him and rested her head on his chest. They stood awhile and held each other.

Sweeping his eyes from Russell and Heather's sweet moment, Dex asked, "Who's going to convince the witches?"

"We'll leave that to you, Gramps," Matthew chuckled.

"I told you not to…" Dex broke off.

"Actually," Dell said. "We may only need one group of witches, and we were headed over to Melvita's just before you guys got here."

"Great, let's go," Matthew said. "We'll take my van."

*****

Matthew's van pulled into Melvita's driveway. All piled out and immediately greeted by Melvita, her sister, Lydia, and brothers, Craig and Thorn. Melvita led Dex and the group into the den, offered drinks and insisted that they stay for dinner. After dinner, Thorn, the oldest of the Burkison siblings led the conversation for Heather's concern about the possibility of Holly setting a trap.

I wouldn't put anything past her," Thorn said. "Holly is a product of her sister and witches don't come any more clever and wicked than Corina."

"It was always her element of surprise that got *us*," Matthew said.

"Thank the gods she's gone," Dex said.

There is a simple solution to Heather's concerns," Thorn said.

"Really," What's that?" Heather asked.

"The Burkisons and the Brewers were quite inseparable in the beginning," Thorn said. "That was before both families rebelled against the Covenant and got kicked out of the Mystic Circle, and before Corina further ostracized our ancestors after they challenged her for the leadership of the new coven."

"What exactly does that have to do with the solution?" Russell asked.

"What I'm getting at is this," Thorn said. "We all had the same mind as Corina. We know practically all of her tricks."

"But Holly is not Corina," Dex said.

"Do not underestimate her, Dex," Thorn warned him. "Holly was well-groomed by Corina. Corina's spirit can only be summoned one time for a few minutes, but Holly knows that's just enough time for Corina's spirit to cast a spell that will release Holly from her prison and restore her to normal size."

"Is it true," Matthew asked, "that the Hunters reduced her to the size of a micrometer?"

"Yes," Thorn replied.

"How the hell are we going to fight a microorganism?" Massie asked. "How are we going to see her?"

"My sister, brothers and I," Melvita said, "have already come up with the obvious solution—we'll have to shrink all of you to her size."

"What!" Matthew said loudly.

"Oh—hell no," Dex snapped.

Russell gasped and Dell and Massie loudly protested.

"All right! All right! Calm down everyone," Melvita said her voice rising above the protest. "How the hell did you think you were going to defeat a microorganism—huh?"

They all looked at each other. "Are you sure that's the only way?" Dex asked.

"If any of you have a better solution, I'm listening," Melvita replied.

There was a moment of silence until Heather asked, "Will we still have our magic?"

"Will the wolves have the ability to shapeshift?" Dex asked.

"Of course," Thorn said. "You think we'd send you into a strange realm after a witch without your powers?"

After hearing that, Dex and the others still uttered words of doubt among themselves.

"How long will we stay that way?" Russell asked.

"Until she's totally defeated," Lydia said.

"I still have to think about this," Dex said.

"Dex, come on," Russell said. "It's nothing to think about."

"The hell it ain't," Dex told him.

"Damn it, Dex. We just went through this hours ago," Russell said angrily. "Remember this is not just to defeat Holly, but to rescue Heather's parents. Can we please keep that in mind before going off on some tantrum and refusing to cooperate because something makes us uncomfortable?"

"Rusty's right, Dad," Matthew said. "If it were you and Mom, I wouldn't care what I had to do." Dex dropped his head and looked up from under his lashes at Matthew. It appeared as a look of understanding.

"So—are we straight about this?" Russell asked, letting his eyes dance over each of their faces.

"I'm down," Dell said. Massie agreed with a nod.

"Dex? Matt?" Russell asked, looking from one to the other.

"I guess I'm in," Matthew sighed.

All eyes focused in on Dex. There were seconds of silence. Dex glanced at each pair of eyes, staring at him. Then he blurted, "Well, did you think I'd let you two half-wits go in without me?" he said, glancing at Matthew and Dell.

"Then it's settled," Heather said. "Now, all we have to do is make sure we're not ambushed."

"That's you witches department," Dex said, "Anybody for a Scotch and water?" Dex didn't wait for an answer but strolled over to the minibar.

"Good idea," Matthew said. He followed Dex to the bar and began filling his glass with ice.

"Well—I like *that!*" Massie snapped.

CHAPTER THIRTEEN

The following day, Russell and Heather rose and dressed. Across town, Dex and Matthew had risen even earlier and were on their way to pick up Dell and Massie. They all headed to Melvita's home where she and her siblings had prepared a shrinking spell.

Russell, who usually drank hot chocolate in the morning, omitted it since Melvita had warned them not to eat or drink anything eight hours prior to the spell casting. She feared, she told them, there was a slight possibility that the food and beverage they consumed would not shrink along with their stomach, and therefore, could cause the stomach to burst.

All arrived at Melvita's, Russell and Heather having arrived twenty minutes earlier, and were told to strip off their clothes, then given white sheets to wrap around them.

"We found the best spell that will keep you shrunk the longest," Melvita said.

"How long?" Russell asked.

"Some shrinking spells have a time limit. This one doesn't," Thorn said. "It will last until we reverse it."

"Will there be a problem growing us back?" Dex asked.

"There's always a problem with any spell," Lydia answered. "But we foresee none at this time," she assured.

Walking midway into the room, Melvita pointed to the sheeted six and said, "I need you all to stand here against the wall." They gathered the bulk of their white sheets so they could move more easily, and stood where she suggested. Melvita then went to the round table where six candles, her Athame, and an opened grimoire were placed.

Dex took a deep breath and rolled his shoulders to get rid of his nervousness.

"You okay, Dad?" Matthew asked.

"Yeah, sure. How about you?"

"Oh...I'm fine," he lied, wiping the beads of sweat from his brow.

Dell thought about being anywhere but there but after convincing a frightened Massie into going through with the shrinking spell the night before, he felt like a pussy backing out now. Russell and Heather were no less nervous or frightened than the others but appeared too focused on rescuing Grant and Rita to worry about the consequences of being shrunk.

Melvita sat at the head of the table, Thorn to her left, Lydia to her right, and Craig sat across from Melvita. She flipped the page to the shrinking spell she had chosen and gently ran her right hand over the page. Then suddenly, she thought of something and turned to address the six who nervously lined the wall.

"Oh, there's something I need to warn the wolves about," Melvita said.

"You're kidding me, right?" Dex spat. "*Now* you're warning us?"

"I'm sorry; it just slipped my mind," she said focusing on Dex. "Once you shapeshift, you'll stay that way until we grow you back."

"And how are we supposed to communicate with Heather and Massie?" Russell snapped. "Four-legged wolves can't talk."

"I'll fix that right away," Thorn said. "I can give all of you telepathic capability."

"What if *Holly* has that capability?" Heather asked.

"She didn't when we were cohorts," Melvita said. "But in case she has somehow acquired it, I'll have you speak a language unknown to most witches, including Holly. It's the language of the Original Witches. My ancestors had the good fortune to speak this language fluently."

"And since I'm the only one of my siblings," Craig interrupted, "who also speaks that language fluently, *I* get to cast that spell," he said smiling.

"If you guys could hurry it up," Dex blurted. "We're starting to get a little chilly over here."

Matthew ignored his father's griping and asked Melvita, "You sure that's it? There is no way we can contact you from inside that zone."

"Yeah, if you've forgotten anything," Russell warned. "We're up shit creek without a paddle."

"No, there's nothing more...I can assure you," Melvita said.

"What about your sister and brothers?" Dex asked, nodding toward them.

Craig answered. "Melvita and Thorn have covered everything. We've given you all the tools you'll need. It's up to you to do the rest."

"Okay," Russell said. "Let's *do* this!"

Melvita lit the six candles that represented each of the ones to be shrunk. The candles bore different colors with their names written on each. Melvita and her siblings raised their Athame above their heads and spoke the same incantation. Then they brought the Athame down and ran the sharp blade across their palms. With blood dripping from their hands, each placed their open cut over the cut of the hand next to them and clasped it squeezing tightly. Melvita spoke the shrinking spell loudly while holding Lydia's hand to the right of her and Thorn's hand to the left of her. Straightaway, a thick gray fog snaked upon the floor, slithered around the table legs, the base of the walls, and around the sheeted six. The room dimmed, and the drapes danced to the rhythm of an ice-cold breeze. A green mist filled the room, and the candle flames turned a bright red and floated above their wicks in midair. Melvita's voice rose higher as Thorn, Lydia, and Craig joined her. As their voices grew louder, the floor vibrated.

Russell and the others began experiencing severe pains in their joints. Bent over holding themselves, they winced and grimaced at the sharp jabs in their knees, elbows, hips, shoulders, ankles, and wrists. Their bodies twitched and shook violently. Their skin felt as though a thousand needles were being driven into it. They became lightheaded and vomited. The room spun so fast that they lost focus. Then there was blackness, except for the glare of the floor under the candles' light. Everything grew bigger and bigger. They experienced a falling sensation as the floor shot closer to their faces. Finally, they found themselves smothered in endless white that were the sheets they had wrapped around them. All were naked, but the wolves would soon be covered with fur. Heather and Massie, however, spotted a backpack with dried foods and water, two pairs of shoes, two pairs of jeans, T-shirts, and jackets. The clothes were their exact size, and they hurriedly pulled them on.

The Burkisons looked on, but the six were no longer visible to the eye. Melvita could only pinpoint where they were by communicating using telepathy.

"Get ready to be transported," she told them. She spoke the incantation that whisked them away. Their tiny world twirled and spun around them extremely rapidly; *now* they weren't falling but being lifted higher and higher like a stone flying out of a sling, a shooting star racing through the cosmos, a spaceship rocketing to the moon. A hissing sound flooded their ears as they shot upward and outward, violently snatched to the left, violently snatched to the right—dropping like there was no bottom and then shooting upward again—repeating over and over like a never-ending roller coaster ride.

Suddenly, everything stopped as they tumbled into blackness and silence. But *was* it silence? Was it the ringing in their ears, or the normal sounds of that strange dark world? Standing in the stillness of the Withersphere, the wolves immediately shapeshifted into miniature four-legged wolves with needle-point fangs and sharp retractable claws. They stood in stock contrast to one another; Russell's fur was white, Dell's tannish-brown with splashes of black and black trimmed ears, Dex was bold-grey with a white belly, while Matthew bore a shiny silver with a black streak down his back to his tail. The wolves used their K-9 vision to scan their lightless surroundings.

"See anything yet?" Heather asked Russell, who walked by her side.

"No—nothing to speak of," he said.

"This place is huge," Matthew gasped. "We may as well be roaming around in outer space."

"It probably *is* huge," Massie said. "But remember, the inside of a toolbox would look like the cosmos to *us*."

"You're right. This is going to take some getting used to," Matthew answered.

Russell saw that the sphere contained floating debris that resembled shredded black and white cardboard. The sides and upper view was like watching the cosmos from a space ship except there were no clearly visible planets—just twinkles of stars in a black sky. The surface under his feet was hard and smooth.

After nearly half an hour of creeping along and relying upon wolf vision to interpret their surroundings, Heather blurted, "Oh, this is foolish...us stumbling around in the dark. I'm going to give us light."

She attempted to cast a spell when Russell shouted, "No. Wait! Holly will see us coming."

"Well, let her, damn it!" Heather snapped. "Isn't that why we're here?"

"Excuse me, Heather," Massie said sarcastically, "but aren't you the one who was so worried about an ambush? Now you welcome it?"

"Massie's right, Heather," Dell said. "You conjure up light, and Holly could see us before we see her."

"Honey," Russell interjected. "It'll waste our element of surprise."

"All right already," Heather spat. "I'm a little anxious, I suppose. It's just this waiting is killing me."

"I get it," Matthew snapped. "But we've sacrificed too much to be here just to blow it because you're anxious."

"Watch your tone when you're talking to her," Russell warned Matthew.

Matthew sensed the old animosity creeping back into their relationship, and he quickly reversed. The others froze and the tension was thick. "I apologize, Heather. I guess we all are a little anxious," he said hoping that would appease Russell. The last thing they needed on such a dangerous undertaking, Matthew thought, was bickering among themselves.

Dex looked on, furious at Matthew's appearing to kiss Russell's butt in order to keep the peace. But he decided not to voice his opinion, just yet, for the sake of the mission.

"Honey, the night vision of the wolves will have to do for now," Russell said to Heather. Heather smiled at him. She brushed his white fur with her hand, bent, and kissed his snout.

They continued walking slowly in the pitch blackness of the Withersphere for nearly an hour until Heather stopped abruptly and grabbed Russell's fur around his neck, signaling him to halt.

"What is it?" Russell asked.

Heather's witch sense had picked up something. "We're not alone," she said.

"You're damn right you're not!"

They spun around at the sound of Holly's voice. The adrenaline within their tiny systems rose.

"How did she know what we were saying to each other?" Dell asked frantically.

"Holy shit!" Matthew spat. "Either Craig forgot to zap us with that original language or the damn spell didn't work."

"That doesn't matter *now*," Dex said. "This is it! Get your asses ready to rumble."

Suddenly, the darkness lifted into a glowing light. Holly, with her limited magic (and no match for Heather and Massie), lit up the entire sphere; and standing before them was a platoon of what appeared to be silverfish but were deadly microorganisms—a little taller and wider than the wolves. Holly was nowhere in sight. The organisms were a light, bluish-silver consisting of three parts: a small bulb— the head displaying several dark, red dots on what appeared to be its face; the larger bulb of the body that had a gold-hued back, and finally a wide, long tail. It stood on thousands of antenna-like legs—if one could imagine fifty brushes walking. They made not a sound but appeared to be looking directly at Heather, Massie, and the wolves.

Heather and Massie rose into action. They stood with their hands outward to cast a spell that would obliviate the microbes. Neither witch knew what spell the other would cast but had confidence, that together, they would destroy every microbe standing before them. As they proceeded to speak an incantation, a huge bubble seeped out of thin air. It descended upon the witches—vacuuming them into its clear compartment. They struggled to break out. The bubble stretched and gave in every direction, but the witches couldn't break free. That was Holly's plan. Her magic *was* weak, but with Heather and Massie trapped, the wolves would have to rely on nothing but their K-9 wits and strength to survive. Fifty killer microbes against four wolves— Holly was definitely her sister's evil paragon.

The wolves kept their eyes focused on the microbes. At first, they were too astonished to move.

"Shouldn't we be doing something?" Dell asked nervously.

Russell, wide-eyed, glared at Dex awaiting an answer. But Dex and Matthew, who had faced worse enemies, never broke their concentration.

"Wait," Dex said. "Let's see what they've got."

Dex didn't have to wait long. The microbes bolted toward them with great speed. Their brush-like feet sounded like the swooshing of horses' hooves plowing through grass.

"Go for those red dots! I think that's their eyes!" they heard Dex's thoughts blast inside their brains.

One bulldozed Russell sending him tumbling backward. It hit him with such force that Russell flipped over three times before landing on his back. The microbe quickly tackled him again. Russell swiped, clawed and bit it profusely. It shot out a razor-sharp tongue that missed Russell's eyes several times but sliced into his nose and ear. Ducking and dodging, Russell waited for it to lower its head just a little more; when it did, he drove his fangs and claws into its face, ripping it to shreds. Russell gasped when he noticed a gold substance oozing out of every busted red dot. The microbe, greatly wounded, clumsily and blindly scuttered about bumping into and blocking the way of other microbes. The rest of its body appeared to deflate as the gold fluid continued to pour out.

Russell looked at Dex, Matthew, and Dell. Their furs were soaked and sticky with gold. They appeared to have lost some of their own substance, with leaking bloody cut marks on their faces and snouts. Matthew also had an injured paw that bled heavily. He bit down hard on the wound to apply pressure.

Despite the injuries caused by the microbes, it seemed Holly's plan was flawed. Gouging out the microbes' eyes pushed the scent of their substance through the air. Her letting the organisms starve so they would be more deadly against her foe backfired when the microbes turned and attacked the injured ones starting a feeding frenzy.

The microbes no longer paid any attention to the wolves which meant the wolves could concentrate on freeing

Heather and Massie. They leaped, clawed and bit into the bubble, trying to rip it, but nothing could penetrate it. They simply had to rely on Holly's magic being so inadequate that the bubble wouldn't hold for long—and they were right. By the time the feeding frenzy was at an end, the bubble gave way to Heather and Massie's weight; the wolves watched as the two spilled out onto the surface.

Sitting on their sore bottoms, Heather and Massie watched their cellophane trap suddenly disappear. The witches stood and turned toward the remaining microbes that still fed on each other. They held out their hands; a bolt of energy shot from them and blasted the microbes into floating debris. Then Heather and Massie went to each wolf and attended to their injuries with a substance from Massie's potion vial necklace.

"Hey!" Russell blurted flinching from the sting of the potion.

"Oh, be still, you big puppy," Heather said, cleaning his cut nose.

"If this is all Holly has, defeating her will be rather easy, don't you think?" Russell asked, still flinching.

"Never underestimate a witch," Dell said, "no matter how weak she appears."

"What's next, I wonder?" Matthew asked.

"Your guess is as good as mine," Dex said. "One thing for sure, we can't stand around here waiting for her to come to us. We've got to play offense."

"How the hell do we play offense when we don't even know where she is?" Russell asked.

"That's why you have us, honey," Heather said. "Witches can find anybody and anything—you know that. We just have to be smarter and not let Holly trap us again."

"How come you and Massie didn't locate her before those things attacked us?" Matthew asked.

"Because we had to use light, and you guys told me that would make Holly see us," Heather replied.

"Okay—well, go to it, ladies," Dex teased. "Don't mind us."

Heather pulled a bubble glass medallion from around her neck and placed it on the surface. Then she and Massie sat cross-legged in front of one another with the medallion between them. They held hands and summoned help from beyond for several minutes until the glass bubble lit up revealing Holly's location.

"There she is!" Massie said excitedly.

The wolves gathered around to look. Holly had managed to structure a fortress out of fallen cosmic debris and surrounded it with a different army of microorganisms that looked like giant chocolate-colored ants with cone-shaped heads and jagged black teeth. Dex turned away and took off trotting, his snout still slightly swollen.

"Dad! Where are you going?"

"To Hollyville," he said.

"Well—wait up." Matthew chuckled, trotting behind him. Russell and the rest scrambled to catch up.

CHAPTER FOURTEEN

Russell grew uneasy about what diabolical scheme Holly would pull next. The first microbes had been easy and quick to destroy. What were the vulnerabilities of these new ones, he wondered? The guarding microbes appeared more monstrous and deadly: they had razor-sharp spikes on their backs and swung whip-like tails; their protruding teeth dripped with a yellow foaming substance. And just as the medallion had revealed, the fortress was well-built; the thousands of fractured star materials Holly magically assembled seemed impenetrable.

Dex, the most senior and battle experienced member of the group, was chosen to command. "Let's not make a move just yet," Dex said. "She knows we're here. We'll travel a quarter of the way back, do some planning and bed down for a time. Heather, you and Massie keep us from a possible surprise attack?"

"I'll place a protective shield around us while we're there," Massie said.

"Good," Dex said. "Let's move out."

After traveling back and setting up camp, and with the magical shield in place, the group spent long hours finalizing a plan and later, slept comfortably. While the others continued to sleep, Dex slipped away and sat alone in deep thought. Matthew, after catching a quick nap spotted him, rose paced over, and sat next to him.

"All right, it's just me, now," Matthew said. He spoke in broken Coptic, a variation of an ancient Egyptian language he and Dex had learned from his grandmother. "What are our chances?" he asked.

"We're screwed," Dex said.

"So, basically every word you told them about the plan was a lie?"

"No, not all of it, but I had to say something," Dex said. "Dell and Russell are just teenagers. They've never been in a battle with a sorcerer before. I don't even know how to command them."

"Dad, you and I are old pros at this, and Holly's magic is nowhere near Corina's."

"Yeah, but we didn't actually defeat her," Dex said. "The wolves won battles, and the witches did all right, but it was the Shadow Hunters who defeated her and shrunk Holly into this hell hole."

"Well, Dad, the Shadow Hunters are not here. All we've got is wolf strength and limited magic. And it's going to have to do. Great Zeus, I've never heard you talk defeat before."

"I've never had two young wolves to look after before. Look, if I make a mistake with just you and me, that's one thing—you and I have gotten out of worst situations than this. But those two kids over there are not you and me. And though Heather and Massie are stronger than Holly, they're not Jewel and Naomi."

"And Holly is not Corina. Great Goddess, Dad...we can *do* this. Listen, I'm Russell's guardian whether he likes it or not. I'll keep him by my side and you keep Dell at yours. Whatever they see us do, they'll mimic."

"So you think it's that simple...huh?"

"Well, yeah," Matthew said.

"I hope you're right, son."

"Dad, stop being so protective. They've got to get fighting experience, and they may as well get it now."

"And you're confident we can get them back to their mom and dad safe and sound."

"I'm confident if you lead us, Dad."

Dex smiled at Matthew's faith in him. "All right, son. If you believe that strongly, then this is what I held back from telling the group. I'm not sure we can easily defeat those stronger microbes; I think that yellow stuff is acid. If it is, we don't stand a chance against it on our own. But if Heather and Massie's magic is strong enough to stop it, then the microbes are made of matter just like us and the wolves can at least hold them off, while Heather and Massie use their craft to penetrate the building. I believe that's where Holly is."

"Now, there's the dad I'm used to," Matthew said.

"Hey," Dell called. "You guys mind speaking our language?"

"Yeah," Massie said. "We've been listening to that gibberish in our heads for over ten minutes now. What's so important, you can't tell us?"

"It's nothing," Matthew said. "We were just speaking about my becoming a dad soon, that's all."

"Hey, congratulations," Dell said.

"Thanks."

Dex and Matthew rejoined the group and Heather passed out rations, while Massie applied more of the potion to the wolves' wounds. Later, Dex ordered the shield removed and the group headed out.

*****

When they reached the fortress, it was dark and quiet as if staged. The fake sun had set. It was as though earlier, Holly had wanted them to see her fortress and the monsters that guarded it. Once the mystery had unfolded—she welcomed them into her unfathomable abode.

All knew it was a trap. They once again stood before the alluring citadel. But that time, they were taking the fight *to* Holly. Determination took over nervousness; courage—terror; uncertainty became a spark of adventure.

Dex waved them forward. Massie had placed a different protective shield that moved when they moved. But they couldn't fight or cast a spell from behind it. The shield would only be used to bulldoze their way through the guards to the building. Dex's plan was to reach the building and with their backs against the stone structure, he felt they stood a better chance of defending themselves against the microbes. Then once inside, Heather and Massie would defeat Holly and force her to set Heather's parents free.

The force waited in the eerie silence. Dex was careful not to move. Then suddenly, out of the dim atmosphere, the mist parted and dark ant-like shapes stood gazing at them. The biggest shape shook its head as if to command the others. The microbes sprang toward them with accelerating speed.

"Brace for impact!" Heather shouted.

"Will the shield hold?" Dex asked.

"Don't know," she said. "So prepare to battle."

Five microbes bowed their coneheads and hit the shield with a loud thud sending it flying backward. The violent slam shook the group, but the shield held. The coneheads hit again lifting the invisible shield from the surface and landing the group up-side-down. Another massive hit flipped the shield several times—causing it to land right-side-up. Each hit sent the group farther back.

"This isn't working," Heather said. "Hold on to each other tightly." Heather cast a spell that drove the shield forward with lightning speed. It hit several microbes and knocked them apart allowing an opening for the group to halfway advance toward the building. The microbes recovered quickly, surrounded the shield, and spat a yellow substance that began to dissolve it. Massie spelled the shield to lift so they could crawl out from under it forcing them squarely into the open. The microbes abandoned the shield and surrounded them. Before Heather and Massie could cast a spell, a microbe whipped its tail around Dex's waist, lifted him, and threw him several feet into the air. Another whip caught Russell around the chest and began to constrict with the might of a python. Matthew bit its tail off freeing Russell who fell to his knees gasping for breath. Matthew gazed around and spotted Dex several feet away scrambling to his feet. Heather incanted to obliviate the microbes, but nothing happened. Then she incanted again and iron muzzles flew over the mouths of the microbes. But one microbe whipped Heather into the air. Massie tried to run but another's tail smacked her into the ground. She scrambled to her feet and the tail whacked her again sending her skidding across the surface. While the microbes violently shook their heads trying to throw off the muzzles, the wolves made it to the building where Massie sat dazed after hitting the hard wall. Heather ran up, lightheaded from *her* fall and helped Massie to her feet. Holly's voice filled the air, and the muzzles fell off. The microbes quickly advanced toward them. Massie incanted and sealed their mouths closed. "I don't know how long that will hold," Massie said. "Holly may undo it."

"Holly's magic seems to be getting stronger," Russell said.

"Yes, we know," Heather said. "I think she's absorbing *our* magic. We didn't want to say anything, but Massie and I have been feeling weaker since we've encountered her."

"Well, in that case, use all the powers you have to get us inside this building. We'll handle the microbes," Dex said.

The silent microbes bowed their heads— signaling a coming attack. They advanced and stood before the wolves, their tails thrashing from side to side. Matthew's powerful claws took off half the face of its leader. Russell raked his claws across the face of another. Beside them Dex and Dell stood side by side—their razor-sharp claws flashing like lightning—swiping off limbs, but as many fell, more followed. Then the microbes turned their backs and whipped their tails at them. The wolves ducked, swiped, and dodged the best they could—biting and clawing off tails, but also lashed by many more.

"Hurry up with that damn spell!" Dex yelled.

"We're hurrying!" Heather shouted.

Holly's voice filled the air, and the microbes opened their mouths. A bucket load of yellow substance spilled from their jaws. Steam rose from the surface where it pooled and fizzed.

"Holy shit! Matthew said. The wolves backed up against the wall as tightly as they could— fangs and claws at the ready. Dripping acid, black jagged teeth moved in so close the wolves sickened from the stench. At that very moment, a large chunk of the building caved inward and the wolves tumbled through. Heather, Massie, and the wolves took off running down a dark hallway with nearly thirty microbes on their tail. Heather and Massie had to magically float in order to match the galloping speed of the wolves. Turning a corner, they sped halfway down the hall and found a locked door. With the microbes moving fast upon them, Heather quickly incanted and the door flew opened. They ran inside and Heather spelled locked it. But Massie made the door disappear. Though the room seemed safe, Heather wasn't taking any chances; she placed another shield around them so they could catch a breath until their next move.

The room was cold and bare, with not even a carpet or scatter rugs to warm their bottoms. There were no windows and thanks to Massie, no door. After attending to the wolves' wounds as well as their own cuts and bruises, Heather and Massie cast a locating spell. The medallion lit up revealing a square outline of a shadowy figure with long, ragged hair. "I believe I've found Holly," Heather said. "But for some reason, the Medallion isn't showing clear images."

"Holly is probably interfering," Massie said.

"What the hell are we going to do about those things outside?" Russell asked Heather, nodding toward the hallway.

"I tried an obscurity spell, but it failed," she said.

"The main thing," Dex said, "is to follow the medallion to the shadowy figure." He rose from the floor and the others followed. "All right," Dex said. "Heather, get rid of the shield. Massie, bring back the door."

With the shield removed, the door appeared and flew open. A huge cone head, dripping acid, stood in the doorway and was pushed by other microbes from behind that were eager to get into the room. A muzzle flew over its mouth, and Dex ripped open its face. Two microbes shoved the injured one out of the doorway and tried to enter at the same time but got stuck. Massie spelled a flaming cloak that wrapped around their heads. The flaming microbes yanked their heads out, rolling and squirming on the floor and knocking the other microbes away from the doorway. The group saw the opening, ran through the door, and into the hall. They were met by several microbes that dashed over the burning ones and bolted toward them. Heather cast a wall of flames that blocked their path.

The group made their way up the hallway then turned a corner. The wolves constantly looked behind them as Heather and Massie, led by the medallion light, walked slowly ahead of them. They turned another corner and the medallion mysteriously began flashing. Suddenly, a blur of a shadow flew in front of Heather and Massie and tried to spell-freeze Heather who responded by flinging a sleeper at it. It missed but the shadow disappeared.

"What the hell was that!" Dex yelled.

"We must be getting close to where she's trapped; she's getting desperate," Massie said.

"That wasn't *her*?" Russell asked.

"No," Heather said. "That was her magic. She's just a trapped body with a voice. She found a way to do damage from her confinement. And she's getting weaker."

"And we're getting stronger," Massie said. "I can feel it. What she zapped from us has returned."

"Thank the goddess for that," Dex said.

Slowly they turned another dark corner. The darker the hallway, the brighter the medallion shined. Up ahead, they observed a set of stairs leading downward. They rounded the spiral staircase onto a round floor that led to a heap of debris. Out of thin air, shadowy figures attacked them, throwing balls of flames, frost cloaks, and paralyzing spells at Heather and Massie. But all were met with a powerful whirlwind cloak that wrapped around the shadowy figures and banished them into thin air.

"Holly, we know you're here. Your magic is weak. Show yourself," Heather said.

They continued to search when Massie spotted a strange looking box among the debris. Observing further, she saw a pathetic looking Holly—weak and barely breathing. The Shadow Hunters had confined her to a transparent container with holes for her to breathe. There was no escape. How Holly managed to do so much damage from her confinement proved just how powerful and dangerous a witch she was. Her face was a bluish-grey; her lips were cracked and bleeding; she was rubbery skin and bone with matted hair and doll-like eyes that flashed from side to side as she looked into their faces.

Holly's voice once again filled the air. "Set me free," she said, "and I'll set your parents free."

Heather spoke from her mouth. "You want us to take your word?"

"I'll set one free before you free me. You choose which parent," Holly said. "And if I lie, which I won't, at least you'll have one parent."

"You want me to choose between my parents!" Heather shouted at her. "Why, you miserable piece of shit! You're going to set both my parents free. Or I'll find a way to do it myself while you lay here and rot."

"You'll never undo that spell," Holly chuckled. "Never."

"Ohhhh!" Heather blurted, raising her hand to attempt an oblivion spell. But Massie grabbed her arm.

"Don't," Massie said. "You'll never get your parents back if you incapacitate her. We've got to think. We didn't come this far to screw up. And we're not leaving here without freeing your mom and dad."

Russell approached Heather's side and lifted her dangling hand with his head. She looked down and repeatedly slid her hand along his furry white head to his neck and back. It calmed her.

Then Massie spoke. "We don't trust each other—that's clear. So, listen to this. We'll spell you someplace that's more comfortable, an improvement over this filthy hole you've been in for the past six years. And you let her parents go. Or you can stay here in this waste, and we'll contact the Shadow Hunters and let them know what you've been up to."

"No! No Shadow Hunters," Holly said dreading the thought. "I'll consider what you say. But where exactly are you sending me? And why should I trust you?"

"Because you have no choice," Heather said. "Think what the hunters will do when we tell them your plan to set Corina's spirit free to absorb her magic and head your own evil empire."

Holly was silent for a moment trying to come up with some trick that would get them to release her, but keep one or both her parents as collateral for future bargaining.

"You're wasting time, Holly," Heather said.

"We're not playing games here," Massie snapped. "If you don't release them this minute, we will summon the hunters and let them know that shrinking you wasn't enough."

"Yeah, think what they'll do this time," Heather smirked.

Holly saw no way out. Still, wherever they sent her, she thought, in time, she could conjure enough magic to spell her way out—even if it took a thousand years. That was nothing to a witch. "All right," Holly said. She spoke an incantation that took less than a minute then said, "You're mom's free."

"What the hell do you mean my mom's free?" Heather spat.

"Holly, so help me..." Massie warned through clenched teeth.

"Wait! This is not a trick. I just wanted you to know I would do what I said. Go check and see that she's free," Holly said. "And I promise I'll set your father free after you hear me out."

"You believe her?" Massie asked.

"No...but I'll check it out anyway."

Heather sat upon the floor and Massie followed suit; they performed a locating spell on her mom. And sure enough, Rita was back at home, but frantically looking and yelling down at her husband who still lingered upon the page. Heather couldn't hear what she was yelling, but her mom looked terrified.

"All right my mom is free, you breathing corpse. Speak...and this better be good."

Holly took a moment. "I know how your particular coven honors your goddess."

"Yeah...so?" Heather snapped.

"You never lie in her name," Holly said.

"Get on with it," Heather said. "You're trying my patience."

"I want you to pledge in the name of your goddess that you will release me from this entrapment, put me back to normal size and send me somewhere clean, warmly weathered, with green grass, lakes, flowers, vegetable gardens, and fruit trees."

Heather and Massie looked at one another. "Are you insane?" Heather said. "You have one minute to set my father free or so help me, so help me, Goddess..."

"And your father?" Holly asked. "What happens to him after the hunters finish with me?"

That garnered a few seconds of silence. "You really think you're clever, don't you?" Massie griped.

Heather turned to Massie. "So, what the hell do I do?" she asked.

"I know what *I'd* do, but they're your parents. I think it should be your call."

Heather took a deep breath then turned to Holly. "All right, I pledge in the name of Asase Ya to grant you what you asked.

Satisfied, Holly kept her word. "It's done," she said.

"It better be," Heather snapped. She performed another locating spell and found her mom and dad locked in a strong embrace. Her mom was crying and kissing her dad's face wet.

Massie and the wolves looked on dreading what Heather was forced to do next.

"Are you ready?" Heather asked Holly who took a deep breath and nodded.

"Yes," Holly said grinning.

Heather spoke a rather long incantation in Hungarian and Holly was whisked away instantly; she tumbled through space and time then landed on a soft, green surface. Holly stood surrounded by a beam of light. Then the light dimmed and faded as her new abode became clear.

No one spoke for a few moments then Russell asked, "Where did you send her?"

Heather just grinned and waved them in to observe the medallion. It revealed a normal-size Holly in a fabricated paradise. Heather had indeed kept her word. But Holly would never endanger anyone again. She banished Holly to the 14th century and had greatly enlarged the box, turning it into an empty castle in Costanocia, Spain—a sleepy little town where the weather was favorable all-year-round. Heather placed an invisible wall around the castle—no one could get in or out. Parts of the inside castle resembled the outdoors with its fruit trees, vegetable and flower gardens, an artificial waterfall and lake. It had multiple rooms with indoor plumbing and a 21st century kitchen. Heather had zapped all of her magic, so Holly would forever be a slave to her new environment with mop buckets, brooms, dustpans, rags and shelves full of chemical cleaners. The wolves laughed and Massie presented her a high-five.

When Melvita got word from Heather's family that Rita and Grant Marshall were safely at home, she celebrated the success with her siblings. Then the Burkisons immediately prepared the spell that would bring the group home and back to normal size.

CHAPTER FIFTEEN

The sun appeared brighter. Even the artificial lighting inside the apartment seemed to match God's glory. What other hints did Russell need that life would be a little more pleasant and bearable from now-on? Not perfect, certainly, but for the first time, he felt being a wolf wasn't the end of the world. He had fought monsters and a powerful sorcerer. Not to make light of war, but not even soldiers in any battle with all its horrors had faced what he'd faced. He had never known that such evil existed except in fiction books and movies. But there he was, in his earlier life, right smack in the middle of that existence; supernatural evil lurking all around him and he hadn't a clue. He'd discovered there was also a supernatural good that could fight it and win—and he was a part of that good. He was a werewolf. He belonged to a race of beings that could transform and take down powerful evils.

All wasn't forgiven, however, and Russell still believed he had been cheated of a normal life. Hatred was no longer an issue, but a matter of principle ruled in its place. He hadn't chosen his own destiny. He felt to embrace his inner-wolf openly yielded credibility to Jewel and Matthew and got them off the hook. Yet, he wanted to bury the bitterness until he knew how to confront it with a more mature nature. Plus and foremost, he couldn't shake the awesomeness he'd felt observing and fighting alongside, Dex, Matthew, and his buddy, Dell. His beautiful Heather and Massie were amazing in the vital part *they* played in defeating Holly. Even though Holly's powers weren't nearly what they once were, her witchcraft, however, was overwhelmingly challenging.

There was a whole other world packed with supernatural good and evil, and Russell felt torn for being one of its many victors. The defeat of an evil genius and the return of Heather's parents would forever be a part of his legacy. Not to mention that he was now a powerful ally. He could protect his family and friends. After all—what was a mugger, rapist, or school bully to him? Certainly, he couldn't transform openly, but he was a more powerful entity.

Heather poked her head in the living room doorway. She had just finished a call from Massie. "Honey, Dell, and Massie want us to join them at the Neather Gardens for a little party. I went ahead and told them we'd come; hope that was okay."

"Yeah, that's fine."

"I said yes because we haven't left the apartment since returning from the Withersphere weeks ago. I thought getting out would do us both some good," she said.

"Honey, you don't have to explain. I think joining Dell and Massie is great."

The night was warm and the crowd at the Neather Gardens grew surprisingly large. Instead of the usual teen and young adults, it seemed all the Northern and Southern wolf pack and their wives were in attendance. The three-man-band sounded fresh and vibrant. People stood with drinks and plates of finger foods in hand while Massie moved through the guests. After she greeted Dell's parents, Dex and his wife Jan, Matthew and a six months pregnant Kayla, Dell gave her a reassuring kiss on the cheek for being the perfect hostess.

Everyone was dressed to the teeth in evening wear. Heather was absolutely stunning in a pumpkin yellow tight-fitting dress and matching six-inch sling-backs. One shoulder and arm were bare; the other arm of the dress hugged her arm down to the wrist. The wrist hem was surrounded with bright gold sequences that flattered her long dangling earrings and tiny gold purse. When Russell and Heather made their entrance, the room lit up in smiles. Dell came over and ushered them to the middle of the room.

"Are we late?" Russell asked. "It seems we're the last ones here."

"No," Dell said. "I gave you a later time because we wanted everyone to be here when you walked in."

"But why?" Russell asked. "Have I done something wrong?"

"No," Dell chuckled.

"Then—then what?"

"Rusty," Dell said as if making a formal announcement. "The wolves thought it would be a good idea to take advantage of this gathering to officially welcome you, not just into the junior group, but into the entire wolf pack. We know you've had a very difficult time adjusting—and I embarrassingly admit some of us," he cleared his throat, "me excluded... made it even more so."

"Your courage was reported to us," interrupted one of the senior wolves, "and we were told that in the face of horrible odds at the Withersphere you were nothing short of amazing for a first-time-battle. Dell was amazing as well, and not to make light of Dell's performance, but he was born with his skills and at least had some training. You, of course, had none. From myself as well as everyone here, you've earned our utmost respect, son." The room exploded with applause. Heather with her gold purse clasp tightly under her arm clapped profusely—her flashing, white smile and sparkling, green eyes danced and twinkled with admiration. Russell blinked several times to hold back the sea that welled in his eyes. When the applause ended, the adult wolves raised a glass to him while the junior wolves, though a few still looked reluctant, made their way to him, smiling and patting him on the shoulder. Heather managed a wet kiss on the lips. "Did you know about this?" Russell asked.

"No," Heather said surprisingly.

As soon as Heather broke her embrace, several junior witches came up giggling. Each pecked Russell on the cheek and eyed him up and down. One cute red-head wet her lips before hip-swaying off.

As the room returned to normal, Russell mingled with the crowd. Matthew kept his distance, but Dex walked to Russell and gave him a quick bear hug. "I told River about how well you and Dell fought, and he said he couldn't be prouder of you both."

"Tell him I appreciate it very much."

"I will," Dex said. Dex returned to Jan who stood talking and laughing with several other wives.

"Isn't it wonderful, honey?" Heather said excitedly. "They've finally accepted the wonderful person I've always known you to be. Now, they know it, too."

Russell faked a smile and even though he had been near tears during the applause he thought, yeah... *but why should I accept 'them' or want to be accepted by them*? But Russell knew, like it or not, this was his new reality—his new world. He had been reborn into a species of wolves with human intelligence and unbelievable skills. He looked across the room and spotted Matthew. He knew what he had to do. Russell put his drink aside, excused himself to Heather, and made his way across the room.

"Matt, I just want to say to you and Mrs. Porter congratulations on your new baby and hope he or she is a healthy one."

"Why, thank you, Rusty. That's very sweet," Kayla said.

"Thank you. That means a lot to me. It really does," Matthew said.

The evening continued beautifully with lively chatter, music, and dancing. Heather kept quite a fixed eye on Russell who had unintentionally garnered much attention from the cute and sexy teen witches. She wasn't jealous and only a few years older, but had never experienced him receiving so much female attentiveness before.

Around ten o'clock, the affair ended, and outside in the dim parking lot lights, people hugged, kissed, and said their goodbyes before getting into their cars. On the ride back to Heather's apartment, she talked on-and-on about the evening and about how delighted she was that Russell had officially been accepted by the wolves. She thought it was a big deal. Russell was still torn between who he was and who he used to be. He guessed it would always be that way with him. He felt his finding out he was a werewolf was like the original five stages of pre-death: shock, denial, anger, bargaining, and acceptance. Russell had indeed wrestled with the first three, but who the hell would he bargain with? Maybe that's why totally accepting what he had become proved so difficult—he had been stuck on anger for such a long time.

When they entered Heather's apartment, she suggested they shower together. The two kissed, fondled, and made love under the steam and rushing water. Their shoes and clothes left a trail leading from the apartment entrance to the bedroom door. The next morning, the maid spotting the trail just shook her head and mumbled under her breath as she bent and gathered the shoes and garments in her arms.

The day after, basking in joy, Heather folded the last piece of Russell's clothing and placed it in the top chest of drawers. School was officially out, except for summer school, and Russell would stay with her in the apartment until September.

Tray and Caroline Sooner were off on a six-week vacation. It was the first time Russell hadn't gone with them. Caroline worried about her baby, but Tray felt Russell was responsible enough to take care of things while they were away and left a long list of things that would keep him busy, such as, mowing the lawn, trimming the hedges, taking in the mail, watering the plants, and the list went on.

Russell stood in the kitchen honing his chef skills when the phone rang.

"Dell."

"Hey, Rusty, have you heard the news?"

"What news?"

"Will Casey, a Southern wolf, was found shot to death this morning...a silver nitrate bullet in his brain."

"What the...oh, my God. Are you kidding me?"

"What! What is it?" Heather asked frantically.

Russell turned to her. "A southern wolf, Will Casey was found shot to death this morning...ah, silver nitrate bullet to the head."

"Oh, my stars," Heather said.

"How did they know specifically it was silver nitrate?" Russell asked.

"Dr. Lorac did an autopsy," Dell said.

"Do they know who did it?" Heather blurted.

"Wait, honey, wait," Russell told her straining to hear the rest of what Dell was saying. He put the phone on speaker. "Dell, Dell, hold-up," Russell wanted Heather to hear. "Do they know who did it?" Russell asked.

"It had to be a human," Dell said. "Who else can be around that stuff?"

"I'm aware of that, Dell...but do they know the person who did it?"

"Dude, you honestly think I'd be on the phone with you if we had the name of the bastard who did it?"

"All right...keep me posted."

"Sure...if I know any more, I'll get back to you," Dell said ending the call.

"Great Zeus...we've never had problems with humans before...not unprovoked, that is," Heather said.

"I feel funny hearing you guys saying the word human. It's like you're talking about something outside of me."

"We *are*, honey. When are you going to accept the fact that you are no longer in that gene pool?"

"When hell freezes over," Russell snapped. "Anyway, whoever shot him is not from around here...has to be an outsider."

"It could be an isolated case," Heather said. "Maybe they found out Casey was a werewolf and killed him thinking he was the only one of his kind?"

"That makes sense. Sure hope you're right. Whoever shot Will is still out there and we've got to find him or them before any more wolves are targeted."

"True," she said. "But how the hell do we find the person or persons who did this? I can't do a locating spell without knowing who I'm looking for."

"I may have to swallow my pride and reach out to Sheriff Tilbert," Russell said.

"Why...what can *he* do?"

"I don't know specifically. But I'll figure it out before I reach Sheerfield." Russell grabbed a hooded jacket and started for the door. A light rain fell from the dark clouds.

"Want me to go with you?" Heather asked grabbing for her purse.

"No, honey, I won't be long." He closed the door behind him and made his way to the elevators.

*****

Russell tapped on Tilbert's open office door. Tilbert looked up from writing on a thick note pad. "Russell?" he said with raised eyebrows. "Come in...have a seat."

"Thank you," Russell said taking the visitor's seat opposite Tilbert's desk. "I know I should have called first, but the news is rather pressing. Hope this isn't a bad time."

"Not at all. What exactly is so pressing...it's not your parents?" he asked.

"No. My parents are fine. In fact, they're vacationing in Florida. We go there every year."

"How come you're not with them?"

"I'm staying with my girlfriend...just until school starts."

"They'll be gone that long?" Tilbert asked frowning.

"They'll be back long before I have to attend school."

"I see," Sheriff Tilbert said. "Well, so, you're spending the summer with your girlfriend. I gather that's Heather?"

"Yes," Russell said dreading that fatherly concerned look on Tilbert's face.

"Wow. I tell you...time flies. It seemed just a while ago—you were just a little kid of ten."

Russell looked down then up with a half-smile. Sheriff Tilbert scooted around in his chair. "You're seventeen now?" he asked.

"Yes, sir."

"Isn't Heather a bit older? Has she met your parents?"

"Sheriff in all due respect, Sir, I didn't come here to talk about my personal life."

"Of course, son," Tilbert said straightening in his seat. "What can I help you with?"

Russell told Tilbert about Will Casey and how he was shot with a bullet filled with silver nitrate. He told him that Doctor Sally Lorac performed the autopsy and how concerned the wolves were about not knowing who the perpetrator or perpetrators were.

"Silver nitrate?" Tilbert's voice rose. "But that's impossible." But Tilbert caught himself. He'd started to say that the only supply of silver nitrate he knew of was the supply he and Bob Wilson had received from the Shadow Hunters which they stored not far from the station. Tilbert knew that that particular piece of information would be seen by Russell and the wolves as making him and the entire sheriff department suspects.

"Do you know of anybody in this town buying silver nitrate?"

"Why—yes, son. People use silver nitrate for all kinds of purposes. But are you sure it was silver nitrate?"

"Doctor Lorac is a pretty good doctor. I'm sure she'd know silver nitrate when she found it."

"You're right, son. I'm sure not going to question the expert opinion of Doctor Lorac." Tilbert went on to explain that ordinary people could buy silver nitrate across the counter for getting rid of warts, nose bleeds, and other minor discomforts. Though reluctant to confirm his knowledge of the amount of silver nitrate it would take to kill a werewolf, he explained that those amounts had to be bought in larger quantities to have any effect. The only facilities licensed to buy that compound in large quantities were almost exclusively hospitals and medical labs. Hospitals used it as a topical solution to treating wounds and burns; other facilities used it as an anti-infective agent in treating drinking water. Being exposed to small amounts, Tilbert continued, only resulted in stained skin of purple, black, or brown. Constant use resulted in painful burns and damage to the eyes. The MO of silver nitrate was a skin and eye irritant.

"Then it would have to be someone working for a facility that uses this stuff in large quantities—wouldn't you agree, Sheriff?"

"I suppose so, Rusty." Sheriff Tilbert could see Russell's determination on his worrisome face, and he tried to let the boy know that he took his concern seriously.

"Could someone put together enough nitrate...say...if they bought it across the counter for a wart or nose bleed and then put it in a bullet?"

Tilbert scratched his short beard. "It's...ah, possible, Rusty. What exactly are you getting at and what do you want me to do?"

"First, I have to ask, did you or your deputies have anything to do with killing Casey?"

"Certainly not."

"Then I need you to investigate this. I need you to make this a priority—just as you would for a murdered human." Russell couldn't believe he was now using the term—almost as if being human was foreign to him. "Will you do that, Sheriff Tilbert?"

The sheriff leaned back in his chair and fingered his beard. "You said that like you were talking about a whole other species, son."

Russell's desperation found him in a non-denying mindset. He couldn't explain it; he just acted on it. "All right, you know what I am, and I've come to terms with it. "Now can you help us?"

Tilbert leaned forward in his chair and his eyes widened. "Are you saying that...?"

"Yes!" Russell interrupted. "I'm a wolf...*will* you help us?"

"Very well, son," Tilbert said quietly. "I'll do what I can."

Russell left the sheriff's office fully satisfied that Tilbert and his deputies had nothing to do with the murder. He saw Tilbert as an honest man who just wanted to keep the people of his town safe. On the way to his car, Russell phoned

Heather who got in touch with Dell. Dell spread the information that Tilbert would help the wolves. The wolves, however, were not pleased.

"Has he lost his damn mind?" Dex blurted. "We welcome him into the pack and the next day he does *this*?"

"Dad, he has a special relationship with Sheriff Tilbert. Who else can go around asking questions and getting pharmacies, hospitals, labs, and other facilities to check their supplies to see if it's been tampered with?"

"Yeah, Dex," Dell said. "Nobody's going to tell *us* that."

"I don't know," Dex sighed. "You know how the wolves feel about outsiders knowing what we are."

"I know, Dad, but Rusty trusts Sheriff Tilbert."

"How do we know the sheriff isn't exacting revenge for what Matt, Rick, and Johnathan did to his deputies years ago?"

"But Rusty said Tilbert knew nothing about Will's murder," Dell assured.

"*Humans* investigating the murder of a *wolf*," Dex said shaking his head. "River is going to hit the ceiling when I tell him."

"Then don't tell him," Matthew said. "Uncle River has enough on his hands with Aunt Jewel's delicate pregnancy."

"So, you're saying we got this?" Dex asked Matthew.

"We don't need Uncle River, Dad. We can do this."

"Yeah, Dex," Dell said. "We're a team."

"A team?" Dex smirked. "Some team. The great *me*...his son and one knucklehead," he said grinning at Dell.

CHAPTER SIXTEEN

It was late in the afternoon, and the waiting area was practically empty. Sheriff Tilbert and Bob Wilson sat opposite a long, gray sofa trimmed in shiny mahogany wood. Two multi-colored chairs trimmed in the same wood sat off to the side. An oblong, mahogany table lined with magazines sat inches from them. Three large, abstract, framed paintings hung on the beige wall behind them.

Suddenly, the inner office door opened; a woman dressed in a dark business suit carrying a black leather case walked out. She passed Bob and Tilbert as she made her way out of the waiting area. Nearly twenty minutes ticked by, and a man in dress shirt and red tie walked through the waiting area, knocked on the office door, and went in.

Not long after, a woman dressed casually in a skirt and blouse came smiling through the door. "Sheriff Tilbert," she said. "Dr. Brighton will see you now." Sheriff Tilbert and Bob Wilson smiled at the woman and walked into the office of Dr. Brighton, Chief of Staff of Holy Cross Medical Center. The man in dress shirt and red tie stood beside him.

"Glad to meet you, Dr. Brighton, Tilbert said, shaking his hand. "This is Mr. Bob Wilson, chief coroner of New Berwick." Bob smiled and shook the doctor's hand. Dr. Brighton turned to the man in the red tie and said, "Sheriff, Mr. Wilson, I like you to meet Mr. Andre Newcomb the head of our medical supply department. I thought you'd be more informed if you spoke with *him*.

"It's a pleasure meeting you, Mr. Newcomb," Tilbert said, shaking his hand. Bob also greeted Newcomb with a handshake and all took a seat. Sheriff Tilbert couldn't be truthful about the murder of a werewolf, so he made up a story about farm animals being poisoned; Bob claimed he'd supervised the necropsy that found large quantities of silver nitrate in the animals' systems. The medical center was their first stop of a series of stops to question if any supplies containing silver nitrate were missing or tampered with in some way. "Thank you for taking the time to speak with us," Tilbert said to Newcomb." I assume Dr. Brighton has explained why we're here?"

"Yes, as a matter of fact, I've already taken the liberty of checking our supply and found nothing missing or tampered with on *my* end. I don't have jurisdiction over our labs or pharmacy."

"Tell us who's in charge," Tilbert said, "and Mr. Wilson and I will go and see them."

"I can do that for you," Newcomb said. "If you can spare a half-hour or so, I can make calls from my office and come back here with the results."

"Well, thank you," Tilbert said. "That would sure save us a lot of time. Are you sure we're not taking you away from your usual duties?"

"No, not at all," Newcomb said. "It's been a slow day. I'll get right on it," he said, hurrying from the office.

Dr. Brighton pointed to a table of assorted donuts and his private coffee maker. "Would you like some refreshments while you wait?" he asked.

"Yes, thank you," Tilbert said.

After nearly forty minutes had ticked by, Newcomb returned with a report that no department in the medical center had experienced any missing or tampering of silver nitrate products. Tilbert and Bob thanked the doctor and Newcomb for their help and left for the two-hour drive to meet with Ms. Katrina Lowes, head of one of Illinois' largest water treatment centers.

Later, in the week, Sheriff Tilbert added hundreds of people to help gather information throughout Illinois. After several weeks of numerous interviews, checking medical centers, laboratories, and other facilities, Sheriff Tilbert's findings were negative for missing or tampered silver nitrate supplies. Tilbert stated there were facilities that were omitted because of the strain it could have on taxpayers. The wolves, however, were angry that the Sheriff hadn't found anything.

"This is bullshit!" Dex yelled. "I'm telling you, somebody from Sheerfield is behind this and it's Sheriff Tilbert. He and his deputies want revenge."

"But we don't know that," Russell said.

"Really?" Dex said sarcastically. "They have the motive, the opportunity, and the authority. They're lawmen: they can lawfully carry guns; anybody they kill is called justifiable homicide. One group is missing from the sheriff's list. And that's his deputies. Did he check *their* homes for silver nitrate? No! Did anybody check the *sheriff*'s house or office for silver nitrate? Hell, no!"

"I believe you, Rusty," Matthew said. "But, I'm telling you—the Southern wolves had a meeting and it didn't go well for Sheriff Tilbert."

"It didn't go well—what does that mean?" Russell asked.

"It means when wolves get mad, shit happens," Matthew said.

"Well, that shit better not happen too close to *my* family and friends."

"Now wait one damn minute, Rusty," Dex said. "You're a wolf now and your loyalties lie with us."

"*You* made me a wolf. I didn't ask for this life. That's what happens when you tamper with human beings. Let this be a lesson to you in case you want to make any more humans into werewolves. They'll have split loyalties and in desperation will *always* side with family and friends. You created me so now *live with it*."

"Why you ungrateful asshole..." Dex blurted. "We welcome you into our pack and..."

"And that's another thing..." Russell interrupted. "I never asked you to welcome me into your stupid pack..."

"STUPID!"

"Hold up! Hold up you two. This infighting is going to get us nowhere," Matthew said. "Dad, he's right."

"Why are you *always* siding with him," Dex blurted. "You know what? Don't answer. I know why. You've always felt guilty for what happened to him. Well, get over it. It's done."

Matthew didn't answer but looked down at the floor then up into his father's eyes. The loud tension in Dex's clubroom grew quiet then the ringing of Russell's phone broke through. It was Sheriff Tilbert.

"Sheriff," Russell greeted.

"You sons of bitches, how could you?" Tilbert blurted. "I told you we had nothing to do with the death of that wolf."

"What the hell are you talking about?"

"Don't you dare pretend you don't know."

"Know what?"

"One of my deputies was just found clawed, chewed-up and headless on the side of the road a few feet from his squad car. *That's* what!"

"Oh, my God!" Russell said. "It...it could have been a bear."

"Don't give me that bear shit. You tell the wolves if they want war, they've got one."

"Sheriff Tilbert, no, you're wrong. The wolves had nothing to do with that."

"The wolves had nothing to do with what?" Dex asked. "What's he talking about?"

"Sheriff...Sheriff Tilbert," Russell repeated. "Damn, he hung up."

"What the hell was he talking about? What is he claiming the wolves have done now?" Dex asked.

Russell was slow to answer and he sighed heavily before he spoke. "A deputy was found bitten and clawed to death. Something tore off his head," Russell said looking off.

"And he thinks a wolf did it?" Matthew asked.

"Worse than that," Russell said. "He said if the wolves want war...they've got one."

"Holy shit," Dell said. "What are we going to do?"

"Is he insane...wanting war with the wolves?" Matthew blurted.

"Rusty...you better go talk to him," Dex warned.

"I'll see what I can do," Russell said solemnly. He rose and walked out of the room.

*****

At the sheriff station, Tilbert sat steaming as his eyes rolled over the autopsy report of Deputy Ron Daily, an eighteen-month rookie with a wife and six-month-old baby girl. Bob sat across from him shaking his head—his eyes glassy. At that moment, Russell stepped into the doorway. Tilbert's eyes shot up and met his. "You've got a lot of nerve showing up here," Tilbert growled.

"I'm trying to prevent senseless killings," Russell said.

"Yeah, well you're a headless deputy too late," Bob snapped.

"And what about the wolves? They lost someone too," Russell said.

"You want us to feel sorry for a damn wolf...after what they did!" Tilbert yelled.

"They swore it wasn't them," Russell said.

"And what about seven years ago?" Sheriff Tilbert snapped. "I guess that wasn't them either."

Russell lowered his head and closed his eyes momentarily then looked up and straight at Tilbert. "I'm not saying the wolves aren't guilty at some point," Russell said. "I'm saying they didn't kill your deputy."

"And you believe them?" Bob smirked.

"We make it a point not to lie to each other. We may keep things from one another, but...."

"Honor among beasts. How touching," Bob interrupted.

"Oh, this is crazy," Russell said. "You guys aren't *serious* about starting a fight with the wolves? It would be suicide and you know it."

"Suicide for the wolves, you mean," Bob spat.

Tilbert wasn't happy with Bob's slip of the tongue and he squinted at Bob. Russell caught it and shot a puzzling stare at Tilbert.

"What does he mean suicide for the wolves? You're no match for the wolves...what does he mean?"

Bob wanted to kick himself. He sunk his teeth into his bottom lip and stared down at the floor. "What did Bob mean by that? Tell me."

"I think you need to leave," Tilbert said.

"Not until you tell me what you're planning to do," Russell said.

"For the last time get out of here, Rusty. Go on back to your wolf den. You're not one of us anymore," Tilbert told him.

"I'm not going anywhere until you tell me why you two are so confident and willing to fight the wolves," Russell said. "You know, I think I may have the answer." Russell thought for a moment. "All right, where is it?" he demanded, looking around. "Is it here?" he said, walking over and opening a door. The small room was only three times the size of a closet. It had coats, boots, umbrellas, and boxes on the floor and shelf.

"What do you think you're doing?" Tilbert asked as Russell tossed aside box tops and rummaged through the boxes. He didn't bother to return the contents to the boxes but turned and said, "Perhaps it's there," Russell said, heading toward a metal cabinet. He barely got one drawer opened when Bob shot up from his chair and slammed it shut nearly catching Russell's fingers. "Just what in heaven's name are you looking for?" Bob asked.

"Silver nitrate, you damn liar," Russell said.

Bob looked over at Tilbert and there were several seconds of silence. Then Russell's voice broke through the tension like a quiet storm. "It *was* you who killed Will Casey!" Russell blasted.

"Now, wait a minute Rusty," Bob said.

"Wait hell. I went to bat for you," Russell said glaring at Tilbert. "I told the wolves you had nothing to do with the murder. You lied to me!"

"Rusty, sit down," Tilbert said.

"Oh, you want me to sit down now? First, you wanted me to leave...go back to my wolf den...isn't that what you said? Now you want me to sit down. I think I'll stand."

"Son," Tilbert said.

"Don't call me that."

"I didn't lie when I said we had nothing to do with Casey's murder. Seven years ago, the Shadow Hunters refused to help us against the wolves, but sent us a big supply of silver nitrate."

"How big?" Russell asked.

"Several boxes big," Bob said.

Russell's face appeared to darken and his eyes narrowed.

"I decided not to attack the wolves," Tilbert said.

"Not that they didn't deserve it," Bob interrupted.

I felt there was no need," Tilbert said. "The witches, wolves, my deputies, Bob, and Bishop Randall all battled Corina; the hunters added the finishing touches and put her away for good. So, I gave ninety percent of the silver nitrate to various medical facilities and kept the rest just in case we—" Tilbert broke off suddenly.

"Just in case what?" Russell asked, tilting his head to one side.

"Just in case there was a sudden up rise," Tilbert said. "We'd use it to keep the wolves in line. But I swear to you, none of my deputies knew we still had the stuff, and we never used it...I swear."

"You expect me to believe that?"

"Rusty," Bob said, "we spent thousands of taxpayers' money investigating hundreds of silver nitrate using facilities. Do you really believe we'd do all that if the sheriff and his deputies were guilty?"

Russell reasoned in his mind that it did seem unlikely that they were the guilty ones having done all that, but if not them then who? Russell blew his breath out hard and ran his fingers through his thick brown hair. He studied Tilbert's face. There was no darkness in his eyes. He knew the sheriff was basically a good man—an honest man. "It doesn't matter if I believe you or not," Russell said. "The wolves won't, especially after I tell them you have the stuff."

"But why would you?" Bob asked.

"I have to."

"They already think we did it," Bob said. "They'll attack us for sure, and we don't have enough silver nitrate to defend ourselves against them all."

"I won't tell them how much you've got. That'll keep them at bay. That's the best I can do."

"Thanks, son," Tilbert said."

Russell left and headed back to the main highway. He was sure that even if he couldn't convince Dex that neither the Sheriff nor his deputies were responsible for Will Casey's death, the knowledge that the sheriff had silver nitrate on hand would make the wolves highly reluctant to attack. The wolves were stubborn, but they weren't foolish.

Up ahead, swinging in a heavy breeze, hung the big road sign for Greyscott Falls. Turning south, Russell shifted gears after pulling onto Moonhawk, the road that led to Dex's mansion.

CHAPTER SEVENTEEN

Almost as soon as Dex decided that a civil war might be brewing, Russell walked down the stairs and into the clubroom. Matthew tried to read his face. As Russell got closer, not even his eyes bore a single clue.

"Come on, come on, it's killing me. What's it going to be?" Dex blurted. "Is the sheriff friend or foe?"

Russell took his time so that his reply could have just the right dramatic effect. He eased onto the sofa and stared into the faces that were quite frozen with anticipation by that time. "We shouldn't waste our time wondering if Sheriff Tilbert or his deputies murdered Will Casey," Russell said.

"That's it?" Dex spoke out. "What kind of shit is that to say?"

"On the way over to the sheriff's station," Russell said. "I was convinced Tilbert was either bluffing or crazy, because I knew they were no match for us. After I talked with him, however, ah—he's not bluffing or crazy. He means what he says, and he's got silver nitrate to back it up—lots of it.

"Damn," Matthew said.

"That bastard," Dex said. "I knew it was him all along. And Casey was the first of his revenge."

"Okay, they killed Casey, but who killed the deputy?" Dell asked.

"Everybody stop," Russell said. "Tilbert swore they never used it against the wolves, and I believe him."

"Then you're an idiot," Dell said.

"Wait," Dex said. "No, Russell's right to believe him. With deadly odds like that against the wolves, he doesn't have to lie. He could have said, yeah, we did it. Come and get us, suckers, then blast us all to hell."

"That's right," Matthew said. "They have no fear of us now. Wonder how long they've had the stuff?"

"Seven years," Russell said.

"That long?" Dex blurted.

"Yeah, the Shadow Hunters supplied them right after the wolves butchered their deputies," Russell said.

Matthew's eyes danced of guilt. "It wasn't *all* of us," he said. "Poor Casey had nothing to do with it."

"It doesn't much matter," does it?" Russell said. "That deputy who was killed was still in high school when the wolves attacked the deputies back then. He was an innocent victim, too.

"Then we're right back where we started," Dell fretted, "if the sheriff didn't do it, then who? Oh, this whole mess is freaking me out."

"Dell, Dell, calm down," Matthew said. "Until we find out who killed Casey and that deputy..."

"His name was Ron Daily," Russell interrupted.

"...Deputy Ron Daily," Matthew repeated. "We need to restrict all wolf activities within Greyscott—"

"You mean don't go outside of Greyscott at all?" Dell asked.

"Exactly," Matthew said. "And strictly monitor all non-wolves coming into our region."

"Okay," Russell said half-smiling. "Hate to shoot a hole in your plan there, partner, but I don't live in Greyscott."

"That's right you're staying with Heather in Falcon Haven," Matthew remembered.

"And I'll be in and out of Sheerfield taking care of my house until my mom and dad come back from vacation," Russell added.

"Well, just watch your back," Dex warned. "Since you're not staying that far from Dell and Massie, you and Dell need to team up before you go anywhere, especially at night."

"Oh, great—me and my shadow," Russell teased, looking over at Dell. "That'll be fun."

*****

Several weeks passed without incident. New Berwick went about mirroring its routine of small-town life. There were the usual picnics, fishing trips, boat racing, small game hunting and the like. Teenagers left home alone, threw wild parties that lit up Sheriff Tilbert's phone lines with boisterous complaints; and young adults were busted for sexing in the weirdest places.

It was mid-summer. The silent, winter birds had gone— replaced with noisy chirps and fussy bread crumb fights that the elderly had to referee. In that atmosphere those gruesome murders just didn't make sense.

Sheriff Tilbert and Bob Wilson got out of the squad car and made their way up the sidewalk of a ranch house about a mile and a half north of Sheerfield Park. A rookie deputy burst out the door, vomit oozing through his fingers that were clasped over his mouth. Down on his knees, a heavy breakfast gushed out of him onto the grass.

"Get a hold of yourself," Tilbert blasted him. "You're an officer of the law, for Christ sakes."

"Yes sir," the rookie said trying to compose himself. He hopped up from the ground and scurried away from the scene.

Tilbert ordered the yellow tape. Bob took mental notes as he checked each victim. They were an elderly couple, John and Wilopy Kramer and their visiting grandson, twenty-two-year-old Storm Kramer. The elderly Kramers were in their bedclothes inside their bedroom on the floor. Mr. Kramer lay at the foot of the bed and Mrs. Kramer was face-down in front of the bedroom window as if she'd tried to escape. One of her hands still grasped the window sill. Their faces and throats had deep, long claw marks. Their necks were broken, probably from the force of the blows, Bob silently reasoned.

The grandson suffered greatly before death. Being young and vibrant, he had put up quite a fight. His knuckles were swollen, bruised and bloodied—his right hand broken at the wrist. The scene included the grandson in a large pool of blood: pieces of torn garments, clumps of human hair, and dark animal fur lay scattered around him. Several fingers had been bitten off; Bob spotted all three and circled where they lay with a marker. Storm must have heard the fracas coming from his grandparents' room and tried to rescue them. He was met by someone or something at the end of the hall where he was found just a few feet outside his bedroom. Barefooted, his T-shirt and boxers were shredded; his chest and abdomen slashed to ribbons. Deep claw marks marred the side of his face; a large chunk of his neck was missing leaving him nearly decapitated. His light blue eyes were wide open as if he'd seen the very devil himself.

Both men remained speechless as they examined the scene. Wayne Tilbert wasn't going to be professional. He wasn't going to be reasonable. He wasn't going to allow his fondness for Russell Sooner to mean a goddamn thing. He took those murders personally. Those victims were not men and women of the law, though harming *them* was bad enough. Because of the nature of their work, law officers expected some hostility, mistrust and even anticipated becoming targets for some level of violence. The Kramers were innocent, God-loving, law-abiding members of New Berwick. They could have been *his* wife and children. Yes— Wayne Tilbert took it personal. And that time, he'd make the wolves pay, even if it meant turning a small portion of New Berwick into a blazing killing field. He'd make the wolves suffer and Bob Wilson agreed.

It was 3:00 a.m. the next morning—nearly eighteen hours after finding the bodies of the Kramers. Twenty-five deputies surrounded a southern wolf's home. The house was dark. Only a stream of moonlight peeked through the edge of a drape and lit a spot on the wall. An antique grandfather's clock ticked away in the silence. In the master bedroom slept Breck Richardson and wife Juanita. In the middle bedroom was their daughter, Sybil—home from college. At the end of the hall were fourteen-year-old twin boys, Breck Jr. (BJ) and Tori.

Suddenly, a loud crash woke the house. Breck jumped from the bed and waved a startled Juanita to stay back. He opened the bedroom door. The downstairs' light hit his sleepy eyes. He stepped into the hall and was met with several rifles and shotguns aimed at him. Sybil and the twins entered into the hall and Breck shouted for them to go back.

"Stay where you are!" Tilbert ordered. The children froze. Juanita didn't want to be safe—not while her kids and husband could be in danger, and she bolted passed Breck.

"What the hell is this? And why are you frightening our children?" she shouted.

"Don't you mean, your puppies," spat a deputy.

"Sheriff, what is going on?" Breck insisted. "Whatever it is, I'm sure we can talk about it."

"We're done talking," Tilbert said. "Get your asses down here."

"All right," Breck said calmly. "Let my wife and kids go back into their rooms, and I'll come quietly."

"You'll come quietly or otherwise," Bob shouted up at him and aimed his rifle at Breck's head. Breck tightened his jaw and his face elongated as dark fur thickened on his bare chest. "Honey, don't," Juanita whispered.

"We'll walk toward the stairs," he whispered to her. "And pretend to go down, then I'll shove Sybil into her room and you do the same with the boys."

"Whatever you two are whispering about up there, it's not going to work!" Bob shouted.

"Honey, please," she said. "They've got silver nitrate in those guns. Please let's go down and see what they want. This all could be just a mistake."

"They killed Will Casey," Breck whispered. "I don't care what Rusty and Dex said. I don't trust them around our kids. Now do what I said. There's a loaded rifle in the twin's closet. Use it if any of them come up the stairs."

Juanita smiled faintly. "Sheriff, we're coming down," she said. They walked slowly together. Bob lowered his rifle. The deputies kept theirs' dead on him. All watched as they slowly walked the length of the banister holding hands. They continued toward the stairs. Every hair on the back of Juanita's neck was on edge. Her hands were slippery with sweat and Breck squeezed them as a sign of confidence. They stopped—every eye was upon them. Both their feet reached out for a step—then snatched back, they bolted. Breck shoved Sybil and Juanita ran and shoved the boys into their rooms. Tilbert and Bob started for the stairs. By the time they reached the top, Juanita rushed the doorway and fired hitting the banister.

"Shit!" Tilbert yelled and he and Bob bolted down the stairs touching every other step.

Then loud shouting came from the deputies surrounding the house. "Don't let him get away!" one deputy shouted. Breck had transformed, leaped out of Sybil's bedroom window, and was loping as fast as he could across the lawn to the wooded area.

"Shoot the son-of-a-bitch!" someone shouted.

"No!" screamed his wife from her son's bedroom window. Thirty, forty, fifty loud rounds blasted Breck. "Dad!" his daughter screamed. Breck, with nearly thirty holes leaking blood, still tried to make it to the woods. "Stay down, Dad!" BJ yelled to him.

"Don't move!" a deputy shouted to the wounded wolf. Juanita, glassy-eyed, saw her husband breathing rapidly. Blood dribbled from the side of his mouth; then his breathing slowed. The deputies watched in astonishment as Breck's fur slowly disappeared. His paws became hands and feet. His snout grew inward and a human face emerged. They had never witnessed such a thing in their lives. They gasped as Breck lay naked on the ground. Juanita looked on with tears streaming down her face. His yellow eyes turned brown. Breck lifted his head and struggled to say something. His head fell back and his chest grew still. Blood pooled soaking the green grass around him. One of the deputies threw his jacket over him. Sybil leaped from the window and sprinted toward her father. The twins froze and stared. Juanita collapsed and Tori lifted her and carried her to a twin bed.

A deputy ran down the stairs. "Sheriff, Mrs. Richardson's fainted. You want me to call an ambulance?"

"No," Tilbert ordered him. "Bring her to and slap handcuffs on her—charge her with the attempted murder of an officer with a firearm. Round the kids up, too."

"Yes, sir."

Outside, the deputies crowded around Breck and stared down at their handiwork.

"GET AWAY FROM HIM!" Sybil screamed. The deputies immediately stumbled back. Sybil fell upon her father's chest; blood stained her face and soaked her hair and nightclothes.

When the wolves heard the news, it was war. Everyone knew it. Dex was stunned. Matthew—frozen. Russell—numb. Private jets passed in the air as Matthew sent an eight-month pregnant Kayla off to the island to join Jewel, and River flew back to New Berwick.

"Honey, shouldn't you and other level-headed wolves be stopping this?" Heather pleaded. "This will be suicide for the wolves."

"No, baby, this is going to bring the Shadow Hunters," Russell said.

"Why would it bring the hunters?" Heather asked. "Humans have the upper hand."

"The humans, as you like to say, only have enough silver nitrate to wound or kill maybe fifteen or sixteen wolves. After that, there won't be anything left of Sheriff Tilbert and his men but piles of meat, hair, and bones."

"Wait a minute," she frowned. "You said they had lots of silver nitrate."

"I lied."

"What?"

"I lied because I thought if the wolves figured the sheriff had boatloads of silver nitrate they wouldn't attack them and that would buy us some time to find out who on the sheriff's side and who on *our* side were doing the killings. We'd punish both and that would be it."

"But didn't someone say that Shadow Hunters don't view werewolves as evil, that's why they wouldn't come to help the sheriff when he asked for it seven years ago?" she asked.

"True, but if werewolves commit crimes against humans at a level of annihilation, I don't think the hunters will allow it. In fact, I'm sure they won't. From what I've learned from my research, the hunters see themselves as Divine protectors of humans against evil."

"So what you're saying is...if wolves decide to do evil against humans, then that's the one thing that puts them at odds with the hunters?" she asked.

"Exactly."

"We can't sit here and do nothing."

"Well," Russell said, "Sheriff Tilbert has hung up on me eight times, and his deputies shot at me several times when I tried to go to his office. So, my brainy love, what would you suggest I do?"

"Send him a text, you nitwit."

Off and on during the day, Russell did just that. "It's no use," he said. "He's not responding."

"Maybe this calls for a little magic," Heather said.

"No! Keep magic out of this. That'll bring the hunters for sure. They know witches always side with the wolves. We don't want Tilbert calling them again for help. I'll call Dell— see what I can find out."

Several hundred feet from the sheriff's station, Dell peeked out from behind Matthew's van. He pulled out his phone and attempted to dial when he felt it vibrate. "Rusty?" Dell said. "I was just about to call you."

"What's going on?" Russell asked.

"Dex, Matt, River, and nearly a hundred wolves have surrounded the sheriff's station," Dell said.

"Dell, that's suicide."

"No, they're not shapeshifting. They've got assault rifles and are buried behind barricades."

"Hey, that's smart."

"What's smart?" Heather asked. "What's he talking about?"

Russell put the phone on speaker. "Where are you right now?" Russell asked.

"I'm ducked down behind a barricade with Matt. I don't have a rifle. I feel like a war correspondent. I just finished talking to Massie about what's going on, now I'm talking to you."

Just then, thunderous rapid firing from AK47s wiped out Dell's voice. Dell abruptly ended the call as the automatic speed of the bullets tore into every window of the sheriff station. Deputies fired on the wolves from rooftops, cutting down several wolves. The roar of two helicopters moved in and hovered over the far left and far right of the barricade. When the wolves looked up, M16s unloaded on them, killing some instantly and severely wounding others. Tilbert's strategy was to reserve as many silver nitrate bullets by using both silver nitrate and regular bullets. The regular bullets couldn't kill them but they would slow them down by incapacitating them leaving many temporally too wounded to fight back.

The wolves fired back at the helicopters, hitting one deputy who tumbled out and fell to his death. The fight went on for hours. Deputies lay dead on top of roofs and inside the sheriff station on the floor near shattered windows. The helicopters with multiple bullet holes roared away. Many wolves groaned and rolled about on the ground. Some turned blue from the effects of the silver in their bloodstream; others shot with regular bullets suffered shattered knees, arms, and shoulders. Many were shot in the face and neck.

Tilbert had given orders to temporarily stop all outsiders from entering New Berwick, especially those from the news media. He called a curfew. Citizens were told to stay low and away from windows. Only medical personnel, firefighters, rescue workers, law officers, and military personnel with proper ID were allowed to be on the street until further notice.

"Think they'll give up before we run out of silver nitrate bullets?" an exhausted Bob asked Tilbert.

"I don't know, Bob. God help us. I really don't know."

CHAPTER EIGHTEEN

After both sides failed to produce a murder suspect, Russell decided he'd have another face-to-face talk with Sheriff Tilbert.

"What the hell are you doing here?" Tilbert snapped. "This is my home, off-limits to wolves," he said, blocking Russell in the doorway.

"I'm also human, or have you forgotten?" Russell said.

"Not anymore you're not. What do you want? My wife will be back soon, and I don't want her to see you here."

"Does she know about me?"

"Of course not."

"Don't shut me out," Russell said. "You're the only person from my former life I can trust."

Tilbert searched Russell's eyes and saw the innocent gleam of that little ten-year-old boy his deputies had rescued all those years ago, and it touched his heart. He moved aside and Russell walked in. Tilbert closed the door and walked past him beckoning Russell to follow him into the family room. Both took a seat.

"All right make it quick—not that it will do any good," Tilbert said.

"Did it ever dawn on you that maybe someone either hates the wolves, or you and your deputies, and is trying to pit you against one another?"

"And who would want to do that?"

"I don't know. I'm just asking you to consider a third entity in this whole mess."

"I have a feeling you can't talk any sense into the wolves, so you're trying to use your human connection to get me to back off. Well, I won't. Son, you're going to have to make up your mind if you're going to side with the wolves or your family and friends. You can't have it both ways, you know."

"You sound like the wolves. I don't have to choose because I have a unique claim to both, and you and the wolves are just going to have to get used to it. Look, Sheriff, I didn't come here to argue about my state of being. Do you or don't you accept my theory of a third entity or not?"

"Rusty, I don't know," he sighed. "It's possible. But who would want to do that?"

"Can you think of anyone you pissed off lately or in the past?"

"Are you kidding? I put people in jail—send them off to prison for years. I'm a law officer. Of course, there are people pissed at me. But what does that have to do with anything?"

"I believe you when you say neither you nor your deputies had anything to do with Casey's murder, and I know for a fact that the wolves are not killing innocent people."

"Well, somebody is."

"I know, but have any of the people you've put away threatened you? Screamed they'd make you pay or anything like that?"

Tilbert fingered his beard and thought momentarily. "This is a small town. I've never had to deal with a hardened criminal here—maybe years ago when I worked the big city. Son, I think you're barking up the wrong tree. But I see how passionate you are, and I'll keep an open mind. That's all I can promise you."

"All right, Sheriff. I'm just trying to stop this bloodbath between you and the wolves."

"I know son, and I regret that you're caught in the middle."

"So am I," Russell said. He stood to leave. "I know this doesn't mean much, but I'm really sorry about your deputies. I truly am."

"I appreciate you saying that."

Tilbert walked Russell to the door then watched him enter his car and pull off.

*****

Just a few hours later, Bruce Middleton, a twenty-nine-year-old Northern wolf, thought he heard something over in the bushes. With his wolf vision, practically nothing could escape him, not even on the darkest of nights. It was after nine at night, and he had just closed his antique shop and was heading home. As he walked to his car, he suddenly got the feeling he was being watched. He turned quickly but saw nothing. As he continued to walk, a dark figure suddenly appeared in his peripheral vision. Bruce turned his head; again, there was nothing. As he climbed into his car, he noticed he'd forgotten to turn off the light in the supply room. He walked back, unlocked the door, walked to the back of the shop and flipped off the light. Something darted in front of him then disappeared as quickly. Bruce hurried out of the shop and climbed into his car. He looked around, locked himself in, and fastened his seat belt.

Bruce pulled off into the highway traffic which was heavy during that time of night. He checked his rearview mirror and noticed a black Jeep Cherokee with heavily tinted windows. On the road up ahead the traffic light turned red. Bruce's fingers danced impatiently on the steering wheel as he waited for the green light. He pulled off and for several miles, noticed the same black-tinted window car.

Bruce stopped to get gas, and the tinted window car pulled to the shoulder of the road and stopped. When Bruce got back into his car, the car pulled back onto the road and followed him. He turned off on a few less-traveled roads to see if he could shake the car, but it stayed on him. Bruce sped up, and the black car sped up as well. He called a fellow wolf and told him what was happening. The wolf asked Bruce his location and said he and several wolves would meet up with him.

"Don't get out of the car," the wolf told him.

Bruce wanted to pull onto the more heavily trafficked highway but realized his fellow wolves wouldn't be able to find him unless he stayed on the dark road. Suddenly, the black car rammed him from behind. Bruce hit the accelerator and shot to eighty-five mph. The black car rammed him again then pulled up beside him. The two cars raced side-by-side. Bruce looked over but couldn't make out the driver through the heavily tinted windows. Then the black car cut him off causing Bruce to ram it in the back. Bruce put the car in reverse, but the bumpers were stuck. He raced the motor, but couldn't force the cars apart. He called his fellow wolf and gave him an update on his situation. The wolf said they were twenty minutes away. The driver's side of the car door opened and a man in dark clothes, black leather gloves, and sunglasses stepped out and slowly made his way to Bruce's car and stood motionless. Then he bent, pulled the bumpers apart, lifted the front end of Bruce's car like it was a toy truck and flipped it upside down. The roof of the car caved and sharp edges of it cut into Bruce's head. Blood streamed down his face. He struggled to get to his gun in the glovebox, but his seat belt prevented him from reaching it and he couldn't get the belt unhooked.

The man kicked in the driver's side front window, bent down and peeked through. Bruce finally saw his face but didn't recognize him. "Why are you doing this?" he yelled to the man. Down on his knees, the man reached into the window and grabbed Bruce by his hair, then pulled out a long, silver blade and stabbed him in the chest. Bruce fought and kept grabbing the man's wrist. Each time, the man broke his grip and continued to stab Bruce in the chest, head, face, and eye several times then cut his throat so viciously, only a few strings of flesh kept his head from falling into his lap.

Just minutes later, a van screeched to a halt and several wolves spilled out. They ran to the flipped-over car and found Bruce with one, dead eye glaring. The black car had gone.

*****

Heather lay back in Russell's arms smoking a joint and laughing at a comedy movie. She looked at Russell, and he seemed far away in a galaxy of his own making. She passed the joint to him but he refused it. "Honey, you've got to give your mind a rest or you'll go crazy," she told him.

"Huh?"

"Great Zeus, you didn't hear a word I said."

"I'm sorry, baby. What show is this?" he asked trying to appease her.

"Never mind," she said. She lay back in his arms and continued watching the movie.

A few miles from Russell and Heather in Sheerfield, county, Dr. Sally Lorac prepared for bed. She walked over to her minibar and poured her usual tumbler of brandy that she claimed helped her to relax before sleeping. She took it into the bedroom and climbed between the sheets, rested her back against the pillow, and sipped on her brandy.

Hours later, deep into sleep, Sally was awakened by her doorbell. At first, she thought she was dreaming, but someone was pressing on the bell. She cursed a little under her breath, slid her feet into her slippers, grabbed a robe, and made her way to the front door. She peeked through the peephole and couldn't believe what she saw. She opened it and half-smiled.

Charlton Daniels, the onetime pathologist at Holy Cross Medical Center from seven years ago stood on the top step smiling.

"Charlie," she said. "Well, my goodness. I thought I'd never see you again."

"I seem always to disturb you this time of night, but I'm leaving early tomorrow morning and wanted to see you before I left," he said.

"Oh! Well—sure. Please come in," she said moving aside. "I don't usually go to bed until at least eleven, but I had a really full day at work and thought I'd get some early shut-eye."

"I can understand that. I won't stay long. Just trying to see everyone I can before leaving."

"Would you like a brandy?" she asked.

"Yes, make mine a double if you don't mind."

Sally frowned at the similarity of this strange encounter as if he was trying to duplicate that night when he'd told her about his testing ten-year-old Russell Sooner's blood and discovering it was inhuman. He had shown up that night—treated her as an ally, only to have her betray him. She handed him the brandy and saw that he sat in the same chair he used that night. Sally sipped on her own brandy and noticed that things were about to be different. Charlton seemed more relaxed, not nervous like he was that night. She detected a bit of sinister in his smile.

"Charlie, you can't know how happy I am to see you."

"Really?" he answered, lifting the glass to his lips. His eyes peering over the flask sent chills up her spine.

"So, where are you working now? I tried to locate you, but it seemed you'd fallen off the end of the world," she said.

"Locate me?"

"Yes, to tell you how sorry I was about what happened to you," she said.

"Happened to me?"

"Let me get you another drink," she said feeling uneasy. She grabbed his glass, walked over to the minibar, and poured a hefty swig of brandy. When she turned, he was standing behind her. "Oh!" she gasped startled. "Charlie, I...I was going to bring it over. You didn't have to follow me." But he just stood there looking at her, his eyes a shade lighter than before. She hurried around him, walked back to where they had sat and placed his drink on the glass table. He followed her, flopped in the chair and just stared at her.

She lifted her glass, but Charlton just sat and watched her as her hand shook bringing the brandy up to her mouth. "You remember that night don't you, Dr. Lorac?"

"Charlie, I swear I didn't know what they were going to do to you. They just wanted the tube of blood, that's all. I told River that they were wrong for running you off the road that way and scaring you by having the wolves transform right in front of you. You must have been terrified. I'm...I'm so sorry," she stammered.

"Is that all you think happened?" he said, staring at her. His eyes had turned even lighter than before and his dark pupils were tiny dots.

"I lied and told you there was a short cut when there wasn't one. They told me they were only going to make you think they were robbers and take your wallet and the brown envelope with the boy's tube of blood in it. They were just trying to keep you from taking the blood to the lab. They didn't want anyone to discover that the boy was a werewolf. They promised me they wouldn't hurt you. And...and they didn't. They just...just scared you a little that's all." Sally began to perspire. "Well, look at you, you're fine. Right?"

Charlton laughed loudly and shook his head. "Sally, Sally, my dear friend. Someone I trusted and admired as a fellow medical professional. You betrayed me."

"Charlie I...I..."

"Shhh," he said. "Let me tell you *my* side of the story. I was once a pretty happy fellow: young, single, a pathologist, dating lovely ladies. You know, just a typical Joe. I went to work that day, thinking it was just another day and tested some children's blood—just a routine check. Two of the labels fell off, so I went to the children's floor and took the blood again. One child's blood, a little girl, was normal, but the other child's blood wasn't human. I tested it again—same results. Then I informed you. You made it seem like I was crazy..."

Charlie, wait..."

Charlton shot up from his chair, reached, and backhanded Sally across the face. Sally let out a scream, and blood trickled from the corner of her mouth. He struck her so hard she nearly blacked out. Sally coward in the high backed chair and watched him calmly ease back in *his* chair.

"Now, where was I? Oh, yes," he said. "After you made it seem like I was crazy. My feelings were hurt. I resolved myself to take the sample to the lab. But I never got to the lab, did I, Sally?"

Sally's eyes darted back and forth watching his every move.

"You told me about a short cut. Ben told me there wasn't one. But I took you up on the short cut anyway. But some people, or should I say some werewolves, were waiting for me at that short cut. They had this beautiful, blue-eyed blonde pretend she had car trouble...that was to get me out of the car so they could take the blood sample. But I smelled a rat and took off for which they nearly killed me running me off the road. I still wouldn't give up the blood, thinking I was dealing with a group of men like myself. Only they weren't men, were they, Sally?"

Sally shook and her heart pounded in her chest. "I never got their names. Anyway, those creatures shapeshifted into huge wolves, and one pranced over to take the envelope intentionally cut my face with his sharp fang. After I pissed and shit my pants, they let me go with a warning. I left town, got a job elsewhere and thought I could put this whole mess behind me. I even thought about forgiving you.

But aw...life just isn't that simple. Is it Sally? You see, I found out later that if you die with saliva from a werewolf in your system, you come back to life as a werewolf. Well, I died in a car accident about five years ago. My wife's religion didn't allow for embalming, and I was buried two days later. I woke up in a *goddamn* coffin, six feet underground, gasping for air. In my desperation, I shapeshifted, had the strength of ten men, and fought my way up and out of my grave. Of course, I'm dead, so I couldn't very well show up at a family reunion, join my wife on her birthday, or play Santa Claus for my kid. So this is my life now."

"I'm so sorry. Please don't hurt me again, Charlie. Just te...tell me what you want me to do."

"Can you turn me back to a human being? Turn back the clock so I can be with my wife and kid—my mom and dad? No," he said. His eyes turned completely yellow and his fangs gleamed under the ceiling lights.

A man walking his dog thought he heard a woman scream. His little dog stopped and looked into the distance. The man pulled on the leash, and the dog turned and went back to sniffing until he found a suitable place to pee and unload. The man scooped it up in a plastic bag. He and the dog continued their nightly walk.

CHAPTER NINETEEN

River and Dex sat five rows behind Dr. Lorac's loved-ones in her family's little, white stone community church. "I can't believe Sally is dead." River whispered to Dex. "Who would do such a thing? It doesn't make sense."

"Nothing makes sense about these murders," Dex whispered back.

Pastor Martinez adjusted his glasses. "Dr. Sallia Elizabeth Lorac," he said ending the eulogy, "a beloved daughter, sister, aunt, and my dear friend. She left an indelible impression on us all. Her practice as a physician and her skills in medical research were impeccable and will definitely be missed." Martinez descended the pulpit and made his way to the aisle.

Everyone stood as the minister and family filed out to waiting limousines. All Dr. Lorac's colleagues attended her memorial; afterward, they watched her cremated remains scattered over her favorite lake.

Later in the evening across town, a puzzled Russell pondered to make sense of the doctor's murder. She had been ten-year-old Russell's attending physician after his rescue. Tilbert ordered the boy sent to the medical center for a victim examination. Russell remembered how kind the doctor had been to him. But was her death a random serial murder, or was Lorac the key to the whole killing spree?

"Honey, where are you going?" Heather asked, placing two plates of food on the table.

"I've got to see Sheriff Tilbert right away."

"But I just cooked dinner. Can't you call or go in the morning?" Russell didn't answer. She watched him grab his car keys and hurry out the door. "Damn it, Rusty!"

Once on the road, Russell phoned Sheriff Tilbert that he was on his way to his home. Tilbert had eaten and just settled in his recliner to catch up on the latest cable news. Rose, his wife, lay in bed watching a movie. "All right," Tilbert said. "I'll be here."

Russell stopped to gas up then soared back into highway traffic—his mind still on Dr. Lorac. Her death remained the first murder of someone he actually knew. That seemed too close to home and made him damn glad his parents had gone out of town. Russell made a left at the light. The traffic thinned, and he noticed a black Jeep Cherokee traveling about three car lengths behind him. His suspicion grew because the car fit the description of the one that followed Bruce Middleton. Russell had been leery of all such cars and often hung back and allowed them to pass just to see if the windows were heavily tinted. He tried for several miles to do the same with *this* car, but whenever Russell slowed, the black car slowed as well. He phoned Dell and told him his travel location just in case this was the same perpetrator. Dell alerted River, Dex, and Matthew, and the three of them piled into River's Dodge Ram and headed to Kingston Road. Dell took Massie's van and headed there too.

Twenty minutes of driving and Russell turned onto Koloric Boulevard. That put him well inside Sheerfield County and a few miles from Kingston Road, the main thoroughfare near Sheriff Tilbert's resident. Russell wasn't happy about being on a dark, less traveled roadway. Seeing only a single car behind him made him realize his help was nowhere near. That made Russell a bit nervous. Instantly, the black car sped up.

"Oh, shit! Dell, where the hell are you?" Russell thought out loud. He realized his mistake; the black Jeep only made its move after Russell left the main highway and isolated himself on a less traveled road. He had to get back on the highway. Russell pressed the accelerator to seventy-five miles per hour. Up ahead, a few cars crossed an intersection. With his horn blaring and their brakes screeching, he made it across. The black jeep made it, too, but not before sideswiping one of the cars and roaring off dragging the other car's front bumper. Russell took a hard brake and circled a small residential section—a short cut to the main highway. His eyes flashed up at his rearview mirror and saw the Jeep closing in, still dragging the bumper. Soaring to eighty-five miles-per-hour, Russell took a hard brake—tires screaming but missed the turn landing in a front yard just inches from a tree. He backed out of the yard and onto the street. In the distance, he saw the busy highway intersection with vehicles flying left and right. He had to get there. Looking at the rearview mirror, the black Jeep was nowhere in sight, but Russell wasn't taking any chances. He saw several cars coming toward him from the other side of the road but not the black Jeep. The distance to the busy intersection shortened, and Russell smiled as he soared towards it. A loud bang jolted the car and shook Russell to the core. Like a black bolt of lightning, the Jeep had roared out of a side street where it lay in wait and rammed him. Russell's car flipped 360 degrees in mid-air and miraculously landed on its wheels. The weight of the car blew out its tires when it hit the concrete. White smoke from the engine made the dark tinted windows stand out.

Russell, dazed from the hit, froze and kept his eyes on the Jeep. *Now comes the waiting game,* he thought. He unfastened his seat belt and tried his door—it wasn't stuck. A few cars slowed to gawk but kept going. Russell sat there, looking at the tinted windows, praying the next few cars were Dell and his fellow wolves. His phone rang, but the jolt had knocked it somewhere under the seat. Russell wouldn't look for it. He didn't dare take his focus off the car. Slowly the black door opened, and a tall figure in dark clothing, leather gloves, and dark shades emerged from the driver's side. Russell opened his door and eased out, but kept his eyes fixed on the dark figure as he walked around the car, and stopped. Every nerve in Russell's body stood on edge, but he remembered he had been shrunk smaller than a dot, wounded by deadly microbes, and helped defeat an evil witch. If he was going down, he was going on his feet and not like Bruce Middleton. Russell held his hands out to his side.

"All right—you got my attention. Now what?" Russell called.

The man eased off his shades. "You've grown. The last time I saw you, you were yea high," he said, bringing his hand to his waist.

"Who *are* you?"

"I guess you wouldn't remember me, Rusty. They still call you Rusty?"

"How do you know me?"

"He chuckled. "You...are the essence of my problem." He stepped forward.

Russell's eyes lightened, and his fangs appeared. "Stay back!" he warned.

The man froze. "Come on. There's no need for that. You and I are in the same boat."

"What same boat?"

Well, Sally or Dr. Lorac, as she was better known, did a little explaining before she...let's say fell to pieces."

"Is that what you call ripping a defenseless woman to shreds? It was you, wasn't it?"

"Guilty."

"Why?"

"She and I had a little score to settle," he said. "Allow me to introduce myself. I am Charlton Daniels once-respected pathologist at Holy Cross Medical Center, now fulltime werewolf," he said flashing a sinister grin. Russell stood and listened as Charlton ranted on.

*****

Heather, dozing on the sofa, was awakened by her phone. "Hello," she graveled.

"Heather, where the devil is Rusty? He called over an hour ago. Where is he coming from, Mexico?"

Heather straightened and slipped her feet in her shoes. "Oh, now I *am* worried. I thought he was already there. Did you call or text?"

"Both. He's not answering."

"Great Zeus! I'm going to go look for him," she said, standing and grabbing her purse and car keys.

"Well, when you see him, tell him whatever it is has to wait until morning. I'm going to bed."

"Sheriff, he could be hurt."

"Oh, Christ!" he said, disappointed. "In *that* case, call me when you find him. No matter what time. Okay?"

"Right!" she said, jumping into her car. Out on the road, Heather quickly phoned Russell. "Pick up, baby, please."

Russell heard the phone ringing in the car.

"So, you see," Charlton said, finishing up his story. "They screwed both of us. You and I didn't ask for this existence."

"Is this supposed to make us BFFs now?" Russell asked, frowning.

"Join me, Rusty. We're not like them."

"Join...join you? You freaking maniac. Okay, I get Dr. Lorac. She didn't deserve to die that way, but what she did was wrong. I'll bite my tongue and give you that. But you didn't just butcher wolves; it wasn't just Lorac. You murdered innocent people who had nothing to do with what happened to you *or* me."

Charlton, sighed, fidgeted, and looked at the ground. "Okay, I admit my plan stunk. I—I got a little carried away," he said looking at Russell. "It was just me against the wolves and I thought the quickest way to destroy them all was to..."

"Yeah—I know. To make Sherriff Tilbert and the wolves think the other was doing the killings and watch them turn on each other—hoping Tilbert and his deputies would wound or kill as many as they could."

"Hm...something like that."

"You're deranged, you know that?"

"Look, I admit it was a rotten plan; it was all I had. But...but you can fix that. No more harming the innocent. Just stick with wiping out the wolves. You and me...wha'da you say?"

The soar of River's Dodge Ram screeching to a halt startled Charlton. Dell, not far behind, pulled up. River waved Dell to stay in the car. Hardheaded, Dell jumped out and stood by the van door. River, Dex, and Matthew slowly walked away from the truck and stood a few yards from Charlton. Their yellow eyes, like tiny suns, gleamed in the darkness.

Charlton chuckled. "Well now, the three stooges; ain't *this* a bitch. I hope you K-9 thoroughbreds got your silver-proof vests on." Charlton put his hands behind his back and pulled two objects from his waistband. He locked the objects to each wrist then stretched his arms out to the side. Silver-plated, Reaper blades shot out of the wrist cuffs. He stood there looking like the sign of the cross.

"Charlie? Charlie Daniels?" River asked squinting at him.

"He's not just Charlie anymore," Russell warned. "Apparently, one of you bit him in the woods that day. He's one of us now."

"Holy shit, Charlie. You mean it's been you all the time?" Dex blurted.

"You know this murdering bastard?" Dell shouted.

"You're gonna run out of silver before Greyscott runs out of wolves, Charlie. Give it up," Matthew said.

Charlton glared at Matthew. "You! You're one of the brats that ran me off the road."

Matthew chewed on his bottom lip and looked around uneasy.

"Charlie," River said. "No one was supposed to hurt you that day. We were only trying to frighten you. I jumped in the ass of the kid who did it. I swear I thought it was just a little scratch. I didn't know it went deep enough to infect you."

"Problem solved," Charlton grinned. "Just turn him over to me. And all is forgiven."

"Can't do it, Charlie," River said.

"Well then, we're right back where we started." Charlton flicked his wrists and the blades shot back into their peculiar sheaves. I'll just keep on killing until you change your minds."

"I might have somethin' to say about that," a tremulous voice broke from the shadows.

Every head jerked in the direction of the voice. An old man, seventyish eased into the dull gold of the street light. He was ash-faced, gray-bearded and bald. His drab clothes hung loose.

"Hey Gramps, shouldn't you be beddy-bye," Charlton called to him.

"Shut your wolf-ass up," the old man snapped and quickly raised the muzzle of a semi-automatic rifle.

"Whoa! Easy now," Russell said. He stood the closest and was in the line of fire.

"Yeah, I know what yawl is." The old man bared a toothless grin. "I always knew they were werewolves in these parts. They said I was crazy. Been waitin forty years for this...said I'd get me one of ya—to show em' I ain't off my noodle. Now, I got me half a dozen." The old man waved the muzzle from one to the other—showing he had them covered.

No one moved a muscle. No one wanted to set him off. The old man kept waving the muzzle back and forth. "Thought you could hide—didn't ya? Been watching ya off and on. Just a shapeshifting. Chasing deer...then struttin' off naked as a *plucked* chicken."

"Mister, look, we're the good werewolves," Dell said in a shrilled voice. "That's the Son-of-a-bitch you want. Shoot *him*." He pointed to Charlton. Charlton folded his lips at Dell and stepped back.

"Take another step, and I'll blast ya," he growled to Charlton. Charlton shot his hands up then said, "What kind of bullets you got there old man?"

"The kind yawl don't like," he said menacingly. The toothless gunman said two more words then suddenly fell forward like a sack of potatoes. He hit the ground face down with a light thud and didn't move. The wolves looked puzzled until Heather emerged from the shadows.

"I thought that freaking, old creep would never shut up," she said. She looked over at the two wrecked cars. "Honey, what happened?" she asked, walking toward Russell. "Why didn't you pick up? And who was that guy who just ran off like a bat out of hell?" The wolves looked and Charlton had slipped off that quickly; his wolf speed had him in the wind at sixty-five miles-per-hour.

"Rusty, who *was* that guy?" she asked again, pointing to where Charlton had been.

"It's a hell of a story. I'll tell you on the way," he said, looking around. "Where are you parked?"

"Back there," she said, leading the way.

CHAPTER TWENTY

The ride back to the apartment proved quite an earful for Heather. Gasping and shaking her head was how she responded to the telling of the mini-history of Charlton Daniels and his killing spree. By the time they reached the apartment, Heather was seething with grief and anger. Earlier, unable to reach Russell, she had pulled over to the shoulder of the road and conducted a locating spell. But who was that man in black with the strange sparkling blades protruding from each wrist she'd wondered? Thanks to the old creep who held the wolves at bay, blood and guts could have been the scene she would have witnessed having arrived late.

"Honey, I can make you a cold, chicken sandwich if you're hungry."

"Are you kidding? I could eat a whole deer after what I've been through tonight."

"Okay, I'll heat dinner then," she said, scurrying to the kitchen.

Outside beneath the moonlight, a werewolf howled and an elderly man sat somewhere sulking with a bruised face and ego. "Almost had me a half-dozen of em'," he would say to his dying day. And Charlton Daniels wasn't finished by a long-shot. Holed up in a small house just inside of the Sheerfield County line, he would strike again.

*****

Although Sheriff Tilbert and Bob Wilson discovered Charlton Daniels as the perpetrator, both felt little sympathy for mistakenly targeting and killing the wolf, Breck Richardson, and arresting his wife, Juanita. They charged her with attempted murder which carried a penalty of life imprisonment. However, Juanita's legal counsel encouraged her to plead guilty to a lesser charge of reckless endangerment, plus assault on an officer and resisting arrest. She received a lenient sentence of eighteen years with the possibility of parole after six. Sybil, her daughter, left the courtroom in tears. She would soon quit college to raise her fourteen-year-old twin brothers.

Bob Wilson felt that the Richardson's fate hardly satisfied the justice he and Tilbert sought for the butchering of Tiara Winters and nineteen deputies seven years ago. Although Tilbert agreed with Bob, he decided to let revenge go, even though the wolves deserved it. Charlton Daniels, once considered one of Sheerfield's upstanding citizens, had become a werewolf and deranged murderer. His focus would turn to Daniels now. But Tilbert felt so isolated in his small town—not able to share the secrets of its strange inhabitants living among them. Without eliciting outside help, Tilbert wasn't sure he could bring Charlton to justice before he killed again. Tilbert could contact the Shadow Hunters. But could the town survive the divine justice of the hunters, which would include wiping out the witches and maybe Russell Sooner too? Notwithstanding, the Sheriff was unaware that he might not have to lift a finger since across town in Greyscott Falls, the leaders of the wolf packs were discussing their brand of justice—a justice that would bring an end to Charlton Daniels.

*****

"Shit!" Sheriff Tilbert blurted careful not to step in the blood. He thought it foolish not to do so since the only reason to resist contaminating a crime scene was to collect evidence. Everyone knew the murderer was Daniels, but the meticulous procedure carried on.

Bob followed Tilbert throughout the house of husband and wife doctors and two children. "Every scene, the same," Bob said. "Bodies torn apart, limbs thrown about, fur, blood, and guts were everywhere. He doesn't seem to have much of an imagination, does he?"

Tilbert shot him a glance. "Do you want him to?"

"I...I didn't mean it that way, Wayne."

The two had their bickering interrupted when a deputy walked up. "Sheriff, you need to see this. I think the bastard has a heart." In the children's room were twin toddlers in separate cribs. One stood teary-eyed, his tiny hands holding tightly to the side of the crib, and the other sat blank. Both had loaded diapers.

"I'll remember to tell them to thank the bastard for making them orphans," Tilbert said.

Bob followed Tilbert back to the sheriff station. "A funeral a week for the last six weeks," Tilbert said. "If we don't stop him, there'll be nobody left in New Berwick."

Bob shifted his weight and hesitated for a moment before spilling. "I hate to throw this on top of what you already have to deal with, Wayne, but I just got off the phone with my assistant, and she informed me that Pete Billings might have killed his wife and made it look like a werewolf killing."

"What!"

"She said he disguised it pretty good, but any professional eye can see it was a person and not a wolf that did this."

"Is she sure?" Tilbert asked.

"She's good, or I wouldn't have hired her. If she says it's going to rain...carry an umbrella."

"All right, ah, I'll put Steve, my top deputy, on this case. Anything else?" he said looking rather wide-eyed at Bob.

"There are a couple more homicides that don't sit right with her, but she said she'd let me know in a day or two."

"Good," Tilbert said, tapping his hand on his desk. "Bob, I could use a night of drinking—how about you?" Of course,

Tilbert was joking; he hardly drank at all accept a beer or two watching a football game, or maybe a Fourth of July picnic in the back yard. If anything, he and Bob would do their usual sitting back, shoes off, listening to some of their favorite jazz artists, and reminiscing about how life used to be in their day.

Bob chuckled. "Yeah, I know what you mean. How about knocking back a few at my place after you get off?" he joked.

Before Tilbert answered, an office assistant called him. "Sheriff, I think you need to take this one," she said. Tilbert clicked the outside call button and raised his eyebrows at Bob. Bob understood.

"Maybe some other time," Bob said grinning. He brushed passed one of the deputies and made his way out of the office.

In Norwick Forest, south of Hamstead Creek, two northern, eight-year-old wolves transformed to play a game of chasing the rabbits. Those were wild, brown rabbits, native to New Berwick. They were twice the size of a cat and could outrun a fox or an ordinary wolf easily. Their meat was tough and not considered good for food unless one was on the brink of starvation. A third little wolf didn't transform, but stood off to the side and cheered them on. The rabbits split up and scattered in multiple directions, so the little wolves targeted one rabbit and stayed on its trail. The fluffy critter was only a brown blur to humans, but the little wolf eyes caught its every move. The rabbit cut and turned, sometimes widening a gap between it and the pups, but soon the little ones would catch up to it. The rabbit cut sharply to pass a tree and ran right into the snout of a large monster of a wolf that bit its head clean off in one snap of its jaws. The terrified little wolves slid to a stop as hard as they could and stared up at the black wolf with its snake-like yellow eyes. Its fangs were just as yellow, and saliva streamed from massive jaws.

The third little wolf transformed and bolted to the high-pitched cries of his playmates. Rounding the tree, he was struck with fear as a wolf, black as coal, bit then pounded the little ones with its paw. After it shot a deep-throated growled at the third pup, it turned and swiftly disappeared into the darkness of the forest. With two pups limping along, the young ones ran as fast as their little furry legs could carry them. Too injured to make it to their own homes, the three fell into the third pups' house frightening his mom and dad. Out of breath, he told his parents what had happened. When the wolf pack learned the news, they called a meeting. The wolves understood that Charlton could have killed the pups and that he was merely sending a message.

"I'm tired of these damn meetings. When are we going to do something dammit!" a Northern wolf yelled.

"We never know where he's going to strike," River said.

"I don't understand why we won't let the witches get involve. They could blast his ass seven ways to Sunday," another wolf said.

"You know why, Carl," Dex said. "Witches' arcane energy alerts the Shadow Hunters. And we don't want those sons of bitches coming here."

"They came before, and we're still here," Carl said.

"It's not the before that counts," Matthew answered. "It's what they said they'd do if they ever came back here."

"Listen up, you guys," Russell said. "We don't need the witches to start an all-out war. Why can't we ask them to put a spell, like a kind of invisible bell on this bastard? So we'll know where the hell he is at all times. That way, we can stop him before he does anything, instead of standing around waiting for him to strike."

"You mean, like a cowbell?" Dell chuckled.

"No, not a cowbell, you idiot," Russell snapped. "You know, a kind of spell that would signal to one of the witches to where he is...then they'd alert us."

"I guess that *could* work," River said, looking around for others' approval. The wolves looked one to another and gave smirking nods.

"I could ask Heather or Massie," Dell said.

"I think we'll put a Covenant witch on this," River said.

Russell felt slighted hearing River dismiss Heather and Massie that way. After what they'd done in the Withersphere, how could he be so disrespectful? But Russell decided he wasn't going to make a big thing of it. He looked at Dell and saw mutual resentment sparkling in his eyes.

CHAPTER TWENTY-ONE

Ignoring warnings from their elders, four young adult wolves picked up some street-walkers, who were unaware that the young men were werewolves. The couples sat around a campfire in Norwick Forest drinking beer, while the wolves thrilled the women with spooky stories.

"Just what do you guys do for a living?" a full-breasted redhead asked.

"I'm an undertaker," one wolf lied grinning.

"No, you're not. Come on—really," a blonde insisted.

"We're *all* undertakers," another wolf laughed

"All right, if you don't want to tell us, fine," the redhead said. They shared a couple of joints, polished off a bottle of Jack Daniels then each couple ran off separately to have sex. One couple, heavy into kissing and removing the bottom half of their clothes, heard a distant howl.

"What was that?" the woman froze.

"Nothing, baby," he said, pushing her onto her back and thinking it was one of his fellow wolves. He mounted her, and after a few moments of enjoyment, came another louder howl that sounded closer.

"Did you hear that?" she said, pushing against his chest.

"Baby, will you relax?" he said humping and burying his face in her neck. Moments later, really into it, she began to moan softly then felt something wet and warm on her forehead. She ignored it and continued to enjoy the moment, combing his hair with her fingers and sucking in her breath when another warm wetness slid from her forehead to her face. She reached up to wipe her face, slightly opening her eyes then they snapped wide open. She froze as another stream of saliva rained from the black snout of a wolf. She cut loose a scream that jolted her lover. His head shot up right into the foul breath of the massive jaws that widened and snapped like lightning. The jaws crushed the young wolf's head causing an eyeball to burst from its socket. The terrified woman let loose an ear-piercing scream as the wolf struck her with its massive paw then ripped her to pieces. Startled by the scream, the other couples, half-dressed and carrying their clothes, ran from three different locations. Awkwardly, they stumbled into each other. They heard something moving swiftly through the dark but couldn't see anything. They searched and called out the fourth couple's names several times. Minutes later, they discovered the butchered bodies. The three women gasped loudly, then screamed, and tried to run but were held in place by the wolves.

"No," a wolf said to them. "Stay by us."

The three wolves backed up, still holding tightly to the hands of the terrified women. They looked about—their wolf eyes scanning the darkness.

"I want to go home," one of the women said, her voice quivering. "I want to go home," she said a little louder, shaking.

"Shhh," a wolf said, jerking her in the process.

One of the wolves kicked out the fire, and the six headed toward the van. Silently, cautiously, they walked through the black of the forest stopping for any little sound and jerking with every slight movement beyond the trees.

"Can't we just run?" one of the women pleaded as she nervously looked about.

"Quiet! A wolf whispered harshly.

Through a line of trees, they saw the moonlight weighing upon the van. As they quietly picked up speed, they heard a twig-breaking sound coming from the darkness. They froze and nervously looked around. Then quietly with even more haste, they made it closer to the van when a deep-throated growl broke through the blackness beyond the trees. One of the women couldn't stand it; she jerked away and bolted to the van. She ran blindly through the darkness, stumbling, falling—bushes smacking her in the face. Whimpering, she ran across the grass and to the van. There, she breathed a sigh of relief, but it was locked. The woman looked around frantically realizing her stupidity; she was out in the open and alone. As she looked toward the forest, something fast was coming at her. Her heart pounded when the sound broke through the light, and it was the wolves and the women sprinting as fast as they could. The woman by the van hopped up and down nervously hoping for the one with the key to hurry. He aimed the key fob at the van, and it unlocked. She hopped in immediately and pushed the doors open for the others.

Safely locked inside, a wolf started the engine. But the inside of the car lit up with ear-piercing screams when the black wolf landed with a thunderous thud on the front hood of the van. Its massive paw broke the windshield, and its claws violently snatched the driver. The women were beyond terrified as they watched, a man, defenseless against a giant wolf, transform and become its equal—both growling and fighting to the death. The two wolves in the car jumped out, immediately shapeshifted, and joined in. The three women couldn't move—couldn't speak. They stared like zombies and watched as the three giant wolves circled the black wolf. They tore into the lone giant—ripping and tearing its flesh. Not wanting to risk further injury, Charlton turned and bolted back into the blackness of the forest. The three wolves slowly transformed and entered in the van naked. The women appeared mummified. No one spoke the whole ride to the women's destination. They were let out and told never to mention what they saw.

"Do you understand?" one of the wolves said sternly. The women nodded nervously and ran.

*****

The next day, Russell sat alone with his head in his hand. It would be two more funerals—one in Sheerfield and one in Greyscott Falls. The bodies were mounting up. Never before had a werewolf hunted another werewolf. But that's what happened when the supernatural crossed the line. It's one thing to curse a generation of men; it's quite another to pluck one out from among his human loved ones and force that existence upon him.

Nevertheless, that still was no cause for Charlton Daniels to murder the innocent. He wasn't just a werewolf, he was a madman. Sure, Russell was angry—still angry when he dwelled on it. He had talked of catching Jewel Porter on a dark road some night, shapeshifting and doing God knows what. And perhaps given that opportunity, he still might. But never did he contemplate hurting innocent humans *or* wolves because of what was done to him—never. Russell's phone rang. It read incoming call without an ID. He answered anyway.

"Rusty," the voice said

"Charlton?"

"You know how to stop this, Rusty. Side with me—tell me who infected me."

"Go to hell." Russell ended the call.

Then Charlton sent him an email that shot a shiver up his spine. It was a picture of Mark standing in front of his house watering the lawn. He quickly called Mark who answered. "Rusty," he said happily. "What's up, buddy?"

"Mark, where are you ...what are you doing right now?" Russell asked frantically.

"I just finished watering the lawn. Why?"

"Are you inside the house? Are the doors locked?"

"Ah, yes, and yes. Rusty, what's wrong?"

"Don't leave the house."

"Okay, I won't leave the house. Mind telling me why? Hello." Russell hung up.

"Heather," Russell said, speeding down the road.

"Yeah."

"Don't ask questions. I need you to do a quick spell and put a protective shield around Mark's house, right now."

"Okay, honey."

But Russell had a hunch. He somehow knew how Charlton's mind worked, and he mashed the accelerator to reach, not Mark but John before Charlton did. John loved the water, and Russell knew he would be out boating that time of day. As Russell approached the lake, he spotted a black wolf among a line of trees. John's backpack was on the ground, and he was slowly backing away from the wolf.

"Oh God," John said in a high pitched voice. "Ni...nice wolfie."

Charlton bared his two-inch yellow fangs. His deep-throated growl turned John pale as a ghost as he steadily looked behind him and slowly backed up. Then the black wolf suddenly stopped and looked past John. John was puzzled until he looked over his shoulder, and a giant white wolf stood several feet behind him, baring his fangs. "Oh, Merciful Christ," John cried out thinking he was about to be a shared meal. The black wolf turned and ran into the forest. The white wolf stood and looked at a terrified John for an instant, and then it too ran off. John blew out a breath of relief. He scrambled to his boat and rowed like crazy out to the middle of the lake and stayed there for hours.

Minutes later, sitting in his car, Russell's phone rang. He clicked on but didn't say anything.

"I underestimated you. I could *use* a partner like you," Charlton said.

"You ever go near anyone I love again, I will *kill* you myself," Russell told him.

Charlton cackled loudly and clicked off. When Russell informed Dell what Charlton had tried to do to John, Heather took away the shield, and Dell assigned junior wolves to secretly guard Mark, John, and their families until something is permanently done with Charlton.

Meanwhile, in Falcon Haven, Naomi cast a spell that could pinpoint Charlton's every move. Many of the senior wolves along with River, Dex, and Matthew and some junior wolves, including Russell and Dell, would carry a handheld device with a map of New Berwick. It would signal a beep when Charlton was on the prowl, and little black walking paw prints would show exactly the direction he was traveling and where he'd stopped.

Sheriff Tilbert was sitting at his desk when Russell walked in. Tilbert looked up. "Rusty, what can I do for you?" Russell handed him two devices, one for him and one for Bob. "What's this?" Tilbert asked. Russell didn't explain fully. He didn't know how Sheriff Tilbert would react to something created by witchcraft. He just showed what it could do. Sheriff Tilbert chuckled. "Why, thanks, Rusty. Is there any chance I could get a few more for some of my deputies?" He asked looking like a kid with a new toy.

"I think I can. I'll see how many we have left," Russell lied.

"Wait until I show this to Bob. He'll get a real kick out of this," Tilbert said turning the device over and over in his hand.

"I've got a couple more stops," Russell said, heading out the office door. "But I'll see if I can come up with a few more for you."

"Okay, and thanks a lot," Tilbert said, still eyeing the device.

Back at Heather's apartment a few hours later, Russell stretched and yawned. "Honey," Heather said, "you've had a really big day today. How about letting me draw you a bath? So you can relax."

"I've got a better idea," he said, hopping up off the sofa. He grabbed Heather and lifted her in his arms. "How about if I draw *your* bath?" he said. She giggled as he carried her through the master bedroom to the bathroom. He put her down and turned on the faucet. She stood grinning as he poured her salts and exotic oils into the bath. He tapped her hand when she attempted to peel off her own clothes. "That's for me to do," he playfully scolded. After undressing Heather, he lifted her and eased her down into the soothing fragrant water. Russell ran to the kitchen, sliced a cucumber, then ran back and placed a slice on each of her closed eyes. As she lay back smiling widely, Russell bathed her with a huge pink sponge then he began to massage and kiss her toes.

In Russell's van, his device beeped like crazy. Black paw prints moved along the map—then suddenly stopped. Yellow eyes blazed through the window and captured the beauty of Heather's soft pink and white body.

"Oh, let them go to voicemail," Heather said of both their phones that wouldn't stop ringing. She didn't want to spoil their moment.

CHAPTER TWENTY-TWO

"Dammit!" Russell blurted, annoyed by the constant ringing of both their phones. He rushed into the living room and spotted Dell's name and number. "Dell?" he said.

"Where the hell have you and Heather been for the past fifteen minutes?" Dell snapped.

"In the bathroom. Why?" What's happened? Is something wrong?"

"Is something wrong, he asks?" Dell repeated to Massie. "Is your device working?"

"Ah,"...Russell looked around. "Shit! I think I left it in the van. In fact, I know I did."

"Damn good it does in the van."

"Dell, will you quit bitching and tell me what's going on."

"The device tracked Charlton to Heather's apartment about fifteen minutes ago. He's not there now, though. He's on the other side of Norwick Forest."

"Here? At Heather's! I warned that son-of-a-bitch not to come near my family and friends. He is really trying my patience," Russell growled.

"Well, I'm just glad you two are all right. Massie and I can turn around now and head back to the apartment."

"You were on your way here?"

"Of course, asshole. You guys weren't answering your phones, and Massie and I thought you were in trouble."

"Dell, I'm sorry."

"Forget it. Goodnight."

"Goodnight, dude, and thanks."

Russell ran out to the van and grabbed the device from the front seat. He checked and saw that Charlton was nowhere near. He returned to the bedroom and found Heather cuddled up to her pillow. He took a quick shower then ate a late-night snack. After bolting the door, Russell walked around the apartment, switching off lights then slipped into bed. In her sleep, Heather scooted over and snuggled up to him.

*****

It was after midnight, and Debra Carter lay woke thinking. She had been sober for over eighteen months. Her son, Raymond could not have been more proud. The drinking started several years ago after her late husband, Kevin Carter, drove a silver dagger through his own heart rather than face another full moon chained like an animal.

Kevin had lived in constant fear of some night, breaking free, and waking in the morning, finding he'd slaughtered his entire family. It had been the nightmare of every werewolf in Greyscott Falls. Debra wondered what life would have been like had Kevin hung on until Jewel Porter produced the moon cure.

While in the deep rows of her memory, Debra thought she heard a noise outside her window. She quickly dismissed it as having been the wind or one of the many small creatures that nightly scurried in that part of the region. Then a loud pouncing sound made her jump. She hurried to the window to find two squinting yellow eyes staring at her—its snout pressed against the glass. Debra snatched the curtains closed and speed-dialed Raymond. Across town, having spotted Charlton on the tracking system, Raymond and a group of wolves were already on their way there. "Raymond!" Debra screamed.

"Mom, we're coming. Stay in the house. Use whatever magic you can!" Raymond knew Debra's magic was limited. Being a minor witch, she could only perform basic spells that had a temporary effect.

On the highway, a Sheerfield motorcycle deputy who had followed Raymond and the group for miles pulled them over. He loudly scolded them and attempted to give each driver a speeding ticket until Raymond explained the situation.

"Well, why in Sam's hell, didn't you say so," he said. He hopped on his motorcycle and led the caravan of cars, trucks, and vans to the Carter home.

Debra eased to the window and slowly peeled back the curtains, but the yellow eyes had vanished. She placed a spell on the window and bedroom door. She heard glass shatter from a nearby room. Minutes later, the wolf hit the door with a loud thud and began to claw through the wood. It bit down on the doorknob with its massive jaws and yanked the knob off the door. Its yellow eye peeking through the keyhole sent an ice-cold chill up Debra's spine. Then the wolf stepped back several spaces and ran forward hitting the door with its weight and loosening the hinges. Another hit and one hinge broke loose. Another hit and another and the door fell like a descending draw bridge. The beast stood glaring at Debra. It leaped just as she shot out her hand with a spell that drove the black wolf into the wall with such force, it nearly blacked out. She ran out of the room, and it followed her swiping her legs from under her with its claws. On top of her, it bit the side of her head, but another spell lifted it and sent it tumbling backward twenty feet. Quickly rising to her feet, Debra ran down the hall and into Raymond's bedroom, putting a spell on the window and door. Debra constantly turned from window to door, not knowing which spell would give way first and prompting herself to be ready to dash in either direction in a split second.

On the road, six patrol cars joined the motorcycle cop. With sirens screaming, they led the wolves down the highway stopping all traffic as they zoomed at nearly ninety miles an hour. Raymond, biting his lower lip, felt his heart pounding, not knowing how his mother fared and not wanting to distract her with a call or give away her hiding place.

The black wolf hit the window with its paw, and a long crack appeared. Debra knew the window wouldn't hold. She looked at the door, then back at the window. The yellow eyes were not there. Charlton played his game. Debra knew if she stayed in the room, it would crash through the window. If she opened the door, it might be there. She had to do something. The sirens screamed from a distance, but Debra didn't hear them. "I've got to take a chance," she thought out loud. Debra took a deep breath and snatched open the door. She shot her head out and took a quick peek. Not seeing the wolf, she ran down the hall as fast as she could. *If I could only get to the attic,* she thought. She jumped and got hold of the ceiling access door. She heard glass shatter as the seven-foot attic ladder slowly descended from the open ceiling door. She rushed up the ladder as the sound of heavy paws pounding the hall floor got closer.

The black wolf skid to a halt and looked up just as she pulled the ladder into the ceiling. The wolf leaped; its claws scraped the metal surface, sounding like fingernails on a chalkboard. Its claws couldn't penetrate the metal, and it fell to the floor. Debra reached to pull the ceiling door all the way closed when the wolf leaped again, almost catching her hand. She shot her hand out again and the wolf leaped, driving its claws into her arm. Debra screamed as she tumbled forward and spilled onto the floor. The wolf stood over her—yellow eyes gleaming and saliva streaming from its fangs. Before she could cast a spell, it bit into her head.

"Get away from her!" Raymond growled—his body half wolf—half man. As the black wolf backed away from Debra, Raymond transformed fully and leaped on Charlton. The two wolves aggressively clawed and bit each other. Silver, gray, and black rolled over and over like one huge fur ball. The thunderous growling and flying fur filled the air. Blood splashed against the walls and ceiling as the death-fight ensued.

"Back away, Raymond!" a deputy shouted. "Let me have him," he said, aiming his silver bullet loaded rifle.

"No!" Debra yelled. "You might hit Raymond."

The speed of the fangs and claws ripping and tearing appeared a blur to those who watched. Charlton's claws caught Raymond's side taking out a large chunk of flesh. Raymond bit into the side of Charlton's face, cutting off half his nose. Another swipe of Charlton's paw dazed Raymond causing his vision to blur. But he could still see well enough to swipe Charlton across the side of his head and ripping off an ear. Both wolves bit into each other and wouldn't let go as they tumbled—their fur soaked with each other's blood. Then Raymond drove his fangs into Charlton's neck. He bit down until his fangs touched bone; the blood pumping from the black wolf's artery filled Raymond's mouth and dripped out of its side and along his silver and black fur. He felt Charlton grow weak as his paws dropped, and his head dangled from Raymond's mouth. Raymond let go and watched Charlton lay with his yellow eyes looking up at him. Blood poured from him as he slowly transformed. "You think I'm the only one, you fools?" he said with a faint voice and a crooked grin.

"Let me have him," a deputy said, aiming his rifle.

No! Wait!" Raymond said to the gunman. "What do you mean?" Raymond asked Charlton gasping for breath.

Charlton's voice weakened to a whisper. "What do you think I've been doing all these years? I did to others what you did to me," he said.

"You mean you've turned others?" Debra asked, blood covering the front of her clothes.

Charlton just lay there grinning up at them.

"How many are there? Where are they?" A deputy asked frantically. Charlton gave a faint chuckle and coughed up dark blood.

"Are they here? Are they coming?" A wolf begged. "Daniels! Daniels!" Charlton fell unconscious. The deputy aimed and shot him in the head.

Charlton lay still with his eyes and mouth wide open—his brains and blood oozing down the walls and ceiling. Raymond transformed and took a sweater his mom handed him and tied it around his lower body.

"You think he was telling the truth...about there being more like him, I mean?" A deputy asked Raymond.

"I don't know," Raymond answered with a worrisome stare.

Immediately, Charlton's remains were taken out into a field and magically burned. The wolves and Debra watched until a light breeze scattered the ashes.

CHAPTER TWENTY-THREE

After the final death of Charlton Daniels, one could say, 'And things got back to normal.' It was more likely that for days, weeks, and months, there seemed a nervous peace among the supernatural and the enlightened portion of the human population. Despite all the blood, brains, and guts Charlton spilled during his reign of terror, something good inadvertently came from his planned decimation. The wolves and the lawmen found a mutual trust and were no longer at each other's throats. Had Charlton said those dying words to punk his enemies, or was there indeed a group of angry werewolves out there somewhere planning to wield their own brand of terror over New Berwick?

"You know, in a way, I kind of feel sorry for Charlton," Russell said.

"Bite your tongue," Heather griped.

"No, I mean it," he said.

"I know you mean it, and I'm appalled.

"What I'm saying is I know how he felt being forced into this lifestyle. At least I can be around my family. It's just a matter of keeping it a secret. But Charlton died in a car crash. He had a funeral and was buried. He could never show himself to his mom and dad, his siblings, or his wife and baby. It was enough to drive *anybody* insane."

"You wouldn't be talking that way if he had chewed up Mark and John."

"Now, why did you have to say that?"

"I'm sorry, honey, but it's true."

"Certainly I'm not agreeing with what he did," Russell said. "It's just a shame, that's all."

"Well, I say good riddance, and if I had anything to do with it, I would have burned him alive."

"Christ! How can someone so beautiful be so cold?" Russell said, grinning and pulling Heather onto his lap. She giggled, and the two fell onto the floor and rolled around playfully, kissing and laughing.

*****

Months after Charlton's murderous rage, Greyscott Falls, north and south, celebrated several new babies into their clan, including Jewel's baby boy, Bridge Porter, and Kayla's baby girl, Beatrice Morrison Porter, named after Kayla's beloved grandmother. Because no one could be sure if Charlton had been bluffing or not, River thought it best to send the wolves younger children to boarding school away from New Berwick; the wolf-pack agreed. Jan had kept her promise of seeing to it that Dria and Becca join Jewel on the Island.

Sheriff Tilbert, aware of Charlton's dying last words, ordered a large supply of silver nitrate. Even though the wolves and Sheriff Tilbert were on good terms, the thought of law enforcement with supplies of silver nitrate understandably made the wolves extremely nervous. But until Charlton's words proved true, the wolves would grin and bear it as River explained at a recent meeting.

The summer ended, and Russell, who had moved some of his clothes back into his parent's house, picked up his mom and dad at the airport. On the ride home, they told him what a wonderful time they had and how much they missed not having him with them. Caroline kept insisting that Russell go with them the next time.

"Mom, I may not even be here next year. You want me to go to college, don't you?"

"Of course, but you'll be home for the summer," she said.

"That means I can take Heather," he said knowing what her response would be.

"That grown woman...I should say not," she said snubbing her nose.

"Mom, Heather is only four years older than me. You act like she's as old as you," he chuckled.

"Oh, honey let the boy alone," Tray said. "Let him grow up for Christ's sake."

"And who's stopping him from growing up? You know what—."

"Mom! Dad! Cut it out, will you? Or so help me, I'll stop the car and let you guys walk home," he teased.

"You do," his mom said smirking, "and we'll take back the gift we bought you."

"What? What?" he said like a little boy.

"Oh, just something you've been wanting," Tray said looking at him. Russell couldn't guess what it was, and his mom and dad teasingly refuse to tell him. The three playfully bickered to their front door. Russell pulled up to the house and couldn't close his mouth. He looked at his mom and dad, and they were ear-to-ear grinning. "Don't just sit there, son," Tray said. Russell got out of his car and stared at the light gray and black Toyota Camry TRD. Tray and Caroline had it delivered while they were at the airport waiting for Russell. "But, but Dad, you always said it was un-American to buy foreign cars."

"I know what I said, son. But I feel like, well, they *are* made in the USA by US workers...so what the heck!" Tray tossed him the keys, and Russell opened the door. The seats were soft gray. The inside doors were gray with red stitches—the dashboard trimmed in silver. And the shift knob was gray leather with red stitches. Russell got out, gave his parents hugs then he helped them unload the luggage from the car into the house.

"I can't thank you enough," Russell told them.

"You deserve it, Rusty. You really do," Tray said.

"And you've been such a good boy...keeping your grades up and all," Caroline said. "We were going to wait and give it to you for graduation this year. But we knew how much you wanted it, so we decided on the end of summer."

"Now, if you go slack on your grades," Tray warned, "it's going right back to the dealers..."

"Don't start on the boy," Caroline scolded.

"I'm not starting anything. I just what him to know...."

Russell watched with amusement as his parents bickered back and forth. He shook his head and chuckled. "You guys iron it out. I'm taking Heather 2 for a little spin," he said still laughing. Russell got into his new car and sped off.

*****

In Southern Greyscott Falls, visiting his mother and father, Matthew's anger boiled over. His baby girl came three weeks early, and he couldn't be there to see that great wonder. "I hate Charlton. I hope he's burning in the after-life. I hope the fires are nipping at his asshole right now," he said.

"Will you stop?" Dex said. "What's done is done."

"That sicko made me miss my daughter's birth. I wanted to cut the cord and let her hear my heartbeat and all that good stuff fathers do."

"There'll be other babies, Matt," Jan said.

"But it won't be the same, Mom."

Dex went to him and gently grabbed his shoulders. "If your little girl should ever ask you why you missed her birth, tell her you were away helping to bring down a monster so that New Berwick could be a safe place for her to live in." Matthew's eyes glazed over as he searched his father's sun-bronze face.

"Thanks. I love you, Dad."

Dex pulled Matthew to him, and the men hugged one another. At that moment, a knock came on the back door. "It's open!" Dex yelled.

Pete rushed in like he was taking a break from jogging. "Dex, you're not going to believe this," he said trying to catch his breath.

"Oh hell, can I get a break! What is it now?"

"Some doctor who knew Charlie Daniels found a notebook belonging to him, and the doctor said that Sheriff Tilbert needs to take a look at it."

"Well, what the hell does the notebook say?" Dex asked.

"He didn't say directly. But he said its proof that Charlie wasn't lying about turning people into werewolves."

"Yeah, but that doesn't prove that he actually did," Matthew said. "Charlton was very clever. He probably left the notebook hoping that if anything were to happen to him, we'd find it."

"I don't know," Pete said. "I'm just delivering the message—is all."

"Does the Sheriff have the notebook now?" Jan asked.

"No, the guy's flying into Illinois tonight. Tilbert is sending a deputy to pick him up at the airport."

"I don't understand," Dex said. "Why couldn't he just tell Tilbert what it says over the phone?"

"Dex, I can't answer that. I'm just telling you what one of the deputies told me. If I learn any more, I'll come straight to you. That's all I can do."

"That won't be necessary, Pete," Dex said. "I'll take it from here. And Pete, thanks."

"Sure thing, Dex." Pete hurried through the kitchen and out the back door.

"What the hell you make of that?" Matthew asked.

"I don't know. I'm going to give Sheriff Tilbert a call. See if he can tell me more," Dex said picking up his phone.

*****

Russell pulled up to Dell's house. Dell had also moved back home to get ready for the school year. Dell poked his head out the door; his eyes stretched so wide, his eyebrows nearly touched his hairline. "Holy Crap! Are you kidding me? You're kidding me. Are you kidding me? A Toyota Camry? Dude, talk to me," he said running out and examining Russell's car. Dell opened the door. "Wow, awesome, Rusty," he said, smoothing his hand along the silver trim of the dashboard.

"I drove my mom and dad home from the airport, and when we got there, this was sitting in the driveway."

"What made your father relent?"

"He said something about it being made in the USA by American workers. But I don't buy it. I think he just knew it would make me happy."

"Aw, your parents are pretty awesome, dude. Hey, let's go in." Russell followed Dell into the house and gestured him to the family room. "My parents are out, want a beer?"

"Yeah, I'll take one," Russell said flopping on the sofa. Dell walked into the kitchen, opened the fridge, and frowned. He joined Russell in the family room and handed him the beer.

"Sorry, it's only one left; we'll share it," Dell said. Russell took a big swig and handed the bottle back to Dell, who downed half and offered Russell the rest.

"No, I'm good," Russell said, and Dell drained the bottle.

"Rusty, I'm kind of glad you're in a good mood with your new car and all because I've got some disturbing news if you haven't heard already."

"Oh, no, what is it now. Don't tell me—Charlton rose from the ashes?"

Dell chuckled. "No, and Jewel Porter didn't fall off her broom and break her ass. In fact..." Dell stared Russell in the eye, "...it's worse."

Russell braced himself as Dell spoke. "A doctor found Charlton's notebook, and he's flying in tonight to hand it over to Sheriff Tilbert. I think they said his name is Dr. Hammerstine or Hammerstein, I'm not sure."

"A notebook," Russell said. "Did he say what's written in it?"

"The doc told Sheriff Tilbert over the phone that Charlton made notes of experimenting with turning people into werewolves."

"You mean medical experiment? There's no medical experiment to it? You just bite 'em, for Christ sakes," Russell snapped.

"I'm just telling you what I heard from the grapevine, that's all," Dell said. "Look, let's put all this talk on hold and go get into your new Toyota Camry, get some beer, pick up Heather and Massie and go for a ride," Dell said. "And I'm driving."

"Whoa! What do you mean *you're* driving?" Russell snapped.

"Give me the keys."

Russell didn't move to hand them over.

"Give me the keys, dude."

Russell just stood with a silly smirk and shook his head. Dell grinned, snatched the keys, and bolted out the door.

"Dammit!" Russell yelled and sprinted after him.

CHAPTER TWENTY-FOUR

Deputy Holloway met Dr. Eric P. Hammerstein at Dowel County Airport at approximately 8:00 p.m. and drove him to Sheriff Tilbert's home. Mrs. Rose Tilbert, watching from the living room window, spotted them and opened the door while the deputy's hand was still in motion to knock.

"Come in, Dr. Hammerstein," she greeted. "My husband is waiting in the den, this way, please," she gestured. The deputy turned and left the house, and Mrs. Tilbert led the doctor to the den, where Sheriff Tilbert waited with Bob Wilson at his side. Mrs. Tilbert left the room and closed the door.

"Dr. Hammerstein, please to meet you," Sheriff Tilbert said extending a hand. "This is our chief coroner, Mr. Bob Wilson." After shaking Tilbert's hand, Hammerstein smiled and shook Bob's hand. "Please be seated," Sheriff Tilbert said to the doctor.

After taking their seats, Hammerstein pulled out a rather thin brown leather notebook. Bob and Tilbert's eyes fell on the book, which Hammerstein placed on his lap.

"I gather that's the book in question," Tilbert said.

"Yes," the doctor answered quietly. "And let me began by saying I am so sorry for your losses. I understand that quite a number of New Berwick citizens lost their lives before Charlton met his own demise."

"Thank you for your kind words," Tilbert said. "I really appreciate it."

"As you probably know," Doctor Hammerstein began, "Charlton was a very sick and troubled man. I don't know how many details of his life you're familiar with since he left New Berwick, but I'll try to fill you in as best I can."

"We know a little," Tilbert said. "But if there's anything more you can tell us, we certainly welcome it." Bob nodded in agreement.

"Well, that's what I hope to do. As I said, Charlton was a very sick and troubled man. He was under the illusion that he was a werewolf."

Sheriff Tilbert and Bob glanced at one another—realizing that the doctor hadn't a clue what Charlton was. *And he was going to fill 'us' in with the missing pieces of his life?* Tilbert thought.

"I served as his psychiatrist for several months," Hammerstein continued.

"His psychiatrist?" Bob blurted.

"Yes, it was a court order, you see. People began to report him as acting strangely. His landlady said he would be missing for days at a time. She couldn't get him to eat or drink anything, and when he was in his apartment, he seldom left his room. After being locked up in his room for days, he'd frighten the other tenants by emerging naked and bloody with animal fur all over him. His landlady said some of her tenants had complained that he would have nightmares so bad, they thought he'd burst right through the walls. Being afraid for her life and her tenants, naturally, the poor woman had no choice but to report him to the police; a judge ordered him committed to Greendale Institute, and that's how I became his doctor."

"Wow, we certainly didn't know that," Tilbert said glancing at Bob. "Exactly how long was Charlton institutionalized?"

"Until he escaped," the doctor said. "He attacked a staff member one night and stole her car. Then a few days later, he contacted me. I begged him to come back for treatment, but he refused. However, later I pretended to believe he was a werewolf so he'd keep me informed about where he was and what he was doing. That's how I knew he was here."

"You knew he was here killing people?" Tilbert shrilled.

"Not at first, of course. He kept claiming he was a werewolf. How was I to know he was actually murdering people? It was a while before I realized he was telling the truth—about the killings, that is. Before I could report it, I learned he was dead. That's when I decided to bring you this book."

"I see," Tilbert said fingering his short beard. "I'm confused. Since you, for obvious reasons, didn't believe he was a werewolf. Then why bring me that book? Charlton's insanity makes every word in that book a lie—wouldn't you say?"

"Insane, yes. His notes bear that truth. But I feel it's what his notes *aren't* saying that's screaming the loudest."

"How do you mean?" Bob asked.

"Charlton was doing something, but I'm not sure what it was," Hammerstein said. "I believe he may have known hypnosis."

"Why do you say that?" Tilbert asked.

"Every person he befriended at the institution—within a short time would suddenly claim they *too* were werewolves. And they all had this mysterious deep cut to their chest. Our medical doctor examined them and couldn't understand how they were still alive. Plus, when questioned about the wounds, they all claimed they didn't know how they got them. It was like some group hysteria. I think he did the same with the tenants at his apartment. Quite a number of them were committed to the institution with wounds in the same spot. After treating them for several weeks, one morning, the nurse and several male orderlies found them all missing, and we haven't seen any one of them since. I'm here because

Charlton told me he had summoned them to New Berwick. I thought, as a psychiatrist, I could be of some help. Have you noticed any strangers in your town lately?"

"Why, no," Tilbert said frowning.

"If they should come," the doctor said frantically, "just persuade a judge to put them in my care. Treatment and medication is the only way of keeping them from repeating the horror Charlton inflicted on your people."

Tilbert nervously pulled on his beard. "Doctor Hammerstein, that's very kind of you. Ah, would you excuse us for a moment?" Tilbert said, not waiting to hear the doctor's answer; he grabbed Bob's arm and ushered him into the next room and closed the door. "Bob, this poor fool doesn't know what he's walking into. We can't tell him Charlton was a werewolf. And we can't let him near the men Charlton has turned."

"Not only that," Bob said, "but can you imagine the massive heart attack this guy would have if he knew this whole town was crawling with werewolves. What the hell do we do?"

"Let's just thank him and tell him we'll handle things from here," Tilbert said.

"What about the book? Think he'll still give us the book?"

"Yeah, I believe so. He thinks it's full of lies anyway."

"Right! Right! Okay," Bob said anxiously. The men faked smiles as they rejoined the doctor. They kept to the script, thanked the doctor, and offered to pay his hotel bill and flight back home, which he politely accepted. The doctor handed over the book and said if he could be of any service to please call him. He said there was no charge. He just wanted to help. Tilbert phoned Holloway to drive the doctor back to the airport. Immediately after the doctor left, Tilbert and Bob read every page of the little book. Just a few pages made it clear to Sheriff Tilbert that it was not the writings of a mad man, and Tilbert felt damn glad he had the silver nitrate.

The first page began:

Monday-September 7th—it is the 4th week since I crawled out of my grave. Infected by the fangs of a werewolf, I now am doomed to be the beast that I am this night. Charlton's first ten pages described the horror of waking up in a coffin and the pain of his first transformation. The next twelve pages he devoted to his ordeal, his anger and sadness of how much he missed his family, especially his wife and child. The following eight pages told of his fears and hatred for Dr. Lorac and the wolves. But it was the remaining twenty-six pages that had disturbed Dr. Hammerstein the most, and now Sheriff Tilbert and Bob Wilson felt that same chill as Bob read the lines aloud. Charlton wrote how he prepared for revenge. It listed everything he had done in New Berwick from the silver nitrate bullet that ripped through the brain of the first deputy and the butchering of Dr. Lorac, to killing several wolves as well as innocent citizens. Plus, page after page described the torture he had prepared for River, Dex, the two teens who had run him off the road, and the wolf who bit him.

It seemed that Charlton had discovered that he could create a battalion of werewolves by drugging young men, biting them in the throat, and driving an eight-inch blade through their chests, killing them instantly. Then after a few hours, they would rise from the dead, a full-fledged werewolf—loyal to him and ready to follow his every command. At the institution, it had been hard getting hold of a knife, so he swiped a long handle serving spoon from the evening food cart. He found a way to sharpen the handle to a fine point, and after biting his victims, he'd stab them in the chest.

At the end of his notes, Charlton composed a poem that had no title. The five stanzas appeared dedicated to his wife though he knew she would never read it.

Grieve for me my sweet

That I may cup your tears

To bathe in the memories

Of our wonderful years

Curse the day I left you

And baby Christi alone

To tread this dark road

For which I now roam

Forced into a world

Men-beasts have comprised

If Christ should come

I cannot rise

From the grave

Which stole my prime

Where immortality

Out shines my shrine

Kiss Christi for me—beg her

Grant Daddy forgiveness

For only then can I bear

This cursed existence.

Tilbert found the poem haunting and sad but felt it seemed unfinished. Closing the book, he and Bob sat silently for a moment.

Then Bob broke the silence. "How will they behave after finding out their leader is dead, I wonder?" he asked.

"Your guess is as good as mine. The main thing is that we can't wait for someone to die."

"We could limit travel and put deputies at every road in and out of New Berwick," Bob said.

"Good idea," Tilbert replied.

The next day, deputies set up checkpoints throughout Sheerfield. Tilbert informed citizens to report any male strangers immediately. Deputies remained stationed around malls, schools, parks, playgrounds, hospitals, churches, closed beaches, and fishing spots as well as the whole residential area. The wolves took care of their region North and South of Greyscott Falls, and the witches had no fear but still placed a magic shield around Falcon Haven. The junior wolves continued to guard Mark, John, and their families. Sheriff Tilbert was nervous. *This would have to happen during the school months,* he thought. Watching the children traveling to and from school, their parents to and from work, plus watching people shop at the mall, doing business at banks as well as attending fun activities like night clubs, the theatre, and bowling alleys would prove a task that the Sheerfield Law officers prayed they could achieve.

Russell talked Mark and John into carpooling with him. He picked them up every morning and drove them to Sheerfield Academy. Dell, however, attended a smaller school with his fellow junior wolves in Greyscott Falls. A whole month went by without incident, but Tilbert didn't lift the emergency. Many of Sheerfield's younger children, whose tender minds were shielded from knowledge of the posing threat, grew angry when Tilbert forbade Halloween activities. The sheriff didn't want his deputies saddled with having to check under every mask to make sure it wasn't one of the enemy wolves. It was a smart move, but when the December snow came, the children were still upset, and they hurled snowballs at Tilbert's patrol car. One got him in the face just as he exited his car, but Tilbert just laughed it off. He'd rather take a few snowballs to the kisser, he told one of his deputies, than to find one of their little bodies butchered and lying next to their deceased parents.

They brought the New Year in with caution; Sheriff Tilbert ordered no fireworks or gunshots. It recorded the quietest New Year's celebration ever. When darkness fell, the streets became eerie and deserted. Only the headlights from the patrol cars cruising throughout the community were visible. Everyone stayed indoors, and deputies stayed alert and cruised until daylight.

The first casualty was the old man. Eager to get him a werewolf, as he had often put it, the seventy-five-year-old was found dead at his little shack about five miles outside of Rhicor's Peak. Hundreds of buzzing flies, like moving black tar, covered the windows. A drinking buddy grew worried when the old guy failed to meet up at their usual spot. He forced his way into his living quarters and found him ripped to pieces. His rifle was empty, and bullet holes peppered the cabin walls. Volumes of blood had soaked into the scatter rugs and in between the cracks of the hardwood floor. His family buried him in his full Marine dress uniform with military honors for his brave service in Viet Nam.

CHAPTER TWENTY-FIVE

Sheriff Tilbert stood in front of his office window. He bit his lower lip and stared at the leafless trees. Fearing for the safety of New Berwick, Tilbert knew he had to do *something*. But where were they? Who were they? How many wolves did the revengeful fangs of Charlton Daniels create?

The office door opened, and Bob Wilson walked through. "Good morning," he greeted.

Tilbert turned and frowned. "You don't have to tell me. Chuck Thompson was killed by a werewolf," Tilbert said referring to the old man.

"Yeah, that's why I didn't call. It didn't take much to figure *that* one."

"Evidently," Tilbert said taking a seat behind his desk. "You've got some other news, or you wouldn't be standing there fidgeting."

"I think I might have a hunch where Charlton's wolves could be."

"Spill it," Tilbert replied.

"You know that old mine shaft about five miles outside South Greyscott?"

"You think they're holed up there?"

"No. It's the mountains behind it. When I went to the bathroom around three a.m., I could swear I saw fire up there in those mountains. I don't think they were locals."

"No," Tilbert said. "They know better than to break the curfew."

"Exactly...so, how do we go about finding out for sure it's them...in a safe way, I mean?"

Tilbert scratched his beard. "I suppose I'll have to call in all of my best deputies and put our heads together."

"Don't forget the Greyscott wolves," Bob snapped. "They're the ones who got us into this freaking shit. Put some of *them* on the front lines. Let *them* lose a few."

"Now, why do that? All that blood, guts, and fur flying when we can do it nice and easy with a silver nitrate bullet to the brain," Tilbert said grinning.

"Yeah," Bob chuckled. "I guess you're about right. But I'd put their asses on the front line just the same."

Sheriff Tilbert handed his assistant a list of deputies to call for a meeting. They were ex-Marines with sniper training and had experienced the horrors of war. Tilbert prayed they could handle this horror as well.

Meanwhile, in Southern Greyscott Falls, a small group of wolves also held a meeting.

"Poor old guy," Dell said.

"Poor old guy, my ass," Dex snapped. "That crazy bastard was going to shoot us that night." Several wolves laughed. "Not funny," Dex said. "You guys weren't there. It was pretty scary."

"Until Heather came out of the forest and bitch-slapped him with one of her spells," Dell chuckled.

"Yeah, that *was* funny," Matthew grinned. "He hit the ground stiff as a thousand-year-old mummy."

Suddenly, the wolves' laughter died as their attention turned to the sound of quick footsteps descending the club's cellar stairs.

"Rusty, what's up?" Dell greeted.

"On my way over here," Russell said, "I got a call from Sheriff Tilbert. He said night fires were spotted in the mountains about five miles from here behind the old mine shaft. He wants us to investigate, but not to do anything."

"What the hell does he mean, not to do anything?" Dex growled. "If it's them, we'll rip their asses. Case closed."

"No. He doesn't want a confrontation," Russell said. "He just wants to know how many there are, then his deputies will go in with silver nitrate and take them out."

"Oh, hell no," Dex said. "A quick death? I want those bastards to suffer...the way Charlie made Sally and our brother wolves suffer."

"Come on Dex," Russell said. "If they want to do it...let them. Why risk some of *us* getting hurt or killed?"

"That's that cowardly human side talking," Dex griped. "Now, let's hear what your wolf side has to say."

"Look," Russell snapped. "I don't give a damn *what* you do. I'm just telling you what the sheriff said." Russell turned and quickly mounted the stairs.

"Rusty, wait...Rusty!" Dex called. Dex scrambled across the floor and yelled up the stairs. "I was only kidding." But Russell never answered. He got into his car and headed back to Sheerfield.

Turning onto Kingston Road, Russell saw the main checkpoint up ahead manned by several deputies. Busy thinking about his tiff with Dex, Russell had missed the exit that would have taken him to the back road he'd traveled earlier. "Damn," he said his eyes darting like a cornered cat. He eased up and braked.

"Get out of the car!" one of the deputies ordered loudly. "Turn around...put your hands on the roof of the car. And don't move."

Steve, the chief deputy who had arrested Matthew for kidnapping Russell seven years earlier, strolled over and waved the young deputy to step aside.

"Rusty, what are you doing out here? You know there's a curfew."

"I know," Russell said lowering his arms and facing him, "but I had some pressing news for the wolves."

"What, your phone broke?"

"No. I'm...I'm sorry."

"Have to take you in, son."

"Please, you *know* my mom and dad and they're alone. I've got to get back there."

"You should have thought of that before you left," Steve griped.

"I won't do it again, I promise."

Steve looked at the ground. The young deputy stood firm with his hand on his handcuffs ready to grab Russell as his superior appeared to ponder. Steve then slowly looked up. He couldn't help but see traces of that innocent ten-year-old in Russell's twin blue pools. "Get your ass out of here," he ordered.

"Yes sir," Russell said scrambling to get into his car.

"See you out here again during curfew, I'm hauling you in, you got that?"

"No problem," Russell said pulling off.

Days later, with everything in place for a possible showdown with the C-wolves, a name they had dubbed, short for Charlton's werewolves, Sheriff Tilbert talked Dex and a small group of his fellow wolves into scouting the area of the mountain where Bob had seen the campfire. Tilbert told them to remain unseen and not attack the C-wolves but to report their findings. Dex reluctantly agreed, and at the last minute, Russell decided he'd go along.

A small caravan of trucks and vans made the forty-five minute trip at nightfall. They hid their vehicles in the thick of a nearby wooded area and traveled the rest of the way on foot creeping within the shadows. Those who shapeshifted made the journey more quietly as their paws made for padded footsteps. Feet and paws climbed diligently up the side of the mountain. The tricky twists and sharp turns on the jagged edges seemed a familiar battle between man, animal, and nature. Paws transformed into hands as they needed them to hold on and to keep balance. Suddenly, a foot, or perhaps a paw, struck a large, loose rock which fell against another cluster of stones creating a scuffle of noise. Everyone froze and pushed their bodies hard against the rough surface trying to hide from eyes that might peer from above as the noise of the rocks scaling down the mountain rose in the air. Though they smelled campfire smoke, the mountain top remained silent.

Dex heard movement coming from above. He signaled the wolves to remain still while he alone checked out the sound. He knew what he promised Sheriff Tilbert, but he refused to let that promise put him and his brother wolves in danger. He quickly shapeshifted and crept along a wide path on the side of the mountain near the top. The footsteps got closer and Dex kept to the path ready to take on whatever he encountered. Then Dex figured out it was playing a game; when Dex moved, it moved and when Dex stopped, it stopped. This went on for several minutes, and Dex held his breath and his heart raced when suddenly the footstep stopped a few feet from him, around a bend on the trail. Dex sucked in his breath and curled his mouth revealing his sharp fangs. Blinded by a thick brush that extended from the edge, Dex growled, rushed around it, and landed hard on the dark creature scaring the poor goat out of its wits. The goat, terrified and flailing, accidentally pierced Dex's shoulder with the tip of its horn. Dex fell back and the frightened creature bolted down the side of the mountain and out of sight. Laughter rained down from the top of the mountain. His brother wolves had watched the whole incident with amusement.

"Come on up," Russell chuckled. "They're not here."

"You guys are sick, you know that? I could have fallen and broken my neck!" Dex shouted walking back for his clothes. The wolves continued to chuckle as Matthew lowered his hand to his father' and tried not to laugh. Dex gripped his son's hand and struggled to the top of the mountain where he looked around and saw the smothered campfires and carcasses of butchered deer, wild rabbits, and discarded cooked bones. "Looks like they had quite a feast," Dell said.

"Hey, Dex...over here!" one of the wolves yelled. The wolf pointed to five stone graves. *These are manufactured werewolves all right,* Dex thought. *Real wolves burn their dead on a pyre and send them out to sea with a prayer to the goddess. Not stack a bunch of rocks on top of them.*

"Let's move those stones and see what we've got," Dex said. Several wolves removed the piles and tossed them aside. The gray faces of the C-wolves stared up at them. "Hey, wait a minute," Dex said. "These wolves got bullet holes in them." Dex pulled out his phone and called Sheriff Tilbert. "Tilbert," Dex snapped. "Did some of your deputies sneak up ahead of us and try to take these C-wolves on? They did a bum job if they did."

"No. What are you talking about?"

"We're at the top of the mountain, and they've cleared out. You guys are the only ones we know of with silver nitrate, and we've got five graves here."

"My deputies wouldn't do that without my orders. I don't know what to tell you."

"All right, let me sort this out. I'll get back with you," Dex said.

"I bet I know what happened," Russell said.

"Okay, genius," Dex smirked.

"That old man."

"What?"

"That's the only explanation. He shot five of them before they attacked and killed him, then they brought their dead up here and buried them."

"Well I'll be damned," Dex said. "You know, I think you're right."

"Why that old geezer," Dell chuckled. "He finally got him a heap of werewolves."

"Never thought I'd hear myself say this, but good for him if he did," Dex said. "Better them than us that night. I'm still kind of glad the guy is gone though. He gave me the creeps." Dex turned toward the mountain path. "Come on," he said. "We better be heading down.

It took them a while to travel down the mountain. In the blackness of the wooded area, many pairs of yellow eyes watched Dex and the wolves climb into their vehicles and pull out.

CHAPTER TWENTY-SIX

Bob Wilson's bedroom window opened onto a balcony overlooking a small park where neighbors frequently walked their dogs. Faraway, the Rhicors Peak Mountain stood dark and still. Bob rotated the focusing wheel on his binoculars but observed no campfire or smoke. He shook his head and sighed, disappointed at the missed element of surprise Tilbert and his deputies might have had against the C-wolves. *No one has a clue where the hell they are*, he thought.

In a phone call to Bob, Tilbert was apologetic. "I'm sorry," he said. "I should have made a move the second you told me about the fire."

"Don't talk like it's your fault, Wayne. We'll get those bastards."

Tilbert ended the call then quickly phoned Dex. Not wanting to suffer another missed opportunity, he told Dex that he and his wolves were free to pursue the C-wolves but to keep him posted especially if they needed assistance. Dex alerted River who informed the Northern wolves and a war room was set up for the Elders from both packs to plan a strategy.

*****

That February was the coldest in thirty years. When it rained, everything, including the water dripping from their noses seemed to freeze. People stayed indoors, and Sheriff Tilbert thanked God for that. It made life a whole lot easier, especially for his deputies who worked double and sometimes triple shifts to keep New Berwick safe. Team spirit among the deputies ran high in the face of things going horribly wrong. It didn't seem like much at first—just a few farm animals missing; then one evening, Begley, a young deputy who had been posted along a strip of highway, came running into Tilbert's office. He wheezed out of breath with news that he'd found a man hanging from a tree with a note attached to his chest.

Later, Tilbert found out that the man was a Northern wolf who had been tortured and left hanging. The note bore the name, Chad Roberts, the fifteen-year-old wolf who had infected Charlton years ago. Roberts was by then a husband and father of three little girls. Apparently, the C-wolves had tortured Chad's name out of that wolf and were letting the Greyscott wolves know that they were going after Chad. But Dex and River knew that those murdering beasts weren't going to stop with killing Chad Roberts—and they were right. The C-wolves may have been manufactured werewolves as Dex had said, but Charlton had made them into deadly killing machines. The pack figured that the C-wolves intended to rain terror over New Berwick traveling throughout the region turning men into werewolves to swell their numbers; then they'd face the Greyscott wolves to annihilate them and anyone else who stood in their way.

Several months later, New Berwick continued to function on lock-down. The people understood the dangers if Sheriff Tilbert loosened up a bit, but still, they loaded the sheriff station's phones and email with hostile complaints. Because of the curfew, the junior and senior proms had been a disaster for parents and kids alike. They'd be damned, angry parents scolded, if they were going to allow the tight reins Tilbert had on the town's activities to spoil their children's high school graduation. With the threat of an angry mob of parents storming the sheriff's station, Tilbert caved and the commencement plans went forward.

On the afternoon of June seventh, Russell's parents sat elated. Dell's private school had held *their* graduation in May with Russell and Heather in attendance. Then it was Dell and Massie's turn to do Russell the same honor. He was all-smiles marching among two-hundred fellow students to Sir Edward Elgar's "Pomp and Circumstance". The Sooner family grinned profusely, and Russell appeared to strut in his royal blue cap and gown; his cap's blue tassel with the gold year charm attached seemed to swing and dance to the slow music.

Although the commencement ensued without incident, Sheriff Tilbert was extremely nervous the whole time. Many of his deputies also had children who were graduating and they wanted to attend—leaving just over a third of the force to keep watch over the entire region. Russell, his family, and circle of friends including Mark, John, and their families, celebrated that night at the Ruston Hotel. It was there where Mrs. Sooner finally made peace with Heather since it seemed unlikely Russell would break up with her. Heather, however, never knew she had disapproved.

*****

Several days later at Northern Greyscott Falls, a hardheaded Chad Roberts had to be restrained in his own home.

"You're not doing this, damn it!" Matthew yelled at him.

"It's me they're after," Chad snapped. "Why should I let the whole pack pay for my screw-up? I'll fight the head of their pack. If he wins, it's settled. If I win, we send them on their way."

"Are you freaking crazy?" Russell chuckled. "That only happens in old Hollywood movies. They're not going to be satisfied with just you."

"That's right," Dell said. "Charlton didn't create a bunch of werewolves just to kill *you*."

"But you don't know that," Chad said. "Why don't we meet with them? See what will satisfy them besides me?"

"Don't you understand, Chad? Those wolves want war. We can't do a sit down with those ingrates," Russell said.

"I think we're making a mistake to start a war without at least trying to negotiate peace," Chad said.

"You can't make peace with wolves that are hell-bent on ripping your head off," Russell griped. "They tortured and killed one of us for Christ's sake. What is wrong with you?"

"Yeah, does that look like they want peace?" Matthew snapped.

"What are you knuckleheads up to now?" River said walking into the family room with a couple of senior wolves trailing behind. In a panic, Chad's wife had called River after she tried and failed to talk Chad out of giving himself up to the C-wolves.

"Stupid here, wants to do a sit-down with the C-wolves," Matthew joked.

"No, first," Russell chuckled, "he wants to do that movie thing. You know, where Alan Ladd and this bad dude are tied together at their wrists and each given a bowie knife in the other hand to duke it out?" Matthew and Dell cracked up.

"What the hell are you talking about?" one of the senior wolves bellowed.

Russell told him about Chad's plan to solve their problem by fighting the leader of the other pack.

"Tell me you didn't say that, Chad," River asked squinting at him. Chad just folded his lips and looked off glassy-eyed. When River saw how serious and hurt he looked, he tried to console him. "Chad, you were fifteen. We know you didn't mean it." River assured him. "We all make mistakes."

"Son, who knew Daniels had gotten infected?" a senior wolf reasoned. "Stop blaming yourself. We'll get through this together. You understand—together?" He touched Chad's shoulder—Chad nodded and half-grinned.

At that moment, Dex rang River's phone. "Yeah, Dex," he said. After a few seconds, River's face turned grim. "What? Goddamnit!" River snapped. Everyone stared silently and strained to make sense of the one-way conversation. "I'm sick of this!" River yelled. "They're picking us off one by one, and all we do is sit around making plans but never do anything. Call Sherriff Tilbert," he ordered. Everyone sat motionless listening. "Tell him to round up his men and all the silver nitrate; the wolves will meet them at Rhicors Peak. We're bringing this shit to a close, now!" he shouted. River ended the call. He took a deep breath and with face flushed, he turned to them and said, "Twelve wolves were found tortured—hanging from trees. Their eyes ripped out."

"Holy shit!" Dell blurted. "These bastards mean business."

"And so do we," River growled.

"When do we move, Uncle River?" Matthew asked.

"After we attend to our dead. We move tonight."

"What I'd like to know," said a senior wolf, "is how are they moving in and out on us without us seeing them?"

"We're not going to know anything about these bastards until we make ourselves targets," Russell said.

"What do you mean—targets?" Dell asked.

"He means," Matthew replied, "we have to take the fight to them by being in the open. That way, they can't sneak up on us."

"Is that it, River?" Dell asked.

"Yes, that's exactly right."

"But we don't even know how many there are," Dell said.

"Doesn't matter," River said. "With the full might of the wolves and twenty-five militarily trained deputy snipers with silver nitrate, if they can come through all of that, we *deserve* to get our asses kicked."

*****

That night, the wolves stood in black pants and black shirts with their familiar red armbands. Behind them, a small group representing the covenant witches stood in black hooded capes—each holding a single lit candle. All watched the twelve flaming pyres float out upon the water under a navy-blue, star-filled sky and each whispered prayers for the goddess to receive them.

Miles away in unmarked cars, Sheriff Wayne Tilbert, and his highly skilled deputies of eight women and seventeen men eased, into the dark wooded area a few hundred feet from Rhicors Peak and turned off their motors. The eerie breeze carried a chill and Tilbert nervously eyeballed his surroundings with unwarranted suspicion. Nervous and impatient Tilbert frowned at his watch a half dozen times during that hour.

"What was that?" Summer, one of the deputies whispered to her male partner who sat in the driver's seat. She thought she'd heard something. Easing the door open two inches, Summer pointed her rifle through the crack.

"No," her partner said. "Wait."

Straight-away, a light flashed on and off three times—a signal to Sheriff Tilbert from River. Tilbert got out of his car; two top deputies with rifles walked with him. Deep within the shadows of the large, wooded area stood River, Dex, Matthew, Russell, Dell, and one hundred and fifty fellow wolves. Fifty had shapeshifted and a hundred carried handguns, shotguns and rifles.

"What are the firearms for?" Tilbert asked. "Lead bullets won't kill them. You know that."

"Of course I do," River said, "I took a page from your playbook. Several blasts of lead will bust them up pretty badly and render them useless against us."

"Aww, yes," Tilbert said remembering his strategy against the Greyscott wolves.

"You and your deputies look like you need some sleep," River said. "Me and some of the wolves will keep watch."

"All right by me." Tilbert turned to one of his deputies. "Tell everyone we're camping here."

"Yes sir," she said gripping her rifle. She turned and hustled back to the group.

CHAPTER TWENTY-SEVEN

The Strike Force, consisting of deputies and wolves, found the early morning disappointing; the near bursting clouds hid the sunlight as the sky grew dull and gray. Because of the coming rain, the tall trees along the valley path stood crowded with different species of birds—their loud squabbling over territory heard for miles. The ground was still wet from overnight rainfall. Tilbert, in the lead van, saw the gaslight come on; the gauge's needle had dipped toward "E" and he seemed amazed at how much fuel the new police vans gobbled up. He stopped to fill his tank from one of many gas cans the department brought along then he raced to his place at the front of the line.

The valley and hills turned green again, and purple mountain peaks stood high against the grayish-blue sky. Clear waters flowed over large, brown rocks and snaked between steep hills lined with clusters of evergreen. Russell squinted and thought he saw movement from a dark wooded area several hundred yards from their point of travel.

"Stop!" Russell yelled waving his hand out the driver's side window.

"Who yelled stop?" River growled looking behind him.

"I did," Russell said.

"Nobody gives that order but me, Dex, or Sheriff Tilbert," River snapped.

"I saw something," Russell said.

"Then you report it to one of us."

"Okay. I get it. You going to check it out or what?" Russell said pointing to the dark area.

Dell jumped from the front passenger seat, ran up, and informed Tilbert why they stopped. Then, at River's order, a small band of four-legged wolves trotted toward the forest to check Russell's suspicion.

The force had spent hours driving through the thick mist with shapeshifted wolves on foot. The grass provided some relief from mud but not from flooding. Russell held his breath for several seconds; his packmates appeared to do the same. Suddenly, roars and high-pitched screams from wounded K-9s echoed from the dark distance—a loudness matched by blood pounding in Russell's ears. River's voice rose above the turmoil. He ordered the wolves to advance. Tilbert and his deputies also advanced. With vehicles surging toward the wooded area, the deputies entered first. Their weapons ready to fire, they paused to allow their eyes to adjust to the blackness. Military training kicked in, and they easily scaled the tall trees like chimpanzees—resting on thick, heavy branches with muzzles aimed. Utter chaos reigned. River staggered and mentally struggled with what he saw. The C-wolves, who proved only sixty-wolves strong, in human form, shot dead several Greyscott wolves with silver nitrate-loaded weapons. With their mastered art of partial shapeshifting, a smaller group tore into four-legged Greyscott wolves with martial arts-like techniques. Standing upright with paws and sharp claws, the C-wolves executed precise kicks and quick clawed swipes that instantly cracked the jawbones and front legs of all advancing Greyscott wolves.

"Sheriff, goddamnit what are you waiting for!" River yelled.

"Fire at will!" Tilbert shouted. He had not been late in attacking the C-wolves; he simply needed to wait until his force was in a safe range. Tilbert squatted behind the opened door of his van and blasted several C-wolves. The deafening roars of assault weapons echoed back and forth across the distance like multiple, mini thunderbolts. Just like River was stunned by the art of their partial shapeshifting, the C-wolf leader was just as stunned at the awesome marksmanship of the deputies whose every shot permanently took down a C-wolf.

Rita, an ex-Marine and six-year deputy, aimed her rifle for the tenth time. She shot at the very moment she felt pain in her right shoulder. At first, she thought it was the familiar kickback of her weapon, but it was a bullet, and blood leaked through her tan uniform. Like a good soldier, she ignored the pain and waited for the target to surface. A smile etched across her face as she slowly squeezed the trigger, and a blast splattered the brains of a weapon-carrying C-wolf against a tree. Rita weakened as her numerous gun blasts sent flesh flying and filled the air with smoke. She remained conscious until her body fell from the tree and hit the ground with a thud. Though her comrades proved superior in the gun battle, many more died.

"PULL BACK! PULL BACK!" Sheriff Tilbert shouted to his deputies.

River's voice melted in the distance as he repeated the same order to *his* group.

"PULL BACK!" Dex's faint voice echoed even farther in the distance.

The deputies in the trees kept the C-wolves dodging the bullets flying over their barricades, so the Strike Force could retreat a safe distance and flee. With men and wolves running, limping, and some carried on backs, they loaded them into vehicles and drove to another near-by wooded area for safety. The silver nitrate took a toll on the wounded wolves. No one had bothered to bring an antidote since none could imagine that C-wolves would have that chemical on hand.

Although Sheriff Tilbert's deputies included an ex-army medic, Dex had to enlist Naomi to treat the wolves. However, Sheriff Tilbert made it clear that Naomi was not to interfere by assisting them with magic. She had brought along a few sister-witches from her coven, and they treated the wolves, left the antidote, and went on their way.

Though the wounded moaned a bit, the night chill brought quietness as Tilbert, his top deputies, River, and major pack members sat around a campfire and planned their next move.

Later, when Sheriff Tilbert attempted to settle into his bedding, a female's loud whisper called to him. He walked to where she lay. Rita, her shoulder bandaged and feeling a little drowsy from the pain medicine, told Tilbert about a strange occurrence during her gunfight in the forest.

"Are you sure?" Tilbert asked.

"Yes," she said. "I'm telling you, I didn't miss, and I know there were at least ten C-wolves who were not affected by the silver nitrate."

"Hm," Tilbert uttered. "I'm sure there's an explanation, but I'll let River and Dex get some sleep and run it by them in the morning."

"Sure thing, Sheriff," she said. "Just thought you should know."

"I appreciate it," Tilbert said. "You rest that shoulder and get some sleep. You're too valuable to be out of commission."

"Yes, sir. Thank you, sir."

By next morning, the sun had practically drunk the ground dry, and the clouds appeared as painted, fluffed pillows on a powder blue canvas. A strong whiff of coffee and fried bacon filled the air. The urgency of battle planning made Tilbert forget what Rita had told him the night before. He had practically dismissed it as soon as she'd mentioned it—citing, in his mind, that perhaps being weak from blood loss had affected her aim and her ego wouldn't allow her to admit she'd missed.

Meanwhile, a group of scouts consisting of two wolves and two deputies hurried back to the force with news of where the C-wolves were spotted. The Force thought it smart of the C-wolves to camp with the mountains at their back and the river facing them—with land on the right and left of them. That way, they couldn't be surprised.

"But they *will* be surprised," River said.

"How's that?" Tilbert asked.

"I think I'm starting to realize how you think," Russell said. "You're going to do the unexpected...aren't you?"

River smiled and said. "We're coming on all sides. They don't expect us to do anything that suicidal, and that's what I want them to think."

"So you want them to see us coming," Matthew said. "I don't get it."

"I do," Tilbert said. "Hitting them on every side will split them into four parts which puts them at a disadvantage since we outnumber them."

"You sure it'll work?" Dell asked.

"We've done crazy things like that before," an elder wolf said. "Most times it worked...sometimes it didn't."

"Well, that's reassuring," Dell complained.

"Of course, we'll strike at night," Dex said ignoring Dell's smirkish remark. "That'll enhance their disadvantage."

With the battle plan set to execute, the Strike Force eased out after midnight. But the plan immediately fell apart. A Ninja-type group of deputies was to creep upon the night-watchers and stab them with silver daggers. Then the force would attack the rest of the C-wolves while they slept. However, silver had no effect and the watchers overpowered the deputies and snapped their necks.

"What's taking them so long?" a wolf asked.

Dex snatched his binoculars from his eyes. "The night-watchers are still there. Something's wrong."

Dex texted the other group leaders, River, Tilbert, and Matthew. They all answered they didn't know what had happened. Then the sound of a horn hung in the air.

"This can't be good," Dex said. And as soon as he had said that, hundreds of bullets rained down from every angle on all four groups. Tilbert and his deputies shot back and killed some but took a terrible beating. Four-legged Greyscott wolves attacked but were cut to pieces by gunfire. River's group also sustained heavy casualties. Dex and his men had situated themselves behind a high bed of rocks which stretched midway the river. Unable to fire back, they barely escaped by diving and then swimming underwater. Bullets peppered the river and turned it red with their blood. Dex looked back only once and saw several of his wolf-mates floating face-down. Crawling onto land, Dex dragged himself up and saw blood leaking from his shirt and pants leg.

The strike force remained fractured and scattered for hours. Small groups stumbled out of the forest, limped down the roadside, or crawled out of shallow waters and continued to regroup with each other throughout the night until daybreak. After reuniting, the force immediately counted their losses and waited on more stragglers; but after a few hours, they realized that Matthew and his young fighters were missing.

"Did anyone see what happened to Matt and his group?" Dex asked frantically. Everyone looked at each other and then shook their heads. Matthew's group had consisted of twenty-two well-trained junior wolves including Russell and Dell.

Dex was right for worrying. Matthew and his six surviving junior packmates had been captured and forced into a cave. The C-wolves were a cruel breed; they delighted in making their enemies suffer the worst possible fate. They decided not to kill Matthew and his packmates. "Tell you what?" one of the C-wolves chuckled. "Eat each other and whoever is left, we'll let go." The C-wolves laughed then rolled a huge, heavy rock that took twelve C-wolves to shove, in front of the cave's only exit.

For days, Matthew, Russell, Dell, and the four other junior wolves languished in their makeshift tomb with useless phones. After day three, they took to cutting themselves with sharp- edge stones and lapping their own blood, but still, they grew weak as the fifth day came and went. No one could rescue them—not without sustaining massive casualties. The young wolves bickered about why it was taking the pack so long to find them.

"Look," Matthew told his young comrades, "None of us are worthy of our pack being wiped out. And that's exactly what will happen when they find out where we are and try to rescue us."

"You think that's what the C-wolves are hoping?" Russell asked.

"I believe so," Matthew told him.

"But what about your dad?" Russell asked. "It's not easy for a father to think that rationally."

"You're right. And that's what I'm afraid of. One of the witches will do a locating spell on us and knowing my dad, he'll try something all by himself. He'll go down fighting, and I'll never see him again." Matthew turned away from his comrades' eyes to hide his cracked face.

Back at the camp, Dex sat with his head in his hands.

"Dex, you've got to eat something," River said. "Matt's smart and he's strong."

Dex sat with a blank stare. "He's dead or somewhere injured," he said.

"Come on—a little food will make you think more clearly."

Dex looked coldly into River's eyes. "Don't, brother. Don't patronize me."

River dropped his head—angry for not knowing how to get through to Dex. "As soon as we find out where they are, we'll pick a small team and go after them."

Dex responded coldly. "I'm going after them."

"Not alone you're not."

"We've been over this, River. We've had enough casualties. It's better for only one person to do this."

"But it's suicide to go alone," River said.

Dex rose and grabbed his gun. "My mind's made up." He made a move to leave but River blocked him.

"You know, brother," River said taking off his jacket. "You and I haven't fought since we were kids. I could kick your ass then, and I can kick it now."

"Really?" Dex said in amazement. "I'm not fighting you, you idiot."

"You're not leaving here without me and some of the wolves," River said moving in a circle with his fist in boxing position.

"This is stupid!" Dex said loudly.

"Whoa, whoa," Tilbert said. He jumped between the brothers. "What the hell is this?"

"Dex insists on going to find Matthew and the group alone, and I'm not going to let him. Simple as that."

"Well, you don't have to fight about it. Just conk him over the head with something and tie him up until we come back with his boy and the group."

"Are you serious?" Dex griped.

"You're not leaving here alone, and that's that," Tilbert said.

"It's my damn life."

"And it's my deputies that are going to tie your damn ass up if you try to leave without us."

"Go to hell...both of you!" Dex flopped down hard on his bedding and shook his head.

*****

Meanwhile—day seven found Dell contemplating cutting off his big toe and eating it.

"Dell, take that shoe off one more time, and I'll shove it down your throat," Russell said in a weak voice.

"Well, at least I'll eat something," Dell slurred. "Hey, wait, aren't shoes made of cows?" Dell began trying to eat his shoe when Russell grabbed it and tossed it aside.

"Idiot! The dye will poison you."

"Well, at least I'll die with a full stomach."

Matthew looked over at the four youngest wolves. Their faces were gray and their tongues swollen. They couldn't stomach licking their own blood and said they'd rather die. Matthew refused to let that happen. He allowed his fangs to grow out then punctured one of his veins; he pried opened the mouths of each one of the young wolves as they lay semi-conscious and allowed large drops of blood to fall onto their tongues. They smacked their lips but never opened their eyes.

"Matt, that's too much blood at one time," Russell warned. "Besides, they made their choice."

"They're just kids," Matthew replied. "Going to keep them alive as long as possible."

Matthew in his weakened state slowly crawled to his side and closed his eyes. Russell couldn't take his eyes off him. He saw Matthew as noble, a creature with a good heart. He wished he could verbally forgive Matthew for the role he'd played in taking his human soul. But Russell knew he could never bring himself to tell Matthew that. He couldn't let Matthew's mind rest from what he had done, so he would just keep his forgiveness to himself.

On day nine, Dex relented, and River with a small band of wolves and deputies joined him in the search for Matthew and his wolf-mates. The valley contained tall hills, and with binoculars they scanned the valley looking for any signs of the group.

Dex got a call from Chad Roberts begging to make an arrangement with the C-wolves to exchange *him* for the missing wolves. But, of course, Dex wouldn't hear of it and wondered if that was exactly the C-wolves' plan—though he had heard nothing to substantiate that.

By day eleven, they had scanned nearly every angle of the valley from several hilltops. Dex felt in his heart that his son and the younger wolves were dead, but he just couldn't let go. More devastating was how to break the news to Jan. He needed to be able to hold his head up when he told Jan that he'd tried everything to find their son. And he needed to do that for the parents of Russell, Dell, and their younger wolf-mates as well.

Back at the cave, seven bodies lay barely breathing on the cold stone floor. Matthew was in the worst shape because of his voluntary, massive blood loss. Russell's health was just as precarious having taken over the duty of feeding his blood to the four younger wolves after Matthew collapsed. Suddenly, the floor began to tremble—just a little at first. It shook everyone conscious though no one had the strength to rise. The vibration intensified and the cave walls began to shatter. The ceiling rained pebbles down upon the wolves. Outside the cave, the earth split and C-wolves fell hundreds of feet into fiery pits; they also fell from the mountain's ridges, breaking their necks and crushed when large boulders fell upon them. The huge rock at the entrance of the cave crumbled into a heap of dust and a stream of sunlight hit the faces of the entombed wolves. Russell only opened his eyes in slits and perceived several tall shadows standing over him. The shadows gathered the half-living wolves in their arms and carried them from the cave.

On day sixteen, Russell woke, but that time he didn't see shadows but rather glares of brightness. He was in a bed in someone's home, except he didn't know whose. He didn't recognize a single stick of furniture. Finally, the bedroom door opened, and River walked in. "Hey, Rusty. Welcome back to the world."

"Hey, River. You—you found us. But how? Where am I?" Russell said his voice hoarse.

"You're in my home. Jewel's been taking care of you for the last five days. You were really out of it."

Oh God! Russell thought. *This can't be happening. Jewel Porter—that bitch...taking care of me? And I guess this is supposed to make everything all right?* Russell did everything he could to not show disdain for River's wife. "Tell her thank you," Russell said rather dryly.

"You can tell her yourself. She should be here in a few minutes to look in on you." River smiled, walked out, and closed the door.

"Shit," Russell said under his breath. He recalled someone had spoon-fed him soup and tea as he lay in a semi-conscious state. He remembered vaguely someone washing him but couldn't recall a face.

Heather phoned Russell and told him how furious she had been at finding out after nearly a week, that he and his group were missing. She performed a locating spell and related the information to Dex, but as usual, Sheriff Tilbert warned her to do nothing. Desperate, Heather turned to Jewel about an idea. Right away she was impressed with Jewel's level of skills and particularly her mystifying bowl; Jewel very cleverly cast a battle spell and redirected it to assimilate a mini earthquake. Even meteorologists were fooled then baffled when it didn't appear on the Richter scale. After ending his call with Heather, the door opened and Jewel entered.

The first thing Russell noticed when she walked in was how incredibly beautiful she was. With her smooth, white skin, long, raven hair, and piercing, blue eyes, she could have graced any number of world-class magazines, he thought. He desperately wanted to shapeshift and rip her throat out, but he had promised Heather he'd behave—for now.

CHAPTER TWENTY-EIGHT

Jewel stood by the foot of the bed and smiled, her twin blues dancing over him. He looked away momentarily, not trusting his emotions; every muscle in his body seemed to rigidify at the same time.

"How are you feeling?" she asked.

Russell felt his skin crawl. "Good, he mumbled." He ignored her small-talk and continued to stare at the bed with eyes that could burn holes in it. He looked through the anger and at a ten-year-old boy, carefree and happy whose future had appeared so certain. He'd hoped to be an engineer, fighter pilot, and astronaut like Buzz Aldrin. Only *his* Apollo Mission dreams would have been 'Man on Mars.' He could probably still reach one of those goals if it weren't for the ongoing conflicts: Holly, Charlton, and the C-wolves. Her abrupt silence brought him back to the moment; he cut his eyes at her, and she stared back at him.

"You haven't heard more than a few words I've said, have you?"

"No. No, I guess I haven't," Russell said.

"I know how you feel about me," she said. "Matt and I talked about it."

"Did you?"

"All I can say is I'm sorry. We were so desperate for a moon cure. The wolves endured three centuries of this curse and they didn't have to—but did so because the Covenant couldn't bring themselves to sacrifice a child."

"Then fast forward three centuries later and you discovered a short cut that turned one into a werewolf...lucky me."

"Rusty, I am so sorry. I don't know what else to say."

He cocked his head looking up at her. "You know how many times I thought of shapeshifting and tearing out your goddamn throat?" He watched Jewel's expression turn icy like the tiny cracks in a frozen lake. "Relax," he said. "So much has happened between then and now. I still have my mom and dad, my friends, and a woman I love more than anything. I guess you'd call that coping. I don't know."

"That's...that's good. I'm so happy for..."

"Don't. Don't tell me you're happy for me," Russell snapped. He turned his head from her gaze and a mischievous smile etched across his face. "You ever heard of Melvita Burkison?" he asked.

"Melvita Burkison? No, not that I can recall."

"Her ancestors got kicked out of the Covenant along with Corina."

"Outcasts. No wonder I didn't recognize the name. What about her?"

"I went to see her about a matter unrelated to me. Somewhere in our conversation, she mentioned the Covenant witches, and I told her about what you did to me. She was taken aback...said your witchcraft sucked...real amateur stuff." Russell watched Jewel's face flush red. He loved it.

"Really," she said coldly.

"Oh, she sided with *you* actually. Said she would have done the same thing except she would have been smarter." Russell could sense invisible steam gathering around Jewel's collar.

"I see," she said.

"I think she called it...sloppy witchcraft," he smirked. "Said she would have never put a teenager in charge of me, to neglect me...leaving me to shapeshift publicly, possibly endangering the secret of the pack...and a few other things... but I forget." Russell quit after Jewel lifted her chin and the corners of her mouth curved downward. He held a grin inside and watched her struggle to keep her composure. She cleared her throat then spoke.

"This may surprise you, Rusty, but in a way, she's right. I didn't know what the hell I was doing, because no one had ever done it before. I made mistakes, I admit. But you can tell your *Miss Burkison* that *any* third-rate witch can improve upon what a genius has originated."

And with that, she strutted out of the room and slammed the door. Russell scolded himself—citing pissing off a witch was how the wolves got into that predicament in the first place. Then he further thought, *perhaps I'd better send out for the rest of my meals... and maybe my medicines too.*

*****

Days rolled into weeks. Russell recovered and returned to duty as did Matthew, Dell, and the four youngest members who survived the cave. The Force suffered staggering losses. Only fourteen of twenty-five deputy snipers and seventy-eight of one hundred and fifty Greyscott wolves survived. Yet, the latest news proved more disturbing: the scouts reported to the camp that the G-wolves had only lost a fraction even though under surveillance they were spotted burying many of their dead.

"I don't get it," Russell said. "Okay, so we turn-tail and ran...*twice*. But we shot the hell out of those bastards. How can they still have that many standing?"

"They're out biting people, I bet," Dell griped. "Turning whole families of men into freak wolves like themselves."

"That and the fact that silver nitrate has no effect on a number of them," Rita said.

"What do you mean no effect?" River asked.

"I mean *no* effect," Rita replied. "Didn't the sheriff tell you? I told him weeks ago."

"Sheriff, what's she talking about?" River asked.

Tilbert, appearing nonchalant, admitted Rita *had* told him but said he brushed it off thinking having lost a lot of blood, it had foiled her aim. Of course, Rita denied it and sounded insulted that anyone would question her marksmanship under *any* circumstances. She reminded Tilbert that she had experienced more pressure in Afghanistan while sustaining minor wounds, and it never altered her performance. She stuck by her claims of having shot at least ten C-wolves that never went down or even flinched.

"She's not the only one, Sheriff," another deputy said. "We've all had that experience. I thought something was wrong with my firearm. I'd hit two or three and they'd go down, then hit two or three more and they wouldn't budge. I'd hit five or six and they'd fall dead then hit the same number again and they'd act like I had thrown a heap of snowballs at them."

"Sheriff, you knew about this and said nothing?" Dex griped.

Tilbert hunched his shoulders. "Rita was the only one who'd said anything. No one else came to me I swear, or I would have told you."

"I thought silver nitrate took out all werewolves. You're telling me some of the C-wolves showed no reaction to it?" Russell asked. "How come?"

River, Dex, and Matthew eyed one another with great concern, and the elder and more seasoned wolves began to grumble among themselves. Russell and Dell looked to Matthew for an explanation. Matthew said what everyone else now knew.

"If what Rita claims is true, there's no doubt that C-wolves have aligned themselves with Lycans," Matthew told them. "Silver has no impact on Lycans.

Russell stood wide-eyed. "Lycans?" he asked.

Dell, like most wolves, knew of Lycans but thought they only existed in Europe and Africa if they still existed at all. No Greyscott wolf had ever come in contact with one, so most assumed they were extinct. "But Lycans hate other wolves...they call us fake wolves," Dell said. "How the hell did Charlton get them to work together?"

"He had to have offered them something," River said. "But what?"

"I think...*us*," Dex said. "You just said Lycans hate us and Charlton did, too. So, they were working together to achieve the same goal."

"Holy shit!" said an elder wolf. "I think you just hit the nail on the head. But those C-wolves don't know that Lycans can't be trusted. I bet they intend to use C-wolves because they can easily duplicate themselves into astronomical numbers, wipe us out, and then turn on the remaining C-wolves."

"What if we get to the C-wolves and tell them they're in danger?" Russell asked.

"I doubt if they'd listen," River said. "Charlton poisoned them against us."

"Then we'll have to destroy them along with the Lycans without them ever knowing they were used. They will have died by Lycan's hands anyway," the elder wolf reasoned.

"But you still haven't told me exactly what a Lycan is," Russell said.

"They're wolves similar to us but with some significant differences," Matthew explained. "Until Aunt Jewel created the moon cure, werewolves like us were forced to transform during a full moon. Lycans have never had that problem. They've always possessed the ability to transform at will. Werewolf means man-wolf...men who transform into wolves; Lycans means humanoid wolf... wolves that can assume human form."

"Where do they come from? And why wasn't I told about them?" Russell asked Matthew. "Weren't you supposed to be my so-called mentor?"

"I wasn't sure they still existed," Matthew said. "And sure didn't think they'd be around *here*."

"Legend has it," spoke an elder wolf, "that the Goddess Luna created the Lycans which makes them the purest breed. They roamed the earth unopposed for centuries. When the first witch poorly copied the goddess's creation by turning men into werewolves, it angered Luna and she cursed the breed, so at every full of her name, they would transform into deranged beasts with no will of their own and would die by the hand of silver."

"Doesn't sound like this Luna is too fond of you guys," Tilbert teased.

"Sounds more like a kid's bedtime story," Russell said.

"Well that bedtime story is about to wipe us all out if we don't do something," Dell snapped.

"Good point," Russell said. "So what else besides silver and the full moon makes them different?"

"They tend to be more muscular than we are," River said, "though not smarter like some believe. And they don't drink alcohol, smoke, or use drugs, not even marijuana."

"Wow, *and* they're boring," Dell blurted.

"Humans can't become a Lycan by being bitten by one," River continued. "Lycans can only reproduce themselves from the womb of their bloodline—which is why they never outnumber werewolves."

"We became werewolves through witchcraft," Dex repeated. "But then, you know that."

"Only too well," Russell mumbled. "Now, you say silver does not affect them? There has to be some way of getting rid of those bastards."

"Only by separating their spine from their body," Dell told him. "And for that, we've got to get up *pret...ty* close and personal. Something I'm not looking forward to."

"So, what do we do, Dad?" Matthew asked.

"Son, I wish I knew."

"I know *one* damn thing," Tilbert said. "We're going to face a tough battle with those wolves unless we sneak the witches in on this. Maybe your wife can make another earthquake," he told River. "I think it fooled the Shadow Hunters, or they'd be here by now."

"After months of ordering us not to get the witches involved, now you want them involved?" Russell asked.

"Well—what the hell else can we do?"

"Okay. Okay," Russell said. "I just wanted to be sure you meant it, that's all."

"I hate to disappoint you," River told Tilbert, "but I don't think the witches should take a chance on another earthquake. They can knock the Lycans around or beat them up a bit, but the mystical energy it would take to destroy them would be too noticeable. Jewel *could* banish them somewhere for a time. But after a while, they'd just come right back."

"Holy Christ!" Tilbert blurted.

"Hey, that'll work," Russell replied.

"What are you talking about, Rusty?"

"Bishop Randall—you said that's how he got rid of the vampires...using the Word of God."

"Yeah, but he had the hunters working with him."

"So, maybe he won't need them this time."

"Rusty, Bishop *despises* New Berwick. He said he'd never come back as long as the witches were here, and I think he meant it."

"Just tell him what we're dealing with."

"He won't care. I know the man. You didn't see how angry he was with all of us before he left."

"So, you really think nothing will get him back here."

"Look, Bishop Randall wouldn't come back here if I told him I'd dug up Noah's Ark. We'll handle the Lycans ourselves. I've been in this town all my life, and I'm not letting anything or anyone take it down."

Russell half-smiled at Sheriff Tilbert's enthusiasm but doubted very seriously if anything he'd do could deter the enemy wolves from their purpose. But Russell did agree with Tilbert about one thing. Victory seemed impossible without the witches.

CHAPTER TWENTY-NINE

The early morning sky remained a thin gray pillowed with clouds. As usual, Sheriff Tilbert and deputy snipers led the caravan. Their eyes, now trained in recognizing the smaller C-wolves from the taller, more muscular Lycans, would guide them in reserving the precious metal for the right targets, and none wasted on the silver-resistant Lycans—though in the heat of battle mistakes would probably happen.

Though wet grass and mud puddles made it difficult, several Greyscotts on all-fours kept pace with the large caravan of vehicles inching toward enemy territory. Weeks earlier, after burying their dead, the Greyscott wolves and the deputies had greatly added to their pitiable numbers, and the Strike Force stood strong again. Additionally, many Sheerfield townsmen who were veterans (some as far back as Viet Nam) joined the deputies. There weren't enough silver nitrate bullets to go around, so the townsmen would use Sheriff Tilbert's plan, which was to bust up the enemy wolves badly with lead bullets, shattering arms, knees, and legs, rendering them temporarily useless then, the Strike

Force would move in and wipe out the C-wolves leaving only the injured Lycans to contend with. Though the Lycans were physically superior to the Greyscott wolves, their limited numbers were no threat to the Greyscotts, and they hoped that alone would prompt the Lycans to rethink their plan and move on.

A few hundred yards from a large, green, open field, Dex pulled the binoculars away from his eyes. "That's exactly what I expected," he mumbled. Dex felt strongly that he understood the battle plan of the enemy wolves. The enemy—outnumbered and outgunned had pulled back deep into the dark forest, using it as a stronghold. That way the disadvantage of their numbers was reduced. Their eyes, already adjusted to the dark, would be another advantage against the Strike Force. Dex's own take on the enemies' battle plan traveled all the way to the front of the caravan. Tilbert, after hearing it, made his way to the rear to talk to River and other wolf group leaders.

"It's not original but it's damn clever," Tilbert heard an elder wolf say.

"Not clever enough," Tilbert replied. "We've got explosives."

"Hot damn!" Dell blurted.

"Explosives?" Dex asked.

"Hell yeah!" Tilbert said. "Maybe silver won't kill them all but none of those sons of bitches can fight with their brains and guts blown out."

"Well, that's one way of separating the Lycan's spines from their bodies," Russell said.

River pulled on his chin and thought a moment then blurted to a scout, "What's in the back of that forest?"

"A small lake full of snakes," the scout answered.

"What's behind that?"

"A steep hill lined with evergreen," he said.

"Sheriff, send a portion of your group with explosives and some snipers around to that hill," River ordered. "The rest of us will ease into the open and use our vehicles as barricades. Anything that comes running out of the forest, we'll cut it to pieces."

"Right!" Tilbert said quickly before making his way back up the line.

A small group of ten deputies and twelve townsmen gathered their firearms, the explosives, and other equipment and were driven back a quarter of a mile; they traveled the rest of the way to the back of the hill on foot.

The sheriff instructed his deputies to pass out bullet-proof vests to the wolves, including K-9 vests, while the leaders stood around finalizing their battle plans. "Dex," River said, "you take your group to the west outside of the forest. Matthew, your group will swing around to the east and cover that part. Sheriff Tilbert and I have enough to cover the entire front. Instead of us going in and getting trapped, the sheriff's unit on the hill will flush them out with explosives."

"Yeah, those explosives was a damn good idea, Sheriff," Dex said.

Tilbert nodded at the compliment but frowned at his watch. Twenty minutes had crept by since his men left. Tilbert waited for the silly tune that signaled an incoming text. When it didn't come, Tilbert text and later, phoned but got no answer. The group failed to notice Tilbert's worried face and continued to talk among themselves, rehearsing the plans repeatedly in their speech and minds.

Another twenty minutes crept by. No text. No answer to text.

A cloud burst and rain poured from the dull heavens. It seemed forty-five minutes since the deputies and townsmen had been dropped off. The mood grew gloomy and the tension thick as the gray clouds. No one breathed it aloud, but all feared déjà vu. Had the group been discovered and were dead, captured, maybe tortured?

Another ten, fifteen, twenty-five minutes slipped by.

"Jesus Christ!" Tilbert whispered. He looked at his watch knowing something was wrong. It should have taken only ten minutes to walk from where they were dropped off. It was well over an hour and Tilbert felt their victory slipping away; all the explosives and nearly half of his best shooters were gone.

The sky grew darker as the raindrops pounded the vehicles. Everyone jumped into their vans and turned on windshield wipers. No one spoke, intently focused on their watches and listened to the sound of the rain attack the rooftops. The dark heaven seemed demonic as if a warning of their demise. A sunken feeling filled the pit of Russell's stomach and a bad taste settled upon his tongue. Dell sat silently next to Russell and watched the pouring rain stream from the sky. Both eyed one another and their expression revealed a twin thought, *the cave*. The enemy wolves proved extremely cruel. There seemed no mercy in them and Russell feared for Tilbert's crew. They were human and wouldn't last as long as the wolves had without food and water. Dell wondered if he should volunteer to go after them. Then the rain stopped as quickly as it began and the sun played peek-a-boo with the empty clouds. Matthew turned to Dex and suggested taking his junior group to look for the suspected missing unit. But Dex said no way he'd let Matthew out of his sight and that the Sheriff would probably send another group of his snipers.

Tilbert nervously drummed his fingers on the dashboard. He agonized over the possibility of his having sent deputies and townsmen to their deaths. He breathed deeply and his heart thumped rapidly. The sheriff turned off his wipers and watched a few drops of water snake down his windshield. Tilbert jumped when his phone rang. Everyone in his patrol van leaned forward. *Perhaps an enemy calling to gloat about what they had done to his unit or a deputy or townsman injured, hiding and needing assistance?* Tilbert thought.

"Yes," Tilbert said holding his breath.

"Sheriff, we're all in place and set up, Sir," a deputy said.

"What the hell took you so long? We've been going crazy here! Why didn't you make contact?" they heard Tilbert shout.

"Sheriff, I'm sorry, but four of the townsmen wouldn't listen and took the short cut across the lake. All four were badly snake bitten including one who carried the container of explosives. We had to drop everything and get to those explosives before water seeped through the container and ruined them."

"Are the men dead?"

"No. Lucky for them Mr. Tucker just happened to have a home remedy of anti-venom. They were making such a ruckus because of the pain, we were afraid they'd alert the enemy. So we took the injured and high-tailed it back down the hill. But we couldn't contact you because the area had no reception for our communication devices. Mr. Tucker said the bit men will be okay, so, we're back on the hill and ready, sir."

"And the explosives?"

"We got to them in time."

"Holy Christ," Tilbert said getting out of his van and shaking his head. "All right, deputy, stand by for the order and stay in a good area."

"Yes, sir."

Tilbert relayed the information to his group and the wolves. They expressed a mixture of *'glad they're okay;'* to *'I'd like to wring the four townsmen's freaking necks.'* But all sighed with relief, and the Strike Force eased into position on the soaked, green, open field, barricading themselves behind large, private vehicles and police vans.

Behind the forest, the lake appeared calm then alive when a ripple stretched across the far side of the lake and came back again. A snake's head glided smoothly along the water then disappeared beneath it. A small bird took a hell of a chance dipping its beak in the middle of the lake, dousing its wings, before quickly soaring off. Above the lake, clusters of evergreen hit by drizzling raindrops helped muffled the sounds of Tilbert's unit bustling about finalizing small details of their set-up, one being two RGP 40 mm revolver police grenade launchers with sighting scopes. It was state-of-the-art stuff given to the sheriff's department by the Fort Winston Army Ammunition Plant stationed at an Illinois military county base. The launchers were semi-automatic and nearly silent when fired. Each launched six grenades in three seconds at 220 yards, the length of two football fields. The cartoonish sound of an in-coming text added to the men's concentration. 'LET HELL LOOSE!' it read.

Tilbert stared morosely at the forest, his hands gripped sternly on his rifle. Beaded sweat lined his upper lip. Each sniper squeezed closed an eye, while their other eye peered through the sight scope—their fingers barely touching the trigger. The wolf leaders stayed crouched behind the vans—their foreheads barely noticeable; they needed only to lift their chins to see over the top of the roofs.

Suddenly, a horrific boom shook the ground. A blazing flash of fire lit the pitch black of the forest. Wailing cries rose from the depths of the shadows. Several four-legged enemy wolves, catapulted by the blast, landed in the open field with a thud—most of their fur gone; the little that was left smoked. With skin blistered and raw, they lay on their sides twitching—eyes wide open, blood gushing from guts spilling onto the ground. Each was nearly dead. The deputy snipers shot them anyway, straight through the head. A distant sound of gunshots rang out from among the trees. Pandemonium among scurrying shadows was noticed when a thundering blast lit up the ground. Several wolves and deputies spotted the enemy running out into the light. The Strike Force peppered them with bullets when they let loose a torrid of gunfire. But not all enemy wolves ran like scared rabbits. Sparks of gunfire unloaded on the force from behind giant trees.

"I'm hit! I'm hit!" several deputies cried out.

"Stay down!" Tilbert yelled.

"Hold your ground!" River shouted.

The clangorous sounds of gunfire and explosions ruled the sky. Like flaming arrows, a confused symphony of crows flapped speedily across the grayish-blue then fell and burned. Matthew's junior group fired on the enemy from the east; Dex's wolves lit into them from the west. A barrage of grenades shot across the lake and took out the barricades of trees along with the wolves that had used them as cover. A storm of return fire roared from the forest. A deputy's ear flew off. Another went down—a bullet in her neck. Several Greyscott wolves fell dead. River staggered bleeding from the face. A townsmen's head was blown off and several more lay groaning. Out of the dark galloped four-legged C-wolves, large as bears, carrying human formed Lycans on their backs with rifles blasting. The Townsmen unloaded on them with shotgun blasts. More than a dozen Lycans on wolf-back barely escaped; those who didn't, crawled about in the blood of the dead. Then out of the dark forest walked Sheriff Tilbert's special unit of deputies and townsmen.

"All clear, Sheriff!" the lead deputy shouted. As they walked into the open field, halfway to where the Strike Force was stationed, they stopped and shot dying C-wolves in the head, and severed the spine of the severely wounded Lycans. Sheriff Tilbert, who seemed glad to see them, also frowned.

"You crossed that damn lake, didn't you?" Tilbert scolded.

"Yeah, but we blasted the hell out of it first, sir." I don't think there's a snake left," he grinned.

Tilbert let out a chuckled sigh. "Good work you guys."

The sheriff turned to check on the wolves and his own group of men and women. Several of Tilbert's medics attended to the deputies and the wolves. River, with the right side of his shirt bloody, groaned as a medic checked his wounds. He lost a lot of blood; plus the casualties of his unit proved staggering. Tilbert lost many of his group as well. A few of Dex's wolves lay bleeding and dying. Matthew's group suffered two dead and several wounded, though not severely.

The forest stood covered in blood with bits and pieces of wolf flesh scattered throughout. Scavengers feasted on the remains as the light rain diluted the blood and the ground lapped it up. Tilbert sent his scouts out to track the enemy. A few men and wolves assigned to take the dead back to be properly buried, immediately drove out; the Strike Force set up camp—patched up the wounded and ended the night planning their next and hopefully, last attack, Tilbert thought.

*****

The following morning, instant coffee, wheat bread, and cheese comprised breakfast. The heavy rain aided to rid the forest of stench and debris.

"What's this?" Dex said squinting through his binoculars.

From across the landscape, Dex spotted the six scouts coming back to camp. Someone he didn't recognize, bloodied and slightly bent over, limped alongside them. A scout shoved him, and he stumbled forward but didn't fall.

"What is it?" River's muffled voice sounded from the tight bandage wrapped around his head and jaw.

"It's the scouts, and they have someone with them. A C-wolf or Lycan, I can't tell. But from the looks of him, he may not last long," Dex said.

"Let's hope he lasts long enough to tell us something," Tilbert said.

"I doubt if it's a Lycan," an elder wolf said. "A Lycan will make you kill him before he'll let you capture him."

The deputies and wolves stood with somber expressions and watched as the scouts pestered the enemy wolf shoving him and jabbing him in the back with the butt of their rifles. One last shove and the C-wolf stumbled into camp and fell to his knees shaking; he looked up at his captors like a frightened puppy.

"Where did you find this rat?" Dex blurted.

"Found him crawling around in the brush," A scout chuckled. "His buddies just left him behind."

"Can you do anything but shake, rat...you got a voice?" Dex asked him.

The C-wolf nodded nervously. "Please," he said searching their faces. "I didn't want to do this...none of us did. They made us."

"Who's they?" Tilbert asked.

"First it was Charlton. He...he said if we helped him he'd give us all the cure. Then when we found out he was dead, the Lycan leader, Daethan said Charlton had shared the secret with him and that the same bargain we had made with Charlton, we now had with him...meaning the cure."

"What cure?" Dex asked.

"You know, the cure that will turn us all back to being just men."

The wolves looked at one another, and the deputies stared at the C-wolf.

"There's no cure," Dex told him.

"Sure there is. Charlton and Daethan said..."

"I don't care what Charlton and this Daethan said. There's no cure," Dex snapped.

"No. No. You don't understand. May...Maybe you guys just don't know about it. Charlton said for us to meet him here in New Berwick and after we..." The C-wolf froze.

"After you what?" an elder wolf insisted.

The C-wolf hesitated then stammered looking off, "He...he ah told us that after we helped him wipe you guys out, he'd give us the cure then we could go home."

Dex glared at him. "Look at me. Stand up. What's your name?"

"Douglas," he said struggling to his feet.

"Douglas, there *is* no cure. They lied to you."

The C-wolf became antsy and irritated. "No. No—there has to be. I...I have a family...ah, a little boy and, and a baby girl. I can't go back like this—I..."

"Look, Douglas, you can cry about your family some other time. We want to hear more about this Lycan leader," Dex griped.

Russell went to Dex and spoke in his ear. "Why don't we give him a little time?"

"We don't have a little time to give," Dex shot at him. "We've got them on the run. We need to find them and crush them before they can regroup."

"You're not going to get anything out of him while he's brooding. Look at him; he's in shock. Just give him a while to get it together."

"Why don't we all take turns rocking the poor dear and singing him lullabies?" Dex blurted before walking off.

Russell went over to Tilbert. "Sheriff let's get him over to one of the medics. He's not going to be any good to us if he bleeds to death."

Tilbert agreed and shouted for a medic to attend Douglas.

CHAPTER THIRTY

Days after sending the enemy wolves into hiding, the force busied themselves with another strategy. Douglas, however, still reeling from the truth of permanently living as a werewolf, needed more time to heal emotionally and physically.

"What's up with Rusty and that damn C-wolf?" Dex spat to Tilbert. "That rat's had enough TLC. It's time he tells us where his pals are and what that Lycan what's-his-name is up to."

"Daethan," Tilbert said.

"Yeah, Daethan," Dex repeated.

"Rusty's okay," Tilbert said. "He identifies with the C-wolf. They were both human at one time."

"Oh, are we back to that again? How many times do we have to listen to his whining about being a wolf? He needs to get over it."

"That's not something one can easily get over. You guys took that kid's normal life away."

"Great Jupiter!" Dex blurted.

"Dex, you didn't know him as a small boy. I've known this kid since he was a baby in his mother's arms. You were *born* a wolf. You'll never understand his mind. Lay off him. I mean it."

"Are you threatening me?"

"No, I'm not threatening you. Just give the kid a break—that's all."

"I suppose you want me to give that rat a break too." Dex didn't wait for an answer; he ripped a path to Douglas' bedding where Russell sat chatting with him. "Rusty, is this rat well enough to talk?"

"His name is Douglas, Dex. He…"

"I don't need you reminding me of his name. And where do you get off being so nice to this bastard? You know how many comrades we've lost? How many of my wolves did you kill you piece of shit!" Dex stepped closer to Douglas.

"Rusty," Douglas squealed hoping for Russell's protection.

"It's okay, Douglas," Russell assured him. "Dex is just angry right now…we all are. It's okay. Nobody's going to hurt you." Russell rose to his feet.

"Oh, is that right?" Dex said. "And who's going to save him...you?"

"Dex," Tilbert said. "We need him in one piece if he's going to tell us what we need to know. Why don't you go calm down and let us handle this?"

"But...but I've told Rusty everything I know," Douglas stammered.

"Is that true, Rusty?" Tilbert asked.

"Yes."

"Then why in the hell didn't you say so?" Dex griped.

"I didn't get a chance to... because as usual, you don't think before you leap into action—always ready to tear someone or something apart," Russell snapped.

"The hell is that supposed to mean?" Dex took a step forward and stood chest-to-chest with Russell.

An elder wolf extended his arms between them and shoved them apart. "Eee-nough, you two." The elder's eyes flashed on Dex. "Take a walk!" he ordered. Dex knew better than to oppose an elder. He turned and silently stormed off.

*****

Around noon, the force leaders knelt around a make-shift map, and Dex, with less steam coming out of his ears, joined them. Russell briefed them on what Douglas had told him. It seemed the Lycans had never heard of New Berwick until Charlton's contact. They lived peacefully and unopposed for over a century in Amahran, a small village in Lasov County, Transylvania. Amahran was noted for its salt mines, wines, primeval dense forests, and Mount Lunas. They spoke five languages including English. Charlton, in his desperation to understand his werewolf condition, stumbled across the original werewolves during his research. Learning how much humanoid Lycans hated werewolves, he took a risky chance and contacted Daethan, the grandson of the late Attisun Dragar, the respected leader of the rebel group called the Medigans—an ancient Amahranian word meaning blood force.

"Douglas said he didn't know how Charlton was able to talk Daethan into joining them. He recalled that Charlton called them all in one day and there Daethan stood with thirty or so other Lycans. And after Charlton died, he said he and his fellow wolves never quite warmed up to Daethan, and that they were afraid of crossing him."

"Okay, the history is for the books," Dex said. "Where are they now and how strong are they...did he say?"

"Dex, I'm getting to it," Russell snapped. Russell leaned over the map and allowed his fingers to slide along the drawings as he spoke. "Now, according to Douglas," he began, "their exit strategy, in case things didn't go to plan, and of course we know it didn't, was for them to all meet up here," he said tapping his index finger on a location of a small wooded area near a little town just outside New Berwick. Charlton's wolves were to help the Lycans regroup by swooping down on this town and turning numerous men into werewolves to swell their numbers.

River strained his voice through his bandages. "Do they know they left Douglas alive? If they do, they may suspect he'd be captured and could have changed their plan."

"Or the rat could be lying," Dex said.

"We'll know for sure after sending the scouts out," Tilbert said.

"I believe he's telling the truth," Russell said.

"Let's make sure," an elder wolf replied. "Tell him you're going to take him with you, if he lied, you'll kill him on the spot."

"And you'll be killing him for nothing if he's telling the truth and plans were changed at the last minute for an unknown reason," Russell said.

One of the scouts who brought Douglas in bellowed, "So what? What are we keeping him around for anyway? He's eating our food and using up our supplies."

"Absolutely," Dex said. "I say we take him out and shoot him."

Matthew and Dell saw that those words didn't sit right with Russell. They watched his jaw tightened, and he bit his bottom lip. Tilbert observed it too and broke in, "I appreciate you wolves working with us, but I'm still the sheriff, and nobody's taking the law into their own hands."

"You don't mean to say you're going to let that piece of shit live?" Dex snapped.

"When we're through with him, he'll be put in jail until the law decides his fate. Killing a criminal in a gun battle is justifiable homicide—taking him out and plugging him in the head is cold-blooded murder," Tilbert ended.

There were a few seconds of silence and harsh stares then the leaders continued with their plans until suddenly a loud voice rang out, "Anybody seen Douglas?" Every head jerked in the direction of Douglas' empty bedding.

"Shit! The bastard's run off," Dell said.

"I'll bet he's gone to warn his wolf buddies," a deputy said.

"He couldn't have gone far," a scout said. He and other scouts grabbed their rifles and bolted to the front opening.

"Here I am." The scouts stopped dead and turned. Douglas stood in the opening at the back intentionally blocked with heavy supplies. "I was taking a leak," he said limping over to the water pan. He dipped his hands in the treated water and searched their steaming eyes while feeling around for a towel.

"You do that again, and I will personally break your neck," Dex said.

"Don't ever leave without permission, Douglas," Russell said quietly.

"Well, I saw you guys were busy and..."

"Don't do that again. Not without permission—you understand?" Russell repeated.

Douglas sensed that Russell was *trying* to protect him. "Sure, Rusty. I'm sorry." Douglas held his left side with his right hand and grunted as he limped back to his bedding and settled in. Tilbert assigned a special guard to watch Douglas' every move even as he slept.

Three days later, the scouts reported that Douglas had been truthful. There were little more than a dozen Lycans left and about twenty C-wolves, but they were heavily armed. From what the scouts could make of it, there appeared no fresh wolves among them. In truth, many were injured so severely that they hadn't the time or strength to increase their numbers even though a small town stood nearby.

Now that they knew the enemy wolves' location, the force leaders vowed that none would escape and none would be held as prisoners. It would be a fight to the death. "God willing," Tilbert said, "only *their* deaths."

The scouts headed out a few hours ahead of the force. They kept binoculars on the enemy wolves and constantly briefed the in-coming Strike Force on enemy activities to ward off an ambush. But then came a briefing that was to be a game-changer.

"Sir," a scout said, "yeah, go ahead," Tilbert replied, "there's movement toward the town, sir.

"How far toward the town?"

"About a hundred and twenty yards."

"All right, keep me posted." Tilbert relayed the message to the other leaders—minus River who had been taken back to Greyscott for medical treatment and replaced with an elder.

"A hundred and twenty yards," Matthew repeated. "Damn, that's a little more than a football field."

"So, *that's* their plan," Dex said, "to stakeout so near the town we can't use explosives."

"Overly used, but a pretty good strategy you've got to admit," the elder said.

"Maybe not so good," Tilbert said. Then Tilbert's mind lit on fire with an idea. He stayed on his car phone until they reached the scouts.

*****

A beautiful flock of tiny birds in arrowhead formation shot across the sky, then all cut at the same time and shot in the opposite direction without one bird falling out of place. It was one of the little miracles of nature. The sun beamed strong and crept between the tall trees in the wooded area where Daethan talked with his wolves. That too was a miracle of nature.

He stood a little less than seven feet in semi-transformation, standing upright on two enormous paws. Unlike werewolves who could speak only when human, Lycans could speak in any form and often scared the hell out of Amahran village hunters when mistaken for an actual wolf. Daethan was muscular in medium light gray fur with reddish-brown streaks running throughout. A thin streak of white ran around and under his mouth and continued to the sides of his face down to his neck. His snout of reddish-brown stopped at the line of his ice-blue eyes with tiny yellow irises. Above the eyes was gray fur with reddish-brown ears trimmed in gray. His fangs showed long and sparkling white and extending from each paw and hand were long, black, retractable claws. His deep-throated voice was amazingly soft, like a harsh whisper of the wind. And when angered, that same whispery tone coupled with drawn back lips and a steely gaze could freeze the very soul.

A C-wolf, accused of acting cowardly during the battle, was brought before Daethan by two Lycans and thrown at his feet. The accused wolf shook with such fright, that his tears turned to blood.

"This is what Charlton presented us with to wipe out the fake wolves in this town," he bellowed pointing at the accused. "This bewitched hunk of pathetic flesh isn't fit to drink the *piss* of a Lycan." He struck the wolf like a flash of lightning. The clawed blow lifted the head and tore it from the body sending it skidding across the dirt. The horrified C-wolves watched in terror as the headless body fell sideways and dark blood poured from the neck. The two Lycans who brought the accused forward were overcome with the splash of his blood.

"Clean up this mess!" he yelled to several C-wolves. Go clean yourselves," he ordered the two Lycans, but in a softer authoritative tone.

When Sheriff Tilbert found himself nearing the location of the scouts, he ended the call. He felt uneasy in enemy territory; still, he and the Strike Force quietly parked and made their way up the hill where the scouts lay peeking through the tall grass with their binoculars.

"Any change?" Tilbert asked easing up beside one of his scouts.

"Not really, sir," the scout answered. "But Douglas had a right to be scared of that head Lycan. We just saw his wrath against one of his own. Ripped his head clean off."

"I don't mean to sound like no pussy," another scout said, "but I wouldn't want to go hand-to-hand with *that* wolf."

"Which one is he?" Tilbert asked peering through his binoculars.

"The big one in the middle—doing all the talking."

"Hm," Tilbert uttered. "He's a big bastard all right. Too bad we can't use explosives. It'll take a lot to bring *him* down." Tilbert lowered his binoculars. "You sure it was one of *his* wolves or a C-wolf?"

"I'm not sure, sir. They were in the shadows."

"This is troubling," Tilbert said.

"Why?"

"I told Douglas if he wanted to avoid prison and see his family again, he had to help us out by going back to his wolves and say he hid from us and just recently managed to elude us. I told him not to say he'd been captured. We even opened up a couple of his wounds so he'd appear convincing."

"You think they'll buy it?" Dex asked easing up beside him.

"For *his* sake, I sure hope so," Tilbert said. "Before we got here," he told Dex who hadn't overheard, "Daethan executed one of his own. Don't know if it were a Lycan or a C-wolf."

"Probably a C-wolf," an elder said sliding up. "Lycans seldom spill one another's blood. They hold themselves too sacred."

"You mean like their shit don't stink," Dell said settling beside him.

"Something like that," the elder chuckled.

"There's movement close-by! Get down! Get down!" the scout whispered loudly. All lay still with their bellies against the tall blades of grass and waited for the lookout scout to give an 'all clear' before they raised themselves. "Oh, wait," the scout said. "It's Douglas. He is really bleeding and he's struggling like he can barely walk."

"That's an act," Tilbert said. "What's he doing now...are they accepting him?"

"I don't know...I can't tell," the scout said. "They've moved farther back behind the trees. It's...it's too dark, sir."

"You think they saw us?"

"I don't believe so."

"We'll just have to wait to hear from Douglas," Tilbert said.

"And hope the poor bastard doesn't give us away," said the elder.

CHAPTER THIRTY-ONE

"I'm telling the truth," Douglas choked out from bloody lips. One eye, puffed shut, resembled a little purple ball covered with skin. He hung from a thick tree branch by his wrists; every line of his rib cage poked through his torso as his feet dangled just inches from the ground. The front of his shirt was covered in blood dripping from a deep gash on his chin. Daethan, along with his generals, sat a few feet away by a campfire stuffing themselves with chunks of roasted meat. They seemed amused by the torture and often smiled in between bites.

Outside the small wooded area not even a shadow stirred. The stars glittered like little seventies disco balls and appeared to wink. At the bottom of the steep hill, wolves and deputies sat sleeping in their vans unaware of Douglas's savaging ordeal.

The next day, Sheriff Tilbert woke first with dawn's light burning his eyes. He yawned, checked his watch, and then exited his van. The sheriff walked until he found a hidden spot to empty his bladder while suspiciously checking his surroundings. The sound of crushed leaves disturbed the silence, and he was soon joined by several wolves and male deputies—all resembling a short line of firemen drowning out a tiny blaze.

"Have you heard from Douglas?" Dex asked Tilbert as they walked back to their vans.

"No, and I'm beginning to think maybe it wasn't such a good idea sending him back," Tilbert said.

"Think they killed him?" Dex asked. He washed and dried his hands then tossed the towel to Tilbert.

A deputy handed Tilbert a foam cup of hot coffee and a big link of beef sausage. Tilbert raised his eyebrows and sipped his coffee before answering. Dex grabbed a sausage and a cup of brew. He bit the top of his link and waited patiently for Tilbert to find an answer. Tilbert took a bite then muffled, "God, I hope not."

Deep within the shadows of the wooded area, Douglas hung unconscious—his chin resting on his chest; dried and fresh blood staining the front of his shirt and pants. Under his feet, a pool of blood covered a scatter of leaves.

"Cut him down," Daethan ordered.

A Lycan pulled a blade from his waist and slashed the ropes. Douglas tumbled to the ground with a soft thud. A C-wolf reluctantly asked permission to attend Douglas. After Daethan nodded his approval, two C-wolves, one at his feet and one at his shoulders, carried Douglas to the far side where the C-wolves camped out. They washed and attended his wounds then placed antiseptic laced cotton where two back teeth had been.

"Douglas, Douglas," one of his comrades whispered. The wolf gently shook Douglas and called his name several more times until he opened his eyes. Douglas looked up into a circle of faces and smiled faintly. He was in fresh clothes and served spoons of herbal broth and teas.

"Hurry up with him!" yelled a ranked Lycan to the ones nursing Douglas. "Attend to the catch!"

Several C-wolves jumped to their feet and pulled their blades; they ran to the catch and began skinning and gutting several deer and wild rabbits. One C-wolf, slow to rise, felt Douglas grip his arm pulling him off balance. "What are you doing? Let me go," the wolf scolded.

"I lied," Douglas whispered.

The frightened C-wolf stretched his eyes and looked about nervously. "What...what are you talking about?"

"We're not alone," Douglas whispered.

The C-wolf pulled away from him and rushed past the Lycan who frowned at his late response to his orders. The Lycan eyed Douglas suspiciously, but Douglas lay still. The Lycan moved on and Douglas opened his eyes. He slowly reached the pocket of his soiled pants just inches from his fingers and eased his hands on his phone.

Everyone familiar with Sheriff Tilbert's text buzz froze when they heard the sound. Tilbert looked down and breathed a sigh. "Douglas says he took a beating, but he's okay and he didn't reveal anything," Tilbert said. The wolves and deputies seemed pleased that the plan was still in play. Russell, however, was just glad Douglas was alive. He and Dell expressed short glances of relief to one another.

Later that evening, the sun at its journey's end, the C-wolves sat about, far from the arrogant Lycans, and stuffed themselves with rabbit—deer was for only the Lycans. TM, the C-wolf Douglas had first whispered to earlier, eased next to him. TM stood for Tall Man a nickname given to him in his earlier human life.

"I lied," Douglas repeated.

Annoyed, TM asked with his eyes darting about, "Lied about what?"

"Stop looking around and listen," Douglas warned him. "There are about eighty Greyscott wolves and deputies just below the hill waiting on a chance to end this.

"What?" TM whispered loudly. "We need to tell Daethan." TM half stood.

"No, you fool," Douglas said pulling him back down. A Lycan looked at them and TM kept his head down and looked away from Douglas. Just talking too secretly could get a C-wolf severely punished—knowing the secret, could get him killed. "You don't understand," Douglas told him. "Daethan lied...Charlton too. There never was a werewolf cure."

"What? No." TM sunk where he sat and his shoulders slumped. He tossed his meat to a plate on the ground and stared down at it. Douglas reached, picked it up, and slapped it back into his hand.

"Eat," Douglas told him. "You'll need your strength."

"For what?"

"To turn on these Lycan bastards and help the law and the Greyscotts...that's what."

"Are you insane?" TM griped.

"Keep your voice down," Douglas warned. "The Lycans will send us out to hunt in a couple of days and..."

"Yeah, they eat like vultures," TM angrily interrupted. "That's all we do is hunt and fetch like...like we're their pet dogs."

"Calm down and listen. Out on the hunt, they let us talk more freely. I'll explain everything then. You pass the word. But be careful."

TM nodded. Shortly after, Douglas texted Tilbert that the plan was moving along.

Three days passed and Douglas felt well enough to go out with the rest of the C-wolves, along with three Lycan overseers, to fish and hunt. Before returning to camp, Tilbert's plan quickly circulated among the C-wolves—though some seemed too scared of the Lycan's revenge to commit to the plan. But when TM told of how they had been grossly deceived about the non-existing werewolf cure, their instant anger nearly cost them the plan. Cooler C-wolf heads prevailed and the angry wolves came eagerly but calmly on board. Later that day, after everyone had eaten, the C-wolves notice swift movement among the Lycans.

"Daethan has called a meeting. And don't keep him waiting," a ranked Lycan snapped.

The C-wolves rose and walked the length of the camp to where Lycans were gathering. Daethan stood before them like a king and spoke his rather lengthy plan; then he ended with, "As you can see, there's not many of us. Somewhere out there are man-wolves and disgusting humans waiting to attack us. So we'll need more of *them*," he said pointing to the C-wolves, "to cause a distraction, while we circle around and crush them from behind." The Lycans all nodded their approval. "I want you, you, you and you," Daethan ordered pointing to Douglas, TM and several other C-wolves. "Go into the town and gather as many men as you can and bring them back here. And don't make a ruckus." The C-wolves nodded and left the camp with two Lycan overseers. They hid deep in the shadows of the wooded area behind the residence near a lake and waited. After two and a half hours, many became restless but knew not to complain. Then suddenly, they spotted a young male; they snuck up on him, muffled his cry, placed a sack over him, and dragged him into the woods where he was gagged and tied. That went on for several more hours. They snatched males from wheat fields, tractors, watering their lawns, cutting grass and from fishing boats;

two snatched coming from church and several conked on the head as they stumbled out of a bar.

At nightfall, the wolves returned with twenty-two strong males in their late teens to early twenties. They forced them down on their knees.

"Excellent catch," Daethan said. Then after a few seconds, he yelled. "Well, what are you waiting for! Get to it!"

Douglas, TM and several of the C-wolves stood in half-transformation above their victims. Their yellowing eyes glared from furry faces and above black, wet noses. Sharp fangs sprang out. Appearing too horrified to scream, the males trembled at the sound of deep-throated snarls. The wolves snatched their victims' heads to one side exposing the thick veins in their necks; then viciously sank their fangs into the veins while their victims kicked and flailed. The males fell backward on the ground—their eyes seemed fixed in another world; the blades sparkled in the furry hands of the C-wolves as they stabbed their victims in the chest and watched them fall limp.

Satisfied, Daethan and his fellow Lycans retired to their camp space to finalize more plans. The C-wolves dragged the males, two at a time, to trees and tied them back-to-back. In just hours, twenty-two new comrades would join their once waning army. The C-wolves sat around a fire where they snacked on cold fish and waited.

*****

Midnight—the smoldering sparks glowed like fireflies as they crackled along the edges of the dry wood. The Lycans quietly snored. Several yards from them, the C-wolves' fire burned brightly and gave light to the leaves hanging above them. They were wide awake and kept a watchful eye on the slumbering Lycans.

Behind the C-wolves, covered in fake blood and loosely tied, unknotted ropes fell from the chests and ankles of the junior Greyscott wolves. The plan worked. Tilbert found a way to protect the town and sneak the Greyscotts into the camp unnoticed. Matthew, Russell, and Dell stayed out of sight. They knew the Lycans would recognize them as the ones they had trapped in their cave, but they felt sure the Lycans wouldn't know the other junior wolves. Tilbert had revealed his plan to the town's minister and urged him to keep the people off the streets. That gave Matthew's group the freedom to stage their own kidnapping with a little acting thrown in for the bite and fake-knife stabbing scene. The twenty-two junior wolves slowly emerged from the shadows; one of the young wolves sent a flashlight signal to Matthew who flashed one to Tilbert and the Strike Force partially surrounded the wooded area. The only other escape for the Lycans was to fight through the C-wolves and Matthew's well-trained unit.

But the Lycans had been alerted. It seemed a young Greyscott who had barely escaped capture was recognized by a Lycan who remembered his unusual tattoo. Though the whole of Tilbert's plan wasn't plain to the Lycans, that discovery proved enough to cause suspicion. Tilbert's element of surprise seemed thwarted.

Suddenly, a gun blast robbed the night of its silence. One of Tilbert's deputies fell—shot through the head. The Strike Force dove to the ground as multiple blasts cut several of their comrades to pieces. Shouts of commands rang from Dex and Tilbert as the force crawled on their bellies seeking shelter. The gun blasts shocked Daethan and his generals out of their sleep, and they leaped to their feet.

Outside the forest, the deputy snipers 'used their gunfire to distract the Lycans so Matthew, Russell and Dell could sneak into the camp to join the C-wolves and the young Greyscott unit.

Every humanoid and man-wolf stood completely transformed. Their deep-throated growls rose and filled the night air—making the terrified town-folk grab their silver-loaded rifles and deadlock their doors. Little, furry, night creatures scurried into their burrows and froze. Frightened owls flew in every direction, and a small pack of animal wolves, sensing strangeness in the air, scaled a mountain top and howled fiercely at the full moon. On the edge of the forest, chaos unfolded as multiple gun blasts and commands bellowed.

Inside the forest, eighteen Lycans stood before the combined force of the C-wolves and Matthew's young task force. Eighteen Lycans were the equivalent of fifty and

Matthew knew only well-executed teamwork could bring them down.

"Man-wolves!"Daethan shouted over the gun blasts. "You're not leaving this forest alive."

The C-wolves and Greyscotts responded with a thunderous growl then bolted toward the Lycans at full speed. The clash sent dirt, fur, and blood splashing into the night air. The growls were deafening like the roars of a hundred lions. It was two to three man-wolves on every Lycan. But the Lycans held their-own as they ripped the heads from several of them sending body parts scattering across the forest floor. Douglas and TM teamed up on the Lycan that had nearly beaten Douglas to death. Douglas' ripped off his nose and ear while TM clawed him viciously from behind, tearing his spine from his body. Many young Greyscotts fought gallantly, losing at the end, but causing irreparable damage to the humanoids. Russell and Dell sustained multiple injuries; Russell's white fur was soaked with his own blood and Dell sustained cracked ribs and could barely see out of one eye, but still, they managed to tag-team a Lycan to death. In the chaos, they looked around for Matthew but couldn't find him.

Meanwhile, outside on the edge of the forest, the Strike Force was bogged down with gunfire that came from high up in the trees. Many of Tilbert's snipers lay dead and the silver bullets originally meant for the C-wolves, of course, proved useless against the Lycans. Tilbert seemed reluctant to use explosives because they were too close to the residential area but believed he had no choice. Dex and his unit were also bogged down with gunfire; some lay dead and some rolled about in agony from the silver nitrate burning within their flesh.

Inside the camp, Russell and Dell spotted a Lycan standing over a dead Greyscott. Dell jumped on his back, and Russell shot from the side and tore at his throat. The Lycan, appearing unaffected, fought on; it raked Russell's chest then reached behind and clawed Dell's face injuring an already punctured eye. The two still managed to bring the Lycan down, and both ripped open his back and clawed out his spine. Russell looked around and spotted Matthew battling to free himself from Daethan's deadly grip. They leaped on Daethan knocking him to the ground. Then the three piled on top of him—clawing and biting off chunks of his flesh. Daethan rose majestically to his feet—tossing Matthew, Russell and Dell aside in the process like they were toys. Dell attacked again, but a powerful swipe from Daethan's paw rendered Dell unconscious; then he kicked Russell in his side and raked Matthew across the face.

Suddenly, from the edge of the forest, came the roar of explosives that shook the ground like a magnitude five earthquake and rocked the homes of the townsfolks. The explosion ripped the trees from under the Lycan snipers and catapulted them into the air. The Strike Force watched as Lycan bodies fell to the ground in multiple pieces. Meanwhile, in each home, the frightened people knelt and prayed.

Inside the camp, fur and blood splattered the trees and covered the ground. With Dell unconscious, Matthew and Russell could barely handle Daethan. He backhanded Russell cracking his jaw then gripped Matthew by the throat. Matthew gasped for breath and felt his eyes straining through its sockets. Russell sunk his fangs into Daethan's leg, but the near seven-foot giant shook him off like he was a Chihuahua. Russell tumbled over several times before landing on his face. He lay gasping in horror as Daethan's python grip had Matthew's eyes fixed in another world. Suddenly, a huge gray paw slammed Daethan on the side of his head. The blow broke his grip on Matthew and sent the giant Lycan crashing to the ground. Daethan shook his head and when his vision cleared, his eyes widened at the sight of Dex standing on all-fours and shielding his son.

Daethan slowly rose to his upright position and towered over Dex.

"Came to save your pup. How touching," Daethan said in a deep gravel voice.

Dex on all-fours was at a disadvantage. Daethan's powerful clawed feet could crack his skull with one swipe. The two wolves circled one another—swiping, growling and baring their needlepoint fangs. The fur rose on their backs. Saliva streamed from their mouths, and eyes blazed at one another as they swiped and growled. Daethan continued to grin—sure of his upright advantage, but Dex saw something in his own favor. By standing upright, Daethan's throat beckoned him. The wolves continued to circle then suddenly,

Daethan went for the face with a swift kick. But Dex moved quickly catching the blow to his side that cracked a rib. Ignoring the pain, Dex swiped Daethan's powerful legs from under him bringing him ass-first to the ground. Daethan looked at his leg and half the muscle hung exposed. He shot up from the ground and the clawed foot whisked passed Dex's ear. The swipe was so powerful the miss threw Daethan off balance. Dex leaped—snapping his powerful jaws on Daethan's throat, forcing him to the ground; but Dex didn't tear out the flesh, instead, clamped down harder—cutting off the oxygen to Daethan's brain. The Lycan clawed Dex's back and kicked wildly to break free. The flesh on Dex's back was peeled back and his muscles were showing. The pain from Daethan's clawing nearly made Dex let go. Matthew ran toward his father and bit into Daethan's wrist, pulling his claws away from Dex's back and Russell did the same with the other wrist. Daethan kicked and jerked his body. His eyes darted crazily as he gasped for breath. Daethan's heart pounded in his chest then he lay unconscious. Dex pulled his fangs out of Daethan's throat; bloody strings of flesh hung from his mouth. With their noses, the three turned Daethan over on his stomach, and Dex ripped out his spine.

Every Lycan lay dead. Douglas, TM, and surviving C-wolves sat on the ground exhausted. Several young Greyscotts sat panting near a tree. Matthew limped over to Dell and found him barely breathing. Dex and Russell watched Sheriff Tilbert, his deputies, and badly injured

Greyscott wolves come in from the outside and stand before them; the deputies' stood with dirt-smudged faces—their uniforms torn and soaked with their own blood and bloody brain matter of their dead comrades.

After everyone gathered their strength, the dead and injured of the Strike Force as well as C-wolves were carried over the hill to various vehicles and transported back to town. Before leaving, Tilbert checked on the town-folk and found many shattered windows, but no one badly hurt. The Strike Force drove back to Greyscott Falls and Sheerfield in total silence. There were no high-fives, talk of celebration or even a smile among them. Everyone appeared exhausted and bewildered that they had even survived the ordeal. It had been an entire year of nothing but fighting with many loved ones lost.

*****

It took several weeks to memorialize and bury the dead and for the injured to recuperate. The scavengers had cleaned the forest of the Lycans. And the town-folk went back to as nearly a normal life as could be expected. Douglas, TM, and the other surviving C-wolves struggled to come up with a believable explanation to their families concerning their whereabouts for over a year. They certainly couldn't tell them about Charlton and what he had done to them. However, the ability to transform at will would aid them in keeping their secret.

Russell drove Douglas to the airport. The two men climbed out of the car and faced each other for the last time.

"Well, this is it," Douglas said.

"Yeah, have a great life. You deserve it," Russell replied.

"You know, I wouldn't have survived this if it weren't for you," Douglas said.

"You had a lot to do with your own survival. Deceiving Daethan wasn't just clever, it was downright dangerous. But you pulled it off...saved all our asses."

"No." Douglas said grinning "I meant saving me from Dex."

Russell chuckled. Oh, well, in that case, you still owe me." The men laughed then embraced, but Douglas didn't let go when he pulled back, and his face had changed colors.

"What's wrong, now," Russell asked.

"Rusty, I don't know. What if my wife doesn't buy this story we've cooked up...thinks I've been off with another woman and lying about it or something?"

"I wish I had a little crystal ball and could tell you everything would work out fine," Russell said, "but unfortunately...."

"I know," Douglas said. He dropped his hands to his sides and stood there like a little boy lost.

"Douglas, you pulled off the most convincing lie that not only saved yourself but me, the wolves and an entire town of innocent people. I won't believe you can't convince a woman who loves you. She'll be so glad you're alive. Just *make* her believe it."

"I'll try my best."

"That's my dude," Russell said grinning.

They embraced again and Russell watched Douglas disappear into the mass assembly of people hurrying about in the bustling crowd. While driving home, where he lived with Heather, Russell appeared delighted when he learned from a phone call that River and Dell were recovering nicely from their wounds.

Meanwhile, at the Sheerfield sheriff station, a happy Sheriff Tilbert stood in front of his deputies with their families and lionized the special ones for their bravery.

He had a gourmet lunch and non-alcohol beverages delivered to the station. In the midst of the loud merriment, Tilbert's phone buzzed on his desk. He leaned from where he was sitting with his fingers barely able to touch the phone and clicked speaker. "Hello," Tilbert said eagerly.

"Did you really think that fake earthquake fooled us?"

Tilbert froze. He hopped up and grabbed his phone. "Campbell. Campbell listen—I can explain. It's... it's not what you think."

"Relax. If we were coming, we'd be there already. And don't give me an explanation, because I wouldn't believe it anyway. Just know this...I like you Tilbert. You're a good man.

But if we detect any more arcane energy coming from your region...well, you know the rest."

"Yes," Tilbert sighed. "I know the rest."

Both phones went silent, and Tilbert stood with his phone dangling at his side.

"Sheriff!" a female deputy called. "Is everything all right, sir?"

"Oh...ah...yes, Carrie, everything is fine."